Not Dead Yet...

Former Title:

A Lethal Time and Place

Peg Herring

Gwendolyn Books: United States

Not Dead Yet... copyright© 2013 Peg Herring
Former title: *A Lethal Time and Place*

Published in the United States by Gwendolyn Books
ISBN: 978-1-944502-15-7

Chapter One

August 16, 1965

Wrapped in a blanket, the naked redhead sat on a sagging chair in the center of a dank, cluttered room as a man called Norman explained his plans for her with large gestures and wild eyes. While she didn't comprehend all of it, she concluded that Norman was extremely clever...and at least half mad.

When he finished his long soliloquy Norman sat back, an expectant smile on his fleshy face. "What do you think?"

After a long pause, the woman spoke. "I think, sir, that you are a pimple on the rump of creation."

A frown passed briefly over his face, but then he laughed. "You're magnificent!" he crowed. "And you're only the first of many." Flecks of saliva crusted at the sides of his mouth. "You can't imagine what I gave up in order to make you mine."

A pale eyebrow rose. "Don't be a fool, Pimple. I am not yours, nor will I ever be."

Still dazzled by his success, the man didn't seem to hear. As he rubbed his hands like some gloating alchemist, the redhead turned to the battered metal door, focusing her gaze as if she might glare her way to the other side. Though not afraid of the strange man, she was concerned nonetheless. If what he said was true, her life would never return to the way it had been. She had to learn to live a new way, in a manner she'd never imagined before this moment.

***

September, 1967

Playing the bum at the Randolph Street Mission amused Leo less and less. Still, he sat patiently among a dozen or so derelicts, hiding his dismay at the sounds and smells around him. They listened, at least some did, to a long, clumsy lecture opposing strong drink and the love of God. Evidently one precluded the other. Maintaining a blank expression, Leo waited as the amateur speaker propounded Christian principles to his captive audience, though he grasped little of the subtleties of his audience or the principles themselves.

As men snored, burped, and muttered, the speaker, rapt with his own voice, went doggedly on. Leo resisted the urge to break into the *Te Deum*, imagining the surprised look it would bring to the man's righteous, acne-scarred face. But that would defeat his purpose, which was the impending meal. Once everyone was busy either serving or eating, he'd steal as much food as possible and then leave. He never spent the night in such places. They were bound to be infested.

With his face lowered, Leo didn't look much different from the others. His longish, flowing hair was shot with gray, and his strong countenance had intriguing life experiences carved on it in the form of deep wrinkles. Hard physical work had roughened his hands, and his scruffy, baggy overcoat made him easily recognizable to the mission staff. When the meal was finally announced, he took a seat on a cockeyed folding chair at a battered table. Pretending to gobble like the others, he surreptitiously stuffed most of his food into large, hidden pockets Memnet had sewn inside the coat.

On this occasion, he was careless. A worker passing with a coffeepot saw two rolls disappear under the table. Though she had a kind face, she frowned. "Clients aren't allowed to take food from the mission."

Leo bent his head as if ashamed. "It's for later," he murmured. "It keeps the cravings down." With a brief nod of understanding she retreated to the kitchen, the empty pot dangling from one hand. A true Christian, Leo concluded, but he resolved to be more careful in the future.

When the meal was over, Leo left the mission and started for home, the food in his pockets bumping against his thighs with reassuring solidity. Having done his part for the communal good, he slowed to enjoy the sights and sounds around him.

Since his arrival two years ago, the streets of Chicago had produced a succession of emotions. First he'd felt only fear and confusion. Later he'd found stimulation, and lately, he'd begun to think of the city as home. As he maneuvered through familiar places, Leo felt a bittersweet happiness.

The buildings of downtown dwarfed the individual man, yet the minds of men had created them. Machinery that rolled, growled, whirred, and whined around him stirred his inquiring mind. Though he didn't understand everything about the city, Leo was interested in every aspect of it.

As the odor of fried chicken wafted up from his coat, he smiled in anticipation. Soon he'd be home, though his home was not what most people meant by the term. Working together, Leo and three friends had carved out a place for themselves and built acceptable though not luxurious lives. Like hunter-gatherers of another age, their daylight hours were spent foraging. Each had discovered and developed talents that contributed to the group's welfare. Leo and Roy put aside their morals, such as they were, and stole. Memnet, who had no talent for crime, earned a small store of cash by singing on the streets. Libby refused to steal, but she made the most of Memnet's money, demanding value for every penny. After screaming like a fishwife at the Greek in the delicatessen down the block, she'd come away with a fragrant cheese or the crispest vegetables. Once she learned not to slap those who irritated her, Libby used her wicked tongue instead, and it paid off.

Walking quickly to avoid the appearance of vagrancy and a chat with Mayor Daley's Finest, Leo made his way down the city's gas-choked streets. A few blocks from the lakeshore, he reached his destination and stopped to reconnoiter.

Set squarely in the middle of the block, the building he lived in was squat and flat-looking, with two rococo balconies on the second story that seemed out of place against the plain gray brick. In an attempt to modernize, bright green awnings had been installed over them, but they only added to the structure's overall oddness. Most people entered and left the building by a lofty entrance where a brushed metal sign proclaimed *Schmidt Museum of Anthropology*. For that privilege, most people paid a fee.

Leo and his friends used an entry not meant to exist and therefore free of charge. A coal delivery chute, necessary in the 1920s when the building was new, had been boarded up when the heating system was updated. The narrow alley between the Schmidt and the building next to it was blocked with a high wooden fence to prevent through traffic. The resulting cul-de-sac was dark, cold, and smelled unpleasant, which made it perfect for unseen entrances and exits. No one knew where the four of them spent their nights. No one was supposed to.

As he approached the alley, Leo noticed a child of undistinguishable gender near the entrance. It wore the uniform of the times: bell-bottomed trousers with hems frayed and dragged to a dirty shade of gray; a tattered denim jacket with signs and signatures drawn on it with an ink pen; and under it a long vest of something shaggy and thick, like sheep's wool. Beneath the vest was a paisley-print shirt in vibrant reds and yellows. Dark hair, heavy and in need of washing, was cut in the style of four young English singers Leo had seen on the television. He decided the child was female only because the bag she carried, which had a ballerina embroidered on it.

The girl's liquid brown eyes gazed hopefully at people passing on the sidewalk, measuring them with a maturity her small frame couldn't match. Leo was cautious lest she see him slipping into the alley, but her glance passed over him disinterestedly. She was searching for someone, but an old man in a baggy overcoat wasn't it. Since his own concerns precluded taking on the troubles of others, Leo entered the alley, ducked behind the trash bin, and headed for an entrance only four people in the world knew about.

A year before, working late at night, Leo and Roy had unsealed the old coal chute, carefully preserving its blank appearance. Its wood-and-wire covering now opened and closed like a door, but only if one knew the trick of a clever mechanism. Roy had moved the alley trash bin to a new position blocking view from the street and further protecting their secret.

When they'd finished the work Libby crowed, "Leo, you've given us freedom!" at which he'd bowed graciously. Commendation from Libby was always welcome, but he was used to being praised for his clever hands.

With a last glance behind, Leo opened the latch and climbed through the door. Once inside, he took a metal staircase down two levels, stepping softly to silence the vibrations. As he descended the air grew stale, but he hardly noticed anymore. If dank meant others stayed away, so be it. At the bottom of the fourth and final set of steps, he turned down a dark, low hall where dusty, wire-mesh-covered bulbs illuminated the way only slightly. At the far end was a rusted metal door marked *Storeroom C* in cracked, fading stenciled letters. Leo closed the door behind him before calling out, "Anyone here?"

Storeroom C was remote from the daily workings of the museum. Ill-kept and clammy, it was stuffed with piles of miscellaneous items, many of them junk. They were stacked with little concern for order, indicating the staff didn't expect anything there would be needed again. Leo followed a rough pathway to the back of the room where they'd made a space for themselves. Here was what they called home.

Roy ducked out of a rectangular hole in the wall, his lank frame bending with the grace of one in the prime of manhood. "Libby and I started makin' supper," he said, the dropped final g's betraying his rural background. He set a mismatched assortment of dishes on a threadbare rug. "We're still waitin' on Memnet, but I got a whole cake and six bottles of root beer."

Roy had a passion for the soda, which Leo found overly sweet but was too polite to mention. Emptying his pockets, he placed his contribution of bread, chicken, and cheese on a chipped plate. "Compliments of the Randolph Street Mission."

Libby emerged from a second, equally odd door with a bowl balanced between hip and forearm and a tomato in hand. Red hair mixed with gray and pulled into a tight bun gave her a severe look. Leo kissed her pale cheek, smelling her Ivory soap, and remarked, "A tomato, Libby. Will you poison us?"

His ancient joke brought a smile that sweetened her haughty expression. "Leo, you must overcome your old-fashioned thinking. I suppose you won't sleep with the window open either, for fear of the night air."

"I might if I had a window," he replied. "Maybe Roy will dig

8

me one."

"Too much concrete for diggin'," Roy observed wryly. "You might could draw you a pretty one. You're good at that." His tone conveyed a tinge of disrespect for effort wasted in the expression of beauty.

Libby stiffened and her mood turned snappish. "If Leo's drawings distract us from the fact that we live like moles, we should be grateful for it."

Leo surmised she'd been thinking about the past, dwelling on it, as she often did. When he put a hand on her shoulder she shivered, adding, "I have always hated damp."

"There's no remedy for it, Libby."

Her nose went thinner. "I don't have to *like* it. Moles, scuttling about in the dark. If they found us..." Resentment crept into her voice. "I used to dance until dawn. Since Norman interfered with our affairs, only Roy celebrates the night."

Roy's expression turned sullen, and Leo searched for a way to deflect the impending argument. "Our life here requires sacrifice—" he began.

"Exactly!" she interrupted. "Secrecy is crucial, but he comes and goes as he pleases, at all hours, never revealing where he goes or what he does."

Unaffected by her tendency to talk about him as if he weren't there, Roy said, "I do as I please."

"As we well know. You return smelling of tobacco and perfume."

Roy took a piece of green pepper from the bowl she held, tacitly daring her to stop him. "I've done my share of layin' low," he said. "A man can only stay in nights for so long."

"But it causes concern for the rest of us," Leo said. "You must see that."

Libby's voice rose. "What if you're caught on one of your outings, half-drunk and loose-tongued?"

Roy waved a casual hand. "I can take care of myself."

"With theft and lies," Libby sneered.

"That's Roy's strength, Libby. People see him as a friendly eccentric with no secrets."

Roy spoke to Leo, neatly turning the third-person gambit around. "You're not so bad yourself. It's Libby who acts like she's got the right to order folks around." He grinned. "We're lucky most people think she's crazy."

Libby tossed her head. "I'm driven halfway to madness by the chances you take. We'll pay when your skills fail you."

Leo tried again. "We each do as we choose, Libby. We agreed to that from the start." They moved about Chicago almost naturally these days, blending into the crowds of odd people any large city attracts. At times Leo almost forgot they were, and must remain, shadows in the city of big shoulders.

Libby's anger faded. "It's no life; that's all I'm saying. No life at all."

"Perhaps soon we'll be ready to leave here."

She managed a weak smile, but they all knew that was unlikely. There was too much they didn't know, too much danger. The Schmidt offered safety and anonymity, and even after two years, they were afraid to make a permanent move.

Done harassing Libby for the moment, Roy changed the subject. "What shall we play tonight, gin rummy or poker?"

Libby sighed philosophically. "Leo's choice. I can guess what it will be."

"Poker." Roy had taught them the game. Leo was a quick learner, so the women always lost to one man or the other. Libby enjoyed chess, though from her first few moves Leo knew what she had in mind. Memnet had long since ceased trying to teach them her favorite game, something with hounds that the others could make no sense of. Still, their evening games were anticipated with pleasure.

Taking a chair padded with an old blanket to cushion a slightly protruding spring, Leo watched as Libby chopped the tomatoes with brisk movements. Though she made many people uneasy, Leo was not afraid of her, and Roy seemed to enjoy provoking her anger.

"Where did you go today?" Authoritative chops accompanied her words.

"Before the Mission? The library."

Libby smiled as if she'd known the answer before asking. Most days, they left the museum in the morning and roamed the streets separately. Leo spent his leisure hours poring over books, grappling with their complexities and his own inadequacies. He yearned to know more about Norman's secrets, though the others said he should accept what he'd done and forget it.

Whatever their chosen path on a given day, they returned between 5:30 and 6:00 p.m., after the staff upstairs had gone home, to share a meal. By tacit consent, their dinner was served in the best style they could manage, and they waited until everyone was present to begin.

Picking up the thread of the former conversation, Libby said, "At least we're safe down here."

"Yes," Leo agreed. "We're safe." Even as he said it, Leo knew it couldn't last. On some uncertain future day, their secret would be revealed. They couldn't predict how it would happen, and they couldn't prevent it. Still, it was good that Libby tried to be optimistic. Tried to behave.

After two years, they were used to each other's ways, but it wasn't always easy. They were so different, yet survival required they function as a group. Norman's interference had forced them together and required them to recognize each other's strengths and weaknesses. Leo had to admit that most of the time they complimented each other.

Libby was the easiest for him to deal with, having known her type all his life, but she also had the hardest time accepting their poverty. They were homeless, jobless, family-less, and friendless, except for each other. It would be a disaster if anyone discovered they were still alive. For someone with Libby's background of wealth, power, and prestige, banishment from the world was a harsh sentence.

As she set out a shoebox with packets of sugar, salt, and pepper lifted from various restaurants, her unsettled mind caused an abrupt return to petulance. "Can that girl never be on time for supper?" Patient with Leo, Libby disapproved of Roy, though she was susceptible to his charm and masculinity. With Memnet she was condescending and demanding.

"Perhaps got confused about the streets again." Roy's tone implied it was normal. His back to Libby, he caught Leo's eye and mouthed, "Women!"

Roy's assumption of male superiority and his low opinion of Memnet's abilities irked Leo, though he noticed the younger man was careful not to let Libby hear his chauvinistic comments. After several fiery diatribes, he was apparently unwilling to accept more from her on that subject.

"She was to fetch fresh water." In theory, they took turns hauling bucketsful from a sink at the far end of the hall, but Memnet took Libby's turn as well as her own. Libby never argued, since she tended to assume everyone should wait on her.

Leo had chided Memnet more than once about it. "My dear, this is the age of women's rights. You are as good as any of us."

"I don' mind," she would reply in her soft, heavily accented voice. "And if I don' mind and it make Libby happy to us, it is a good thing, yes?"

Possessed of a beauty Leo appreciated intrinsically and goodness that shone from her like an internal candle, Memnet was what Leo imagined the lesser angels to be. Soft and yielding, she lacked the will to combat Libby's pettiness. She also seemed unable to contemplate evil, having lived a sheltered life before coming to Chicago. Leo tried to encourage her confidence, but Memnet was Memnet, and what is Man to alter an angelic soul?

Leo had faults of his own, beginning with a decidedly un-angelic outlook on life. He tried to be modern and learn everything he could about the world around him. That was his good side. Opposing that was a stubborn streak. In addition to that he was prone to ignore reality and ponder impractical "what-ifs?" It often made Roy shake his head in disgust.

"Why do you care?" Roy would ask as he pored over books from the museum's reading room at night. "It's over, and there's no changin' it. What happens next is what we need to think on."

Leo always nodded in agreement, but his stubborn mind wouldn't let him leave it alone. A life, his life, had been left behind, and he wanted an explanation. So far, there was none.

***

August 26, 1965

A haggard face hung over Leo when he woke, sore and woozy, to new surroundings. "Jet lag," Norman said with a wheezy chuckle. He had a large nose with veins like chicken tracks running all over it, rheumy blue eyes, and a small, thin-lipped mouth surrounded by several days' growth of gray beard. His breath smelled of onions and what Leo later learned was Scotch.

"How are you?" He shouted the words, as if Leo were deaf.

Dazed, Leo was at first unable to communicate. Light too bright to comprehend shone everywhere in the room. It hurt, but gradually his eyes grew accustomed. Behind the homely man, a red-haired woman watched with something like pity on her face. When her gaze moved to the man, her lips twitched with bitterness. She knew what was happening, and she opposed it.

Norman leaned even closer, inspecting Leo as if he were an unfamiliar bug. "Are you all right?"

Leo pulled his wits together enough to give an intelligent answer. "*Je ne parle pas l'anglais.*"

Chapter Two

1967

While the squatters at the Schmidt Museum shared their makeshift meal, a small-time, slightly-built forger known as Dickie slid into a restaurant booth. His furtive air belied his clean-cut looks, and he wrinkled his nose at the smell of something that had burned in the kitchen. Opposite him, a tense man of about thirty gave the barest of nods before asking, "How did it go?"

Dickie grinned, revealing a wide space between overly large front teeth. "Smooth as glass. He plans to stay at the Palmer House till he finds an apartment, should be checking in around six on the eighteenth. Everything's in here." Glancing around furtively, he slid an envelope across the table. "All you need to become one of Edgar's own."

"Who else knows about this?"

Dickie looked aggrieved. "Nobody, like you said."

The stern face formed a smile that appeared to take effort. Pushing away an acidic cup of coffee, the man rose. "Come with me to my car and I'll get your money."

Though skilled at his trade, Dickie was a poor judge of people. Without objection he followed the man he'd privately dubbed "Stoneface" to the back of the restaurant.

A clatter sounded as they rounded the building, and both men stopped warily. The setting would have turned off most of the diners inside. Stacked crates crowded the area, many half-filled with rotting vegetables. Cardboard boxes had rested there long enough that weather had turned them into amorphous blobs. A few broken dining chairs lay off to one side of the door, and a junked gas stove, grimy with burned-on grease, sat against the back wall. Across the alley, an anonymous Ford sat next to several rusty trash cans. A cautious face peeped out from behind the car's rear fender.

"Come out of there!" Dickie ordered.

A girl rose from the shadows, her escape blocked by the men. She wore jeans, a shaggy vest, and a paisley shirt in need of laundering. Over her shoulder was a pajama bag with a ballerina stitched onto it, and in one grubby hand a sealed cellophane bag crackled. It was full of broken cookies someone had thrown away, and she grasped the bag tightly. Eyes that had seen a lot tried to gauge the threat the two men posed for her.

"Picking through the garbage, huh?" Dickie felt a moment's pity for the kid but brushed it away, sensing his erstwhile employer had no such sentiments.

"I didn't take anything anyone wants." It was half challenge, half plea.

Dickie noticed his companion had turned his back, leaving him to handle the situation. "Runaways," he scoffed. "They hear songs on the radio about free love and take it seriously. Raising his voice he ordered, "Get outta here!"

As the girl ducked past Dickie, he lunged at her with a playful growl. She sprinted away, almost falling on the oil-slicked pavement as she rounded the corner. "Go home to mama!" He called after her. "Dumb kid!"

For a few seconds Stoneface watched the spot where the girl had disappeared. Apparently satisfied she was gone, he moved toward his car. "Time to get paid." As he unlocked the door Dickie leaned in, too trusting, too close.

With a last glance around them Stoneface turned, a flash of metal in his hand. Before Dickie could react, he felt a sharp pain in his gut. A grunt escaped him and he slumped against the car, holding his stomach. More pain shot through his back as the knife penetrated each lung, rendering him airless and silent.

The helpless forger felt himself lifted off his feet by his shirt collar and pants waistband. Pain intensified as he was thrown headlong into the piled boxes. By the time he died, the Ford was already pulling away. Stoneface had hardly broken a sweat, and Dickie's work rested securely in his pocket.

***

When meal was finished Roy patted his belly, commenting, "I thought for a while we'd starve down here. Thought someday they'd find four rotting corpses to puzzle over."

Leo looked up from his book. "We have been lucky." Two years ago, neither he nor Memnet spoke any English, and they'd been terrified of what lay before them. With time, determination, and the luck Roy claimed was in his stars, they'd forged a team that managed both survival and secrecy.

In the quiet of the last two years, they'd grown accustomed to their new surroundings and tolerant of each other, at least most of the time. The language barrier shrank as Leo mastered English and Memnet gained the rudiments. A kind of normalcy evolved, any routine being preferable to chaos.

A sound from above caused them to freeze, but silence followed and they relaxed. "Harley on his rounds," Roy muttered. The museum guards, old men who didn't care to walk much, patrolled just often enough to satisfy insurance requirements. Having learned who was on duty and what their routines were, the unrecognized tenants of Storeroom C seldom worried about the guards anymore.

"What would they do if somebody broke in?" Roy wondered aloud.

"That's not likely," Leo replied. "Few seem to even notice the Schmidt as they pass it on the way to better-known attractions."

"We need a decent curator." Roy spoke as if he were on the museum board rather than squatting in its innards. "Dobbs doesn't care we get fewer visitors every day, and nobody looks sharp on the job anymore."

It was true. The staff grew ever more lax, possibly due to the fact that the present curator was more interested in her status in the city than the day-to-day operation of the museum. Charlene Dobbs spent her time at luncheons with the mayor and meetings of various civic groups, leaving her employees with little oversight and plenty of time for their own pursuits. None of them seemed to involve Storeroom C.

"Charlene's lack of leadership is a good thing for us," Leo argued. "We are undisturbed."

"Undisturbed," Roy repeated thoughtfully, "like the dead. But we ain't dead yet, Leo. Someday we're gonna have to rejoin the human race. We have to be somebodies again."

***

September 2, 1965

"What in the hell?"

Those were Roy's first words when he awoke and learned he was Norman's unwilling guest. In a cigarette-roughened voice, the squat, greasy man explained this new life to his third and newest "boarder." He stood back, apparently, afraid this one, more notorious than noted, might attack him.

The redhead stepped in. "It can't be helped, sir," she counseled. "We depend on him for our very lives."

He looked her up and down, still furious, still terrified. "And just who the hell are you?"

Chapter Three

1967

On Fridays Memnet stayed in the El station on Michigan Avenue until the last of the commuters left. She sat near the entry, softly strumming a lute and singing. Money clinked into the jar set beside her, coins she proudly contributed to the living expenses of the little group in Storeroom C. The lute she played was museum property, a duplicate acquisition left to gather dust.

Though it had taken every bit of courage she could summon to begin singing on the streets, Memnet was determined to do her part. Each day she faced the unfamiliar bustle of Chicago's streets. At first the city's pounding, lively pulse was a waking nightmare, relived in her dreams each night. Over time she'd learned to function, though it was still hard. Crowds of people teemed through all large cities. The number and speed of American cars could be accepted. But the cold of winter she could not become used to.

"Hey, Baby, you sing good." She smiled in response but avoided making eye contact. Libby said Memnet's earnings had little to do with talent and much to do with male lust.

Memnet didn't like being noticed for her looks, but a glance at the man, who turned to stare at her as he retreated, confirmed Libby's statement. She dropped her gaze until he turned and hurried toward his train.

"I love your haircut," said a passing woman whose own hair was a mass of frizzy curls. Cut bluntly at chin level, Memnet's straight, black hair framed her oval face, highlighting dark, compelling eyes and full lips. The cut might have come from a trendy hairdresser on State Street, but in truth Memnet cut it herself with scissors borrowed from an office upstairs.

The crowd dwindled to a few stragglers, hurried and unlikely to drop in a coin. Rising, Memnet put on the sweater she'd left lying nearby, took up her rug, bundled it around the lute, and put it into a cloth bag she then slung across her back. As she walked homeward, several men turned to look at her, but she kept her eyes downcast, pulling the sweater close around her neck.

Just outside the Schmidt, Memnet came face-to-face with a girl of about thirteen. Noting black hair, brown eyes, and dark skin, her first thought was they might have been sisters. No. Memnet had no living relatives.

The girl's gaze locked on Memnet, revealing that she too saw the resemblance. As she passed, Memnet felt the girl pluck at her sweater. "Miss, I need help."

Strangers made Memnet nervous, and she had trouble making herself understood beyond "Please" and "Thank you." Pushing the girl's hand away, she moved on.

"Please."

A month before a boy had scooped up her jar of coins and run off with it, so she'd learned to be wary, even of children. Mimicking Libby's fierce tone she ordered, "Leave me alone!" and hurried on.

Glancing back, she saw the girl watching, a forlorn expression on her face. What does she want? She'd have to circle the block in order to conceal her destination.

Returning a few minutes later, Memnet saw the ballerina bag a half-block down Roosevelt. With a sigh of relief, she ducked into the alley, opened the concealed door, and slid inside. A few seconds after she'd closed it behind her, the girl reappeared at the alley entrance. Her hopeful expression turned to confusion when she saw no one there.

Memnet hurried down to Storeroom C and reported in a tumble of poor English, "A child in the street say she need my help, but I say to her no. I go around and she is leave when I return."

"For heaven's sake, Memnet, we've all been approached by vagabonds," Libby remonstrated.

Memnet knew she'd been their biggest problem in the early days. For weeks after her arrival she'd cowered in corners, and it had taken her months to learn even the most basic sentences. English was so difficult, and Chicago so different from the sand and seas of Egypt!

"Brave as a hedgehog!" Libby muttered just loudly enough to be heard. "You didn't give her money?" Memnet's negative response brought a nod of satisfaction. "That's progress, then."

"What did she look like?" Leo asked. At Memnet's halting description, he said, "I saw that girl earlier. I thought she was looking for someone."

"For Memnet? Why?" Roy wondered, but nobody had an answer.

With everyone home, they sat down to supper. Libby had learned to make a new kind of salad from a television show called The Galloping Gourmet. "The chef's name is Kerr," she told them, "and he speaks English quite decently. Of course, I didn't have all the ingredients he used."

"It's wonderful," Leo proclaimed, and the others agreed. There was also bread, cheese, and a piece of chicken for each, thanks to Leo's visit to the Mission. "The food transports better since you lined my coat pockets with the waxed paper, Memnet."

"Take-out food," Roy put in. "That's what they call it."

"Leo is a wizard," Libby declared, finishing her drumstick.

"But who got us a whole cake for dessert?" Roy protested.

"That was quite a feat," she admitted. Roy craved praise for his exploits, and it was true he obtained things the rest of them wouldn't dream of.

"How did you manage it?" Leo asked. If there was anything Roy liked better than thievery, it was an attentive audience to tell his stories to.

"First," he answered, cutting himself a large slice of the item under discussion, "I stole a shoppin' bag from Hudson's. That was easy. I puffed it out with newspaper so it looked full. I went into the bakery and waited till the clerk was talkin' with a customer. Five seconds, it was in the bag. Then I sauntered out the door, real casual." Roy waved a hand to convey nonchalance. "I lost a little icin' on the sides of the bag, but Libby repaired it like an expert, and it's good as new."

Unused to compliments from Roy, Libby reacted with a smile. "Couldn't be picky about the kind though," he finished.

"Oh, don't worry." Leo said, helping himself. "For today, lemon is our favorite kind of cake."

After supper they discussed the day's events. "Memnet made good money," Libby announced after counting the coins from the jar. Memnet smiled shyly, pleased at Libby's approval.

"Fridays make them generous, being the end of the workweek." Leo's expression became troubled. "Still, summer's exit means fewer chances for her to sing, which will mean less cash."

For the hundredth time, Roy tried to marshal support for his proposal. "We need to at least consider robbing a bank to get us through the winter."

"Oh, for the love of St. Peter, St. Michael, and St. George!" Libby moaned.

Leo gently discouraged the argument they were tired of hearing. "It's too much of an undertaking for us, Roy. Petty theft we do because we must, but we aren't serious felons." He tactfully didn't add the words *like you.* "Our expenses are few, and we will have to rely on foraging."

Seeing he would get nowhere, Roy shrugged and gave up, at least for the time being.

Shortly afterward they retired to their sleeping areas, Leo and Roy through the doorway on the left and Memnet and Libby to the right. Once they were alone, resting on cushions of different sizes and textures, Libby remarked, "That boy has no sense of property. If you have something he wants, he's very likely to take it, unless you can stop him."

Memnet didn't reply, but that was not unusual. She was thinking about Roy, so brave, so handsome, so unlike her he seemed another species entirely. How could he calmly propose robbing a bank, as if they were criminals?

***

Roy lay in the darkness listening to the sounds of the women readying for bed in the other room. *They think I'm the devil's own kin, but I only want to make life easier for them.* A lifelong loner, Roy had been at first reluctant to notice the other victims of Norman's treachery, but against his will and better judgment, he'd begun to care. He liked Leo's keen interest in everything around him and his clever sense of humor. Libby was practical and honest, though uppity and a real terror when angry.

And Memnet? Not his type: too fragile, too pure, too timid. Still, she appeared in his dreams from time to time, and it bothered him some. She was a beautiful woman, and he was, after all, a man.

Sometimes they agitate me, though. We almost starved last winter, and it's comin' around again. I'm good at illegal ways of makin' money, and none of us is good at legal ways. That should end the discussion.

His companions insisted on sticking to petty crime, and thus far Roy had accepted it. These days Leo, Libby, and Memnet were pretty much the whole world to him.

Roy found himself wishing for a smoke. He didn't use tobacco much, but sometimes late at night he thought of those skinny cigars. Wanting one now, he made a mental note to lift a couple tomorrow.

Unlike the other three, Roy enjoyed the thrill of theft and the fun of horn-swoggling people. In a restaurant he could get a free meal almost at will. Stealing food from grocery stores was almost too easy, and even getting new clothes was not much of a challenge anymore.

He was proud of the fact that he'd introduced Leo to "free" entertainment at downtown theaters. "You find a big group of people coming in. School kids are best 'cause you can act like you're one of their teachers. You wait until they're all bunched up at the door, rarin' to get inside, then join them, actin' like you're corrallin' the strays. You smile like you wish you were somewhere else. Nine times out of ten, you'll get through."

The times he was caught and evicted didn't bother Roy, and Leo was willing to take the chance as well. They'd gone together a few times but found it more difficult for two extra men to slip in. Roy liked movies and Leo preferred live theater, they went separately nowadays. Still, teaching Leo something had made Roy feel smart.

Aside from what Leo called "foraging" to provide for their needs, the other three did little that interested Roy. Leo read all the time, and Libby made list after list of things she intended to do if she ever got to go home. Memnet did little tasks: mending, cleaning, or making the place nicer. Sometimes Roy helped if the day was rainy or too cold to be out.

"You are...tool-good," Memnet said when he fixed a chair with a wobbly leg. That had pleased him. Most items in Storeroom C were broken, and he'd begun filling idle hours by making them serviceable again, with Memnet fetching what he needed for the job. She knew how to keep quiet, and he liked it when she clapped in delight at a table that sat solidly again or a crack artfully repaired.

In the evenings the four sometimes walked around the Loop and peered into shop windows, a free activity that attracted little attention. "Like two married couples on a stroll," Libby said once. Memnet had blushed at that, but it made a nice picture, no matter how far off the mark it was. Though she was definitely not Roy's type, it was fun to point things out to Memnet and see her smile in response.

They could survive the winter without a bank robbery, he supposed. It would have been fun to plan it out, though, to see to the details and make it work.

Leo's voice interrupted Roy's mental drifting and he started.

"Shall we take the ladies for an outing tomorrow? It's Saturday, and the weather will turn cold soon."

Typically, Leo had sensed his restlessness. "Sounds good. We can walk down by the lake."

"That will be pleasant."

"Remember how it was after Norman died?" The memory was vivid to Roy, who'd been the only one able to function. While the others hid in the basement, his daring kept them alive.

"I remember." He heard the smile in Leo's voice. "Something Norman had on him allowed you in and out of the museum."

"His staff pass." Encased in a plastic sleeve, the card was a courtesy that allowed an employee of any Chicago museum entry into all the others. "I found a suit in the wardrobe room." Pinning the badge to the lapel of the jacket, Roy had left the Schmidt for the first time. He could admit now that he'd been pretty scared at the time, but someone had to do it.

"I believe you told Libby the trick is to look bored."

"I used to do things like that before a job," Roy said. "People generally ignore you unless they got reason not to." Shifting his pillows, he went on. "First I went into the museum and walked around. Once I figured out how the place runs, I came and went at different times so nobody saw me too often." He remembered the thrilling dread of the first time he'd walked past the guards and out the door, returning in a few hours with a casual wave of his pass at the woman at the entry. Once he knew it was possible to exit and re-enter, he'd become the group's lifeline, needed in a way he'd never been before.

"The city streets must have challenged your courage."

"Yeah," Roy murmured. "Those first few times, I must have looked like a lost tourist. The downtown regulars were good though." He snickered. "Most of 'em are happy to have somebody listen when they talk."

"The map you brought back was a great help." They'd studied it, Leo leaning over Roy's shoulder and jabbering in some foreign language to Libby. "We'd have died had you not stayed to help us."

"Then you found the boarded-up doorway and reopened it." With Leo's clever creation, all of them could come and go undetected, as long as they were careful. Leo had gone first, following Roy around, fascinated by everything he saw.

"Remember Libby's first time? She made such a fuss I had to shush her. Boy, did she get mad!"

"Dealing with Libby requires practice." Amusement sounded in Leo's voice.

"That was the first time I raised her temper but not the last, by a long chalk."

Leo continued their memory walk. "Finally even Memnet couldn't stay shut inside anymore."

"We shouldn't have let her watch the television. She was scared there'd be gunfights on every corner."

"How she hated the traffic and the rattle of the trains!"

"But now she's out as much as any of us." *We've gotten good at surviving, Roy thought, more than I'd have guessed at the start. Still, sometimes I miss the days when they all depended on me. He raised one arm, resting his head on it. These days, all I can do is treat them to stolen cake.*

Chapter Four

The man the now-deceased Dickie had dubbed Stoneface dialed a number the forger had provided. An answer came on the second ring.

"Blackburn." The voice was businesslike until the caller identified himself. "Randy? Man, it's good to hear from you! It's been, what? Five years? I thought you'd forgotten me."

Picturing his cousin's face, so like his own but much more expressive, Stoneface forced himself to smile. They said even a false one carried into a person's voice. "I've been busy, Cuz."

"With what?

"Did a couple tours in Vietnam. After that I got some training."

"Job training?"

"Yeah." He changed the subject. "I'm in Chicago, and your mom told me you're moving back. I thought I'd call and see if I could help with anything."

"That's great! I always think about how much fun we used to have when Dad took me fishing at your place up in Wisconsin."

It took effort to maintain the smile. "Every summer, like the good father he was."

"Yeah, but your dad was a hoot. What a character!"

"Yeah." Stoneface glared at the wall. "A real joker."

"He sure could put it away."

"He sure could." His tone flattened, and the other heard it.

"Not that my old man didn't down enough JB to keep up."

"Yeah. I remember every time you came, you had new fishing equipment. You always let me use it too, just like I was as good as you."

"Come on, man, you know I never thought I was better. It was cool up there. I mean, I like Chicago, which is why I asked to come back here, but your place was a great getaway."

"It might have been great as a vacation spot, but it was a shit-hole to live in."

Blackburn paused, apparently embarrassed to look at the past through his cousin's eyes. "Listen, Randy. I know life with your dad was no picnic, but we had good times, you and me."

Stoneface couldn't let Charles sense how much he'd resented his cousin's comfortable wealth and loving father. "When you get to Chicago, we could get together some time."

"I'd like that, but first I need to find a place to live."

Could it be this easy? "Hey, there's a spot in my building. It hasn't opened up yet, but I was talking to a woman in the elevator who said she's moving out. I could look into it."

"Where is it?" Charles asked.

"Close to downtown, on Jackson."

"That's near the Federal Building."

"You could walk to it." Randy feigned ignorance. "Why the Federal?"

"I'm with the Bureau, didn't you know?"

"Hell no, man. I guess it has been a while. Living close to work would be good, right?"

"Perfect. I can't believe my luck."

"It's no sure thing, but if I can help, I will. When are you coming in?"

"On Friday. Got a room at the Palmer House."

It was time for a small monkey wrench. "Too bad. I work late on Fridays."

"We can do it some other day." Blackburn sounded disappointed.

"Yeah, or...wait. Could we meet later, nine or so? I'll come to your hotel, you can buy me a drink, and afterward I'll show you my place. If you like it, we'll contact the super first thing Saturday morning."

"Randy, I sure appreciate this. It would be great to get an apartment before I have to start work."

The caller smiled for real this time, and it was good that Charles Blackburn couldn't see its feral nature. "No problem. I've missed you, man."

***

The day had turned rainy, so Memnet headed back to the museum at four-thirty. With wind pushing stinging drops into people's faces, no one had any inclination to stop and listen to her music. She'd forgotten about the girl until she turned into the alley and saw the small form hunched against the sheltered east wall. Her dejected posture conjured an image of Memnet's own misery two years earlier.

***

September 13, 1965

She understood nothing they said to her. The building was

different from any in Alexandria, and she felt as if she were freezing. The woman with red hair offered food she didn't recognize. The kindly older man saw her distress and brought things she knew, grapes and an orange, for which she was grateful. Gradually she came to understand that she was very far from home. Someone must have drugged her, for she remembered nothing of the journey.

She thought the smelly man had captured them to sell as slaves, but no one touched her. In fact, he seemed disappointed in her, frowning and shaking his head. He spoke of it to the red-haired woman, who rebuked him fiercely, pointing her finger at Memnet then at the man's ugly nose. The kind-faced man seemed, like Memnet, unable to communicate. A fourth man, young and sulky, paced like a caged tiger, paying little attention to them.

What is to become of me? She asked herself. *Why was I brought to this place?* And finally: *Will I ever return to the things I once knew?*

***

1967

Sensing Memnet's presence, the girl raised her face, taking in the wet hem of her skirt and raising her eyes to the protruding neck of the lute wrapped in an embroidered blanket. She rose, her bluish lips forming a pitifully determined smile. Memnet backed away then turned and moved off, almost at a run. The girl followed. Memnet ducked into the crowds of people headed toward the El in the homebound rush. A kid with a transistor radio held to his ear bellowed, "Watch it!" and a policeman on the corner took note, his expression suspicious.

Heart hammering, Memnet slowed somewhat, trying to

move quickly without appearing panicked. A block away, she turned to look back. The child was walking in the other direction, toward Soldier Field.

She made herself wait twenty minutes before entering the alley. Relieved to find it empty, she hurried to the secret door. As she disappeared into the Schmidt, Memnet asked herself again what the girl wanted with her. What could be done to banish her forever?

***

Leo was concerned when Memnet came home upset for a second time. She insisted the girl had been waiting for her in the alley, which meant she knew where Memnet was headed. The incident set them all on edge.

"All this time we've avoided the police and now we're discovered by a child?" Libby asked sharply. "Memnet must have encouraged her in some way."

Leo interceded to save the tearful Memnet. "We knew this place would not be safe forever. The time for decision is closer now, that's all."

Roy asked, "If the kid is spying on us, what do we do?"

"We mustn't panic." Leo pushed his hair back with a characteristic one-handed gesture. "She might give up her quest if she is unsuccessful."

"Memnet must stay inside," Libby ordered. "The rest of us don't interest the girl."

"Maybe Memnet looks like someone she knows," Roy suggested.

Libby set her lips. "Are we agreed she must remain inside until the street child moves on?"

"All right." Roy didn't seem to notice Memnet hadn't been consulted.

Though Leo gave her a pitying glance, he didn't disagree. If the child didn't know the secret of the alley door, it was vital to keep her from finding it out.

***

Leo made his way down the street the next morning, apparently looking idly into store windows as he went. The fine September day brought sunshine, and a slight breeze off the lake kept it from becoming too warm. Passing a building with blackened plate glass along its front he was surprised, as one sometimes is, to catch a glimpse of a man he didn't recognize at first. The fellow had strong, handsome features, a good build for his age, and appeared good-humored and grandfatherly. When Leo realized it was his own reflection, he mentally changed the word to *avuncular*.

Then he saw the girl again. She stood scanning the faces of passers-by, her posture betraying the vigil's importance. What was she looking for? She resembled Memnet, though lighter-skinned. Noting that her clothing was the same and she carried the same ballerina bag, he guessed she was a runaway. That was good. There was less threat if the child had reason to avoid the police. He couldn't help feeling sorry for her, though—so young, so alone. He hoped the girl had a safe place to sleep and something to eat.

***

October 4, 1965

The three of them were sitting at a scarred table when Norman entered. The woman had been talking, but she fell silent and set her folded hands on the tabletop. Despite their obvious animosity, the tableau made Norman's face light with satisfaction, maybe even happiness.

Opening a bag, he set out white cardboard containers. A strong aroma rose, causing the woman's thin nose to twitch. None of them touched the food. "Eat! Eat!" he said in a jovial tone, but the woman's eyes slid over him as if he were mold. The Italian looked to her in an attempt to understand what was happening. The younger man watched, his eyes hard.

Norman opened the first container and tasted the rich brown sauce with a finger. He set it before the young man. "Roy." Setting a second carton before the other man he said, "Leo. Leo, *comprendez*?" Norman pointed at himself and said, "Norman," then back at him. "Leo."

Uncertainly he repeated, "Leo. Norman."

Norman pointed at the woman. "You're Libby now."

The look on her pale face would have disquieted a person more in tune with human feeling. When she spoke it was first to Leo, in Italian. When she turned back to him, she managed to reduce Norman's choice of new names for them to a request she'd decided to grant. "I agree, Mr. Bohn. We are not who we once were, and it is best if we accept it. If not, we may be even more unhappy in the future than we are at this moment."

***

1967

Leo and Roy began watching for the Ballerina Girl. Every day she wandered the Loop and the lakeshore, searching for someone. Once in a while she spoke to a woman on the street, always one with dark hair. None of them stopped for long, though some seemed sympathetic. A couple of them gave her money. Others seemed angry and shooed her away, and one even grabbed her by the arm and gave her a good talking-to before stalking off. Every day at about 5:00 p.m., she took up a post outside the museum, near their alley.

"Waitin' on Memnet," Roy told Leo, who nodded in agreement. Around 6:30, when the downtown emptied of workers, the girl would go off, always dispirited but always back the next day.

On Thursday, a chance came Roy couldn't pass up. As he was leaving the alley, a slight scuff drew his attention. Looking up, he saw the girl climbing the museum steps. She entered the huge double doors confidently, as if she'd done it before. After a moment's thought, Roy turned around and went back to the secret door. On the street she'd consider him a threat, but inside, as a fellow patron, he might strike up a conversation and find out what the child wanted with Memnet.

Negotiating the interior steps, which were not kept as clear as the fire marshal recommended, he waited until the hallway was empty and slipped into the back corridor. Down the hall, after a short wait by a second door, he stepped out into the central court. A guard, Perkins, it looked like, stood with his back to him. Roy ducked into an exhibit and gazed with apparent interest at the Plains Indians who, being mannequins, ignored him. When the guard wandered off, Roy went looking for the kid.

The main floor consisted of an open central area dotted with cases displaying items visitors weren't allowed to touch: weapons, armor, and themed collections with titles like *Women's Headwear of the Early 1900s.* Arranged around it were dozens of small rooms, each set up to represent a typical home for an era of history, such as a pueblo, a cave dwelling, or an early American living room. Instead of simply looking at displays, as patrons of other museums did, visitors at the Schmidt became part of the exhibits. In the Roman room they could recline on a bench and imagine what attending a feast might be like. In the medieval section, they took their places at the high table and looked down on the poor slobs below the salt. It was part drama, part history, part fun.

Roy found the girl at a display of armor and weaponry in the main hall. The third of six large cases set in a row along the center of the building, it was Roy's favorite spot for rumination. Sometimes at night he sat before the case on a padded bench, thinking about the people who'd wielded and yielded to the various instruments of death. He could almost hear the shouts, grunts, and cries of battle, the seeking and taking of life.

Leo liked all the exhibits. Memnet always headed for the Egyptian room, and Libby clung to anything English. Roy pondered weapons. "Man's the only creature who creates diabolical devices for getting rid of other men," he would remind them. "It is a lesson to sit there and study on it."

The kid stood in front of a complete suit of armor. No more than thirteen, slim to the point of skinny, her dark hair went all directions in the back, like it does when a person gets up and goes in the morning without using a comb. Careful not to spook her, Roy entered silently and stood facing the display case. After a while he observed, "Can't imagine anybody wantin' to wear that stuff." His voice sounded false, but he wasn't used to talking to kids.

She didn't answer.

"*Armor, unknown knight, c. 1300,*" he read. "Guess he wasn't much of a fighter. No dents."

She glanced at him. "It's ceremonial, worn for parades and

stuff. They didn't fight in it."

"Really? It's just for looks?"

Warming to the subject, she pointed. "See those curlicues and designs? In real fighting, they'd catch hold of a sword or lance point and knock a man off his horse."

"You know a lot about armor."

"My teacher gave me a book about it." The soft voice indicated surprise at the gift. How many things had ever been given to her? Not many, he guessed.

"Did you tell her you liked it?"

"I don't—" she reconstructed mid-sentence. "I don't have that teacher anymore." Having avoided both truth and school in his youth, Roy guessed she'd ditched school, possibly for good.

"Look, little lady, I don't want to stick my nose into your business, but maybe it's time you went home. Your momma and daddy are probably worried sick."

"There isn't anyone." Staring at the unknown knight's shell, she squared her thin shoulders. "I'm staying with friends." Her voice sounded weak, the words disjointed. "They're expecting me."

The girl bent to pick up her bag from the floor, and he saw that her face had gone pale. When she stood straight again, her brown eyes looked glassy. Teetering, she tried desperately to maintain her balance, but her eyes rolled back. Quickly Roy stepped forward and caught her as she fainted into his outstretched arms.

***

Stoneface spoke softly into the pay phone, his eyes scanning the bar for anyone who might be listening. The place was almost empty, and even the jukebox was silent. "Meet me outside Trader Vic's around ten. He'll be a little drunk. Join us like you're an old friend of mine."

There was a question from the other end. "Don't sweat it. He knows me, so he won't suspect anything. Once we get him to the park, it'll be easy. We have to do it tonight, though, before he meets the people he'll be working with." Repeating the time and place again, he hung up and returned to the bar. There was time for a drink before he met with the others. He was sure they'd be pleased with his progress.

Chapter Five

Roy thought it through, the way he always did when the unexpected happened. The kid didn't seem to be hurt, and he suspected she didn't want the attention a call for help would attract. A glance told him there was no one nearby.

Picking her up, he ducked through the door marked *No Admittance* he'd come in through a few minutes earlier. The corridor behind it smelled of dust and bleach. Setting his burden down near the stairway door, he peered at the girl's face. His gut said she'd fainted from hunger.

Her eyelids fluttered then opened, and she moaned softly.

"How long has it been since you had anything to eat?"

She mumbled, "Lunchtime yesterday, maybe."

"No dinner? No breakfast this morning? What'd you eat yesterday?"

"I had...chips and a Pepsi and some ice cream. For calcium." Recognition dawned. "You're the Cowboy."

On the streets, Roy's outfit had earned him the nickname. Some teased that he looked like Roy Rogers, but he liked his long-sleeved, double-breasted shirt in suede, the tight-legged jeans, the western hat, and boots. The girl's expression betrayed a negative opinion.

"You scared me there for a minute."

Panic flickered in her eyes, and he knew what she was thinking. She'd fainted in his arms, and had he called for help? No. Instead, he'd carried her into a service corridor.

"I found a quiet spot until we see if you're okay," Roy explained. "I figured you might be avoiding somebody."

Her expression remained wary. "I have these spells a lot." Raising herself onto her elbows she added, "My friends are probably wondering where I am."

Roy gave her a wry smile. "Don't kid a kidder." Her feet shifted on the floor as if she might be getting ready to run. "You've been alone on the streets for at least a week, stopping women and asking for help. It hasn't worked out so far, right?"

Her answer was a shrug. Accustomed to reading faces across a poker table, he guessed she figured it was okay to admit that much.

She tried to sit, put a hand out to steady herself, and made it on the second attempt. "I'll leave your friend alone, Mister."

"What do you want her for?"

Turning her eyes away, she spoke to the floor beside him. "I need someone to pretend to be my aunt for just a little while. I asked the Arab lady because she looks like me."

"You want Memnet to pretend to be a relative of yours?"

You're a little slow, her frown said. "There's insurance money, but I can't get it because I'm just a kid." She licked her lips. "I'd pay her. Will you tell her that?"

It was a relief to know her purpose had nothing to do with their secrets. "Let's get this straight. Your parents died and left you money?"

"My grandfather did, but they'll only turn it over to an adult, like a guardian."

"Won't they find you somebody like that if you ask 'em?"

She shook her head. "I had a friend that went into foster care. The people made her baby-sit their brats while they spent her money on themselves."

Though Roy didn't know much about the current system, he guessed she might be right. Foster care was often iffy for kids.

The girl's hands formed fists. "I took care of my mom when she was dying, and now I can live on my own!"

Though she indeed looked like Memnet's little sister, the child had developed mental armor Memnet never would. Still there was about her the same aura, the sense that evil could hurt but never vanquish her.

Roy sat back on his haunches, settling his hat more comfortably. "Where you been sleeping?"

"In the El station." Another lie, but he didn't call her on it.

"Little lady, you need something to eat and a place to rest. If you'll sit right here for a couple of minutes, I'll get you some food. Do you like root beer?" She nodded blankly. "Root beer, then, and a safe place to sleep. Is that a deal?"

"I guess so."

"You won't run away? Promise?"

"Promise."

"Spit on your hand."

"What?"

"Spit on your hand. I spit on mine, and then we shake. It's an Indian promise."

She did it, but what he thought would amuse her seemed to disgust her instead. With a final assurance he'd be right back, Roy went down the stairway, past a second warning sign: *This Area*

Not Accessible to Visitors. He took the stairs too fast, but Roy was not the type to stumble, like Norman had.

***

October 29, 1965

Hearing the crash on the stairs at three a.m., they left the storeroom, the two men first, the redhead behind them, and the confused Egyptian girl last. Down the metal steps were strewn a dozen or so cans of food, some blankets, four toothbrushes, a clock, and a small table radio, the cord of which they later theorized was the cause of Norman's fall.

On the landing was the man who'd brought them to the Schmidt and made them his prisoners. His head lay at an impossible angle.

"Is he dead?" the redhead asked.

The older man felt Norman's carotid artery. *"Muerte,"* he confirmed.

They stood in the dimly-lit corridor, looking at each other in confusion. So much for Norman's plan, even if they'd been willing to go along with it. Finally, Libby ordered, "Take the things he was carrying into the storeroom. They'll find his body tomorrow, but they mustn't know what he was doing here."

***

1967

Roy rummaged through the stored food, picking out an apple, some cheese, and a bottle of root beer. Searching the cutlery box for an opener, he told the others about his encounter. Popping the top off the soda with a sharp hiss, he faced them inquiringly.

"So what do you think?"

43

"About what?"

"Do I bring her down here?"

Libby fairly bristled. "You can't! We'd be exposed."

"She's just a kid, Lib."

"Our goal is remain stay hidden. You can't endanger that."

"She won't tell on us. She's hiding out too."

"We avoid outsiders to minimize our risk. You can't bring one into our very home."

"She could help," Roy argued. "Explain things we need to know."

"She could also sell us to the nearest policeman." Libby's lips barely parted as she spoke. "I will not be imprisoned again, Roy. I couldn't bear it!"

"I don't want to go back either, Libby. But this girl won't make it on her own." He tried an argument he knew would affect her. "Her mother's dead."

Libby's expression became slightly less belligerent. "Perhaps we could blindfold her."

"And walk her through the streets of Chicago that way?" Leo said with a chuckle. "She'll know where she is because she knows where she is now." He stood up and put aside his book. "Roy and I will talk to her. If we think she can be trusted, do we have your permission to bring her here?"

"It's dangerous." Despite the words, her tone registered defeat.

"Perhaps Fate is telling us it's time to move," Leo said. "We've discussed it for months."

"We need time to plan." Libby looked at the room that was both a prison and a haven.

Leo offered a compromise. "We'll tell her she must stay with us until we're ready to leave. Once we have made our plans, she may do as she pleases."

"One big job, we'd have all the money we need to get a new start," Roy interjected.

For once, Leo didn't contradict him. If they left the Schmidt, they'd need money. "We'll discuss it later. Let's get the girl down here before the shift changes." He turned again to Libby. "You agree?"

She nodded stiffly. Memnet gave no opinion, nor was she asked.

As things turned out it didn't matter, for when they got to the main floor, the girl was gone.

Chapter Six

Having outsmarted the man she'd renamed "Crazy Cowboy," Jake hefted her bag and left the museum. From the shelter of a doorway, she watched to see if the nut came after her. He didn't, but she remained for a moment, looking fondly at the old building. With the chance that Cowboy might be waiting, she could never return, so she gave the Schmidt a nod of goodbye. It had long been her favorite place to spend free time. While her friends liked the art museum, the Field, or Science and Industry, the Schmidt's unique aim was to present everyday life in various historical periods. It was there Jake imagined the thing she most wanted, a real home.

Her first visit had been with her fifth grade class. While some scoffed at the dull theme ("I can look at tables and chairs at home," one girl remarked), Jake loved picturing herself in each era. Reality was a series of awful places with nothing lovable about them, but at the Schmidt she conjured families for herself from the mannequins in the displays. Looking into their eyes, she made up conversations. "How was school today, Jerilyn?" the tall Nordic man would ask.

"Fine, Daddy," she would answer. "I got an A in ice skating."

"Of course you did." He would smile, and Jake would move on to the next exhibit.

Since that first time, she'd often returned on the museum's free student day, the third Thursday of each month. It had been something to look forward to, but she could never go back now. *Spit on your hand! Ick!*

The building beside her had a sign she hadn't seen before,

identifying a newly formed agency for social progress: *B.R.I.C.K.* Looking closer, she saw that stood for "Building Relations in Cooperative Kindness." A smaller sign under the big one claimed: *Employment and community-building activities for people of all races.*

What about kids with no home? Jake thought miserably. *Can you make them pay me my money? Can you give me back my mother?*

Checking once more to be sure Cowboy wasn't coming after her, she headed toward her most recent unsatisfactory home, Grant Park. Once there, she sat on the bench she'd come to think of as hers and pondered what to do. What if Cowboy followed? The park was big, more than 300 acres. Maybe he'd forget about her. There were plenty of other girls to harass. Still, the encounter bothered her. He was too nice, too weird.

In the end, she judged it best to spend the rest of the day out of sight. Choosing a large spirea bush whose branches spread out like an umbrella, she scooted under it, finding shade from the sun as well as a screen from visibility.

Jake was a regular borrower from the public library, though the staff there didn't know it. Since the windows were opened in good weather, she often went in, located a book she liked, set it on a ground-level sill, and left, retrieving the book from outside. She returned the pilfered items by the same method, so no one knew they'd ever been missing. In Jake's opinion, her shelving experience should entitle her to a job as a librarian, but like the insurance money, her age prevented even asking.

This week her book of choice was *Rebecca*, recommended by the teacher she'd mentioned to Cowboy. She was fascinated by the nameless heroine, sweet but treated badly by Mrs. Danvers.

Jake wondered why Max didn't do something about it, but maybe Max was like the father she'd never met, outwardly caring but selfish underneath.

Pausing, Jake thought how nice it would be to discuss Max with Miss Karsten. She'd sensed the teacher liked talking with her about books, even though she had lots of students to talk to.

"Jerilyn," she'd said one day as the students left the classroom, "have you read this one?" She handed her a copy of *Jane Eyre*. "I think you'll enjoy it, since you read on a higher level than most."

"Thanks." Jake opened the book to scan the first lines. "I'll get it back to you in a few days."

Miss Karsten smiled. "No hurry, but I know you will." She began putting papers into a folder on the desk, but stopped as Jake turned to go. "You know, doing well in school can make up for a lot of...other things in life that aren't so great."

"Thanks," Jake repeated, embarrassed at the teacher's perception.

"Don't neglect other homework while you keep up with Jane's activities," Miss Karsten said with mock sternness. "I know you'd rather read than do math."

Jake grinned. Jokes were easier to take than pity. "Okay, I'll do the dumb story problems too."

School was easy for Jake, but she did no more than she had to. Teachers often urged her to "achieve her potential." Jake listened politely, but her mind asked, *What for?* No matter how smart she might become, she was a kid from the projects who looked different, not American.

As she settled under the bush with her novel, she wondered

if anyone, even Miss Karsten, had asked why she didn't return for the new school year. No great loss, Jake told herself, settling her hips more comfortably. Now she could read all day. No questions about fractions or the laws of gravity.

The marital difficulties of the de Winter family sped the day, and when Jake shut the book and looked around, traffic had picked up. *After five*, she guessed. *Everyone's heading home.*

She missed home, though it hadn't been much. She hadn't had to worry about strange men abducting her, and there'd always been something to eat. The Great Society would take care of them, Mom claimed, and it had, until she died. "Why can't I get ADC?" she muttered. "I'm a dependent child, and I need aid." Jake shook herself. *Great. Now I'm talking to myself.*

She felt weak, like she might pass out again. Must have picked up a bug somewhere. It wasn't easy to keep clean in the park, and she probably should eat better, even if it meant spending precious cash. "I'll buy some milk and a sandwich, maybe even dessert," she announced to no one in particular.

When she stood up, there was Crazy Cowboy, coming right toward her. If she'd stayed in her hiding spot a minute longer, he'd have walked right by.

His face registered recognition, but Jake took off like a shot, running as fast as she could toward the crowd heading for the trains, buses, and parking lots. Behind her she heard him yell, "Hey! Hey, miss!" but she ran on, legs pumping. With energy born of panic, she sped all the way to Eighth Street before looking back. He wasn't behind her. Leaning against a building, she gulped air in huge gasps until her breathing slowed to normal.

No returning to Grant, then. She'd have to head north, up to Lincoln Park. It was less familiar, but she had to get away from that pervert.

With a sinking feeling, Jake realized she didn't have her bag. Everything she owned was in it, including her money. Slumping to the pavement, she considered her options. When darkness fell, she'd have to go back and get the bag from under the bush. *Then,* she promised herself, silently this time, *I'll get something to eat and get out of downtown.*

***

The girl had become an obsession for Roy. "Leo," he said, "she's alone, hungry, scared, and in trouble unless somebody helps her out. I am plannin' for us to be somebody."

Leo regarded his young friend obliquely, thinking he wasn't as tough as he tried to act. Still, Leo recalled feeling sorry for the pretty little waif himself that first day.

They split up to search, Leo north of Roosevelt and Roy south. When Leo returned to the Field Museum, he found Roy out front, hands on his knees and out of breath. "Spotted her," he said between pants, "but I lost her in the crowd." As his breathing slowed he added, "She's not done for yet."

"Shall we return home?"

"You go ahead. I'll take a look at her hidey hole and maybe find out who she is or where she comes from."

"I'll come along. I hate to think of the child alone on these streets as the good weather fades." Leo gestured at the leaves, their green beginning to go gold at the edges. Mowers growled across the park grass, possibly for the last time this year.

Returning to the sprawling spirea bush, they found the bag with the ballerina embroidered on it. Roy looked inside—ill-mannered, Leo thought, but necessary for the girl's own good.

The bag held a book, two pairs of white cotton underwear, a chewed pencil, a pad with some notes scribbled on it, a round cardboard tube of Evening in Paris talcum powder, and fifty-three dollars and change.

"She will come back for this," Roy said. "On the street, it's a lot of money."

"Imagine Libby's reaction if she knew we had it for the taking."

Busy scanning the park, Roy ignored Libby's opinion. "I'll wait for her."

Clearing his throat Leo said diplomatically, "Perhaps I should do it. She seems to be afraid of you."

Roy grudgingly accepted the logic of that. "You might be right."

Leo took a seat on the grass. "Go home. Tell the women what happened. I'll wait and have a try at speaking to her."

Roy sighed. "I suppose an older man is less scary." As he turned toward the Schmidt, scanning the park, Leo smiled. For the first time he was aware of, Roy's charm had failed him.

***

At the museum Roy proposed a plan that Libby opposed, as he'd expected. "She's not our concern."

"I've scared her twice now. I just want her to know we'd like to help."

"We can't even help ourselves, lackwit! When she tires of the streets, she can go home or go to one of the agencies that help runaway children in this city."

Memnet, who never injected herself into conversations,

made a surprising statement. "If I speak to her, it is best." Picking up her jacket, she faced them, apparently ready to argue her case.

Roy was ashamed he hadn't thought of it. "Of course! You can tell her we're friends."

Looking from one of them to the other, Libby opened her mouth to argue. Then, in the phenomenon that was always Libby, she changed tactics. "We'll all go," she announced in a tone that warned against disagreement. "Memnet will calm the girl's fears and introduce me. I will convince her to go to the authorities. Once she is safe, Memnet can go back to work, and you can stop fussing about one waif among the hundreds roaming these streets unsupervised. Life can return to normal."

It was the best he could hope for. Pulling on his own jacket and taking up Leo's, Roy promised himself that somehow he'd make sure the girl got decent foster parents.

***

Leo stood as his friends approached, Roy in a deep brown, fringed leather jacket that swayed with his cowboy walk, the hat "borrowed" from a museum display, and the stitched leather boots he'd got in a trade with a hobo from the train yard. "Almost certainly stolen," Libby had sniffed, but she admitted they were fine boots. Roy never said what he contributed to the deal, and it had no doubt been museum property, but Leo simply couldn't watch him all the time.

Memnet wore a corduroy jacket over her colorful skirt, and her arm bangles jingled softly as she approached. Libby's clothing was so dark she almost appeared disembodied in the dusk, her white face and hands the only parts of her visible.

Roy had brought Leo's overcoat. "Warmth is welcome after dark," Leo said, "and it will hide my white shirt as well."

"We aren't exactly inconspicuous as long as Roy is around." Libby's tone was acidic.

"If I wasn't willin' to be noticed," Roy answered, "you'd have starved to death that first month. I helped you, and I am determined to help this girl."

"But you understand that we must remain anonymous."

"Yes. Now stop fussin'." He set the girl's bag under the bush where they'd found it.

"I wish he were more reasonable," Libby said through clenched teeth.

"It is his nature to be flamboyant." Leo scanned the area, looking around for a place they could hide.

"I appreciate flamboyance," Libby replied, "but there is a time for it. By his own admission he deserves hanging, and he seems determined to take the rest of us along."

Leo shrugged, Roy ignored her, and Memnet said nothing, as usual. Libby made a noise of disgust and went silent.

Grant Park stretched along Lake Michigan from the Loop to Roosevelt Road. Though respectable people avoided the park after sundown unless there was a scheduled event, it was peaceful tonight. After the closed-in feel and concrete hardness of the city streets, it was pleasant to walk among trees and feel soft grass underfoot. The breeze swept away the smells of traffic and the sounds of the El rattling around the downtown, and though Navy Pier blocked the view of the lake to the left, it was calming to think that beyond it there was nothing but water for two hundred miles.

Leo located an anemic clump of trees on the stadium's north side. "Here. We can observe her hiding spot unseen."

Settled in to wait, they munched on cheese Memnet had thoughtfully brought along to serve as supper. They spoke quietly, each keeping lookout in a different direction. Libby fussed about the cold, about the discomfort of being squashed together, and again brought up the perils of sticking their noses into someone else's business. Sensing Roy was about to tell her off Leo said, "If you want to return home then go, but I think we must be quiet or she will hear us and stay away."

Libby, who seldom argued with Leo, lapsed again into wounded silence. Their end of the park went quiet and dark. Lights came on, but their incandescence, aimed at the street, didn't penetrate their hiding place. Soldier Field retreated into stark shadows, no event there tonight. Cooler evenings had banished the crowds who came in summer to watch the Buckingham Fountain light show. When no one came through the park for almost thirty minutes, Libby made one more grumbling comment. "We should have worn warmer clothes."

Roy, whose hearing rivaled that of a wild animal, hissed, "Quiet!"

Someone moved toward them, but it wasn't the girl. Three adult shapes approached from Michigan Avenue, the two on the outside leaning toward the one in the center as if propelling him. The man might have been ill, but it soon became obvious he was a prisoner. Leo looked at Roy, faintly visible in the darkness next to him. What should they do?

The question was settled before they could act. The center man pushed both arms outward with great force. His captors staggered backward, and he broke free and ran toward the lake.

The path he took was a poor choice, because in seconds he was silhouetted against the shoreline. One of the men raised both hands, feet spread. A sharp report sounded, and the running man crumpled like a stricken deer.

Although the sound echoed across the water, the traffic noise from the street went on uninterrupted. Memnet let out a whimper of dismay, but Roy put a warning hand on her shoulder. Beside Leo, Libby held her breath, as he found himself doing. It was hard to take in what they'd seen. Leo was familiar with war, sickness, and death, but this was murder.

"Now what do we do?" The second man had stopped not ten feet from their hiding place. The other bent over the still form and checked for signs of life. Apparently there were none.

"What we planned to," he said, standing upright again. "We get rid of the body in the lake, and we go home. He just shortened things by a few minutes."

"What if somebody heard the shot?"

"Do you see anyone?"

After a hesitation, "No."

"What are the bums in the park going to do, run to a pay phone, put in their last dime, and say, 'Officer, I'm a non-tax-paying citizen, and I just heard a gunshot'? They'll roll over in their bug-infested blankets and pretend they heard nothing. Now let's finish this."

He was right. No one in the park at this hour was likely to attempt a citizen's arrest.

Looking over Roy's shoulder, Leo saw movement and pointed. Against the skyline, a slight figure approached. Head down, the girl staggered directly into the path of the killers, who'd begun dragging their victim toward the water.

Roy was up and gone in an instant. Realizing his intention,

Leo followed, unsure of the plan but unwilling to let Roy face danger alone.

The strangers paused when they saw the girl teetering toward them. As Leo and Roy crossed the grass, her slight body relaxed, and she fell to the ground like a stuffed doll. A moment of confusion allowed the rescuers to cover the open space, and they hit their targets almost simultaneously.

Scrambling to his feet, Leo felt something bump against his shoe and realized it was the shooter's gun, sent spinning away by the force of Roy's attack. He gave it a kick before his man recovered his feet and came at him like an angry bull.

Roy knew more about knocking people around than Leo did, and he went to work, pummeling the larger man with his fists. Leo hit his opponent in the neck with the side of his flattened hand, as he'd seen in Hai Karate commercials, but the man staggered back a step and came at him, head down. Leo delivered a two-fisted blow to the back of his head, as he'd seen the man from U.N.C.L.E. do. His opponent went down but almost immediately got back to his feet. *A lesson,* Leo told himself. *Do not accept what television portrays as realistic battle.* As the man came at Leo again, he prepared himself for a real fist-fight, the first of his life.

For several minutes, grunts and other sounds of violence testified to the four-man struggle. Each was knocked to the ground at least once, each managed to recover and rejoin the fray. Leo heard Memnet's cries and Libby's encouragements, but he had little time to think as he parried his adversary's blows. After a time he made a discovery: the man relied on weight and aggressiveness rather than any real fighting skills.

Knowing he couldn't outlast the much younger man, Leo

decided he had to end the matter as quickly as possible. Dropping his hands as if exhausted, he waited until his foe rushed in to finish him off. With a quick movement to the side, he avoided the clenched fist, letting the man's momentum carry him into a solid punch to the jaw. When he went to the ground this time, Leo's foe remained there.

Roy's man was more skilled and more intelligent. In the glow of a security light, Leo saw clearly that he was the one who'd shot his prisoner dead. Roy struck him squarely in the face, a stunning blow, but the man took it and returned one every bit as forceful.

Both men stood reeling, their breath coming in gasps. Roy's opponent crouched low, minimizing his target area and sizing up the possibilities for defeating him. They were evenly matched in size, but something in the man's face revealed a lack of humanity Roy couldn't match. This man would fight to win, and nothing would be held back.

Knowing there was no such thing as a fair fight in this situation, Leo tipped the scales in his friend's favor by shouting, "The police!" The man's attention wavered for a split second, and Roy launched a fierce uppercut that lifted him onto his toes, sending him to the ground with a soft plop.

As they stood panting over their prone adversaries, the women joined them. "Clever, Leo," Libby cheered, her orneriness overcome by the adventure.

Memnet touched the blood on Roy's lip, but he wiped it on his sleeve. "It's nothin'. See to the girl."

She bent over the unconscious form. "She breathes okay."

"Lights coming this way," Leo whispered.

They looked in the direction he indicated, where two

flashlights floated across the grassy center of the park. "It could be friends of these two," Libby whispered.

"Whoever it is, we don't want to talk to them," Roy said in low tones. "I'll lead them off while you get the girl out of here. I'll circle back home when I lose them. Got it?"

"All right." Leo lifted the girl onto his shoulders. Staying low, he moved north, along the lakeshore, while Roy, with a series of cow-calling whoops, set off in the opposite direction. Answering shouts indicated police rather than criminals behind the flashlights. "You there, stop!" Thankfully there was no shooting.

Libby was not with them, which caused Leo concern, but she soon caught up. "I retrieved the bag," she whispered, obviously proud of herself. It was indeed an accomplishment, Leo acknowledged, for a woman who'd spent decades with servants to bring her anything she wanted.

Chapter Seven

For the second time that day, Jake woke to strange surroundings. She lay on blanket-draped cushions on the floor of a narrow room, small and empty of furniture. At the opposite end, another pile of cushions formed a second odd bed. Each cushion-bed had a small stack of items beside it. Near her were a brightly-patterned shawl, a sewing basket, and a small transistor radio. By the other bed were books and a battered wooden chest. Along the wall between, neatly stacked boxes had labels like *Dishes* and *Pots*. Items of women's clothing hung from several nails, and a few feet off the floor to her right, a tiny door like something from Alice in Wonderland stood open.

Beside Jake sat a glass of red liquid and something wrapped in cloth. She sat up slowly, testing her balance, and looked inside. Two chocolate chip cookies. Sticking a finger into the liquid, she tasted it suspiciously. Strawberry Kool-Aid. If she was the prisoner of perverts, the food might be drugged, but she was so hungry it didn't matter. The cookies were delicious, the Kool-Aid a little sour but drinkable.

Food gave Jake the strength to stand. Though wobbly, she took the few steps needed to reach the little door. A tentative peek into the next room was, as school friends would have termed it, a trip.

The room was huge, with pipes and exposed ductwork running all over the unfinished ceiling. It held an amazing variety of stuff: a huge Chinese cabinet, missing a door; six chairs of deteriorating rattan; an old refrigerator; lamps of many styles, some electrical, some not; and other pieces of furniture she couldn't identify.

The weirdest part was closest to her. Four heavy chairs covered with ratty velvet or tapestry fabric were arranged facing each other. Against the wall was an old refrigerator, and a television set atop a sagging bookshelf. It looked like a scene from *The Addams Family*.

People occupied three of the chairs: an old lady with a pale face and reddish hair, a man who looked like Charlton Heston grown old, and the dark-eyed woman she'd been trying to find for a week. They looked up at some sound she'd made, and two of them smiled. The old lady's expression conveyed distrust, maybe dislike.

The young woman rose, indicating Jake should take the fourth seat. She obeyed, and the woman returned to the chair beside her, setting aside the sewing she'd been working on.

"Where am I?" Jake asked.

"In the basement of the Schmidt Museum." The old man acted as spokesman. Putting down his book, he made a graceful, calming gesture. "No one here will harm you." He said "one-a" and "harm-a," like the guy in the deli near the projects. A foreigner. Didn't Mafia guys have accents like that?

"Why?" A dumb question, but she had to say something.

"We live here." It came out "live-a," almost musical.

"You'll have to stay here now." The old lady's tone was imperious and unfriendly, and she made no eye contact with Jake. "You can't tell anyone." She sounded foreign too, but not like Mafia. Her words were clipped, and she spoke without moving her chin very much. She didn't move anything, but sat very straight, like she had a metal spine. If Jake felt like Alice, this was the Red Queen, for sure.

Curiouser and curiouser. She was the prisoner of crazy people who lived in the basement of her favorite museum. But was the park any better? Winter loomed, and this might be a chance to escape freezing to death. Choosing her words carefully, Jake spoke to the old lady, sensing her acceptance was crucial. "I'd like to stay for a while. I haven't anywhere else."

The lemony face didn't warm, but the old man tried to offset her chilly reception. "Well, then. I am Leo. This is Libby, and Memnet. We are waiting for Roy, who won't be long."

"We hope," the old lady said, glancing at Jake to indicate the absence was her fault.

"Roy?"

"The gentleman from before, the one in the hat?"

Jake tensed, and Leo hurried to reassure her. "Roy approached you in the museum because he feared you had discovered our private entrance."

"Entrance?" She caught on and turned to Memnet. "So that's where you went!"

"Leo make a door no one can see." She had a heavy accent, but her voice was soft and low. If Jake waited a second to let the words sink in, the meaning came through.

"He must be very clever," she replied, and the woman, Memnet, smiled.

Though Jake had always seen her in sandals, tonight she wore scuffed penny loafers with gym socks. Seeing Jake's glance, she explained, "My feet cold down here."

Jake felt oddly at home with these people. Like her, they

were outside normal society. And like her, they did what was required to survive. "I've been wearing the same underwear for a week," she confessed, then blushed to have said it. The man and the young woman smiled again.

"You are welcome to our home," Leo said, waving a hand.

"It's not our *home*," the old lady interrupted. Jake had forgotten her name but decided she was a pain, always snapping at people. "If we *could* go home, we'd leave straightaway."

"But this is what we have," Leo said gently.

She made an impatient gesture. "Then she must be taught the rules, Leo." She turned to Jake and added emphatically, "and she must pay strict attention to them."

Once again Leo lessened the sting of the woman's blatant animosity. "Let me show you our secrets." He offered his arm. Having seen the gesture in movies, she put her hand on it like Audrey Hepburn would.

"We hide all this when necessary." He pointed to a bell in one corner. "That rings when someone starts down the stairs. When that happens, we disappear."

"The chairs are pushed together, two atop the others." The old lady's tone was peremptory. "The refrigerator is emptied and unplugged. If we were interrupted now, you would help with that."

"That's improbable at present, since it's the middle of the night." Leo opened the door to the hallway. "Down there is a small toilet, which Memnet will show you when you are ready. I'm afraid it looks a bit uninviting, but we dare not clean it lest someone might wonder how it happened. Upstairs is our door to the alley, our means of coming and going from this place."

"She wouldn't be able to open it," the woman said. Being spoken of as if she weren't there was beginning to irritate Jake. The old bag didn't want her there, but it wasn't like she'd asked to come.

"Someday, I will show you the secret," Leo said. Him, she liked. "See how we hide our rooms."

Between where she'd slept and the main room was the window-like door she'd exited earlier. When Leo closed it, the door disappeared behind a gaudy painting. Smiling, Leo moved a few feet farther along the wall and released a catch behind a second painting. Another door opened that Jake would never have known was there. Behind it was a room similar to the first with cushions and boxes. A man's hat hung on the wall. The room she'd occupied smelled of soap. This one had a different scent, cigars and the earthy smell of men.

"You sleeping in our room," Memnet told Jake. "I gather lot of more pillows."

"I brought your bag from the park," the older woman announced. From her tone Jake sensed she wanted recognition for the effort.

Whatever her faults, Jake's mother had taught her daughter good manners. "Thank you, ma'am. It was nice of you to think of me."

The woman's face underwent a transformation at the compliment, and Jake glimpsed behind the anger a woman who yearned to be appreciated.

"I know you didn't ask me to come here," Jake said. "But I'll keep your secret. I don't tell on people, especially friends." The woman said nothing, but she made no further comments as Leo completed the tour, showing Jake how they hid the television by rolling a dresser in front of it.

When they returned to the chairs Memnet asked, "You found the food, yes?"

"The cookies were great." At Jake's enthusiastic tone, the old lady sniffed.

"Libby is our cook," Leo said. "Roy found her a small device called a toaster oven." Leo pronounced the unfamiliar words carefully. "She does wonders with it."

"Come and see what is." Memnet was gently insistent. "Something you will like." She pulled open a drawer in a three-legged dresser propped on the fourth side with books, and Jake saw an array of foods wrapped in foil, cellophane, and even cloth. Pulling out several items, she offered them to Jake, who chose a piece of white cheese and a Hershey bar. The cookies hadn't quite done the trick.

Next Memnet opened the refrigerator. "This was broke but Leo make it go," she said proudly. The top shelf was crowded with bottles of root beer—She recalled Roy's earlier offer—milk, and a bottle of Ripple.

"Terrible quality," Leo scoffed, but Libby had a different opinion.

"No worse than a lot of the stuff I've tasted in my travels."

Jake accepted a root beer, which Memnet uncapped with an opener taken from a different box, and they all watched as she ate and drank. "Are you feeling well?" Leo asked.

"I'm okay now." She really did feel better. Food, warmth, and safety did wonders for a girl.

Leo recounted what had happened in the park, but Jake didn't remember.

"I was concentrating on putting one foot in front of the other," she recalled. "I didn't even see the men. You say they killed someone?"

"Yes, but the police arrived," Leo replied. "They will find the body and arrest the killers."

Footsteps sounded on the metal stairway, and Cowboy, Roy, as Jake now knew him, entered. The others were happy he'd escaped his pursuers, but she got the feeling they'd assumed he would.

Roy waved carelessly. "Two cops. I led them up Lake Shore Drive then ducked into an alley."

"It is good to know the streets well at night," Leo remarked.

Roy glanced once at the straight-backed Libby, and Jake sensed the subject wasn't a comfortable one. "What I don't know is what happened to those two killers."

"We must discover the answer to that, for our own safety and for this young lady's as well." Leo's face was serious, and Jake thought he actually cared what happened to her. Roy had gone to a lot of trouble to find her. Memnet was kind, and even Libby had helped, bringing her bag along.

They must want something. Even Jake's mother, who'd loved her in a weird way, never spent much time worrying about what her daughter needed or whether she was in danger. Jake had learned caution early on: which of Mom's boyfriends to avoid, which to charm, and which to ignore. She'd also learned to get home early the day the ADC check came, or there'd be no money for bills that month.

These people hardly knew her yet they included her safety in their concerns. And they were going to let her stay with them.

Whatever the price was, she figured she'd get around it. She could always run into the museum and escape if she had to.

"Do you think the police found the body, Roy?" Leo asked.

He shook his head. "I went back to the park. No ambulance, no flashin' lights."

Libby's face drew into a frown. "You two were clearly visible in the lamplight."

"They also saw, uh, what is your name, friend?"

"Jake," she replied.

"Jake?" It sounded like "Jake-eh" as Leo repeated it.

Roy raised an eyebrow. "Your bag says *Property of Jerilyn Kay Marks.*"

"J for Jerilyn, K for Kay, makes it pretty close to Jake."

"I've been known to use a nickname myself, Jake." Roy shook her hand, but this time, she noted with relief, he didn't ask her to spit in it first.

Chapter Eight

The Chicago federal office building hummed with activity as men moved with serious intent to complete their tasks. As the youngest member on staff passed through with a brown paper bag in hand someone asked, "Your new boss eating in his office again, Danner?"

Clay nodded, shifting the bag to his other hand. The smell of fries wafted around him like an aura, and grease stained the bottom of the bag. Glancing at the closed door of Blackburn's office Rhein added, "Does he ever come out of there?"

Clay kept his voice low. "Not very often."

Rhein leaned closer and lowered his voice. "What's with the guy? It's a week now and he hasn't said one word that wasn't absolutely necessary. Is he weird or what?"

"He works hard." Though he wouldn't criticize his superior, Clay had wondered the same thing. Blackburn was taciturn, almost surly, unless the big brass was around. Then he was efficient and respectful, though hardly a barrel of laughs.

Clay figured his boss meant to move up in the Bureau. He obviously thought courtesy was required to those above him in rank and nothing was due those below. Though Clay hoped to move up too, he wasn't as fixated on it as Blackburn appeared to be. Pasting a smile of his face, he knocked lightly on the office door. "Lunch, sir."

***

Jake's first few days in the Schmidt were a mixture of bane and blessing, the bane being Libby. She carped constantly, and though the others seemed used to it and ignored her, Jake resented her pointed comments and the suspicion Libby took no pains to conceal. She tried to make herself useful, hoping the old woman would be grateful. It didn't seem to be working.

One night when she was supposed to be asleep, Jake crept to the door and opened it a crack, curious to hear what they had to say about her. There was discussion of other things, but eventually Roy said, "The kid is good about helpin' out. And she's smart too."

"You mean she enjoys your crude attempts at humor," Libby said with a derisive snort.

"She's always complimenting your cookin'." Roy kept his tone even. "I don't think she ever had much, but she understands about keepin' quiet and helpin' out."

"She's all legs and arms and quite out of control," Libby complained. "Inevitably she'll cause a terrible crash that brings them downstairs to investigate, and we'll all be discovered."

Roy was scornful. "She'll do no such thing."

Memnet spoke, and Jake strained to hear the words. "She is very afraid these weeks. She tell me it is good to be warm and dry and hided away."

Roy's voice took on a rueful note. "After while this place will drive her crazy."

"I don't think she trusts us," Leo put in. "There are truths yet to be told."

"Like how she came to be on the streets?" Libby asked.

Roy shifted his feet to a more comfortable position. "She didn't want to go to foster care when her mother died. That's easy to understand." He paused. "The insurance policy she mentioned.

She might be afraid we mean to steal it from her."

"Do you think she has money?" Libby's tone brightened at the prospect.

"Not likely, or why was she sleepin' in the park?" Roy apparently recalled what she'd told him. "She needs someone to pretend to be an adult relative in order to get it. Since the two of them look alike, Jake thought Memnet might help."

"Let Memnet go to an insurance office and attempt to lie? We could never take such a chance," Libby said firmly.

"No, though I'd help Jake if I could." Leo sounded regretful. "She's seen little good in her life."

"That child deserves some happiness," Roy said. "With her momma dying and her daddy off doin' what he likes."

Jake waited for Libby to disagree. When she heard nothing, she peered around the door to see her staring at the floor, lost in thought. What chord had Roy sounded that left Libby silent?

***

The afternoon of the next day, Roy returned to the museum looking worried. "Barney at the newsstand says someone is asking about Jake."

"I knew it!" Libby exclaimed. "We'll be discovered."

"Who's looking for her?" Leo kept his voice calm, his gaze warning Libby to do the same. Jake moved a step closer to Memnet, who put an arm around her.

"He didn't know. He heard it from someone else."

"Then it might be rumor." Like any community, idle gossip moved among street people. Anything outside their daily tedium was welcome.

"Child welfare? They must know Jake's mother died." Roy turned to Jake, a question in his eyes.

She shrugged. "We had a case worker, but she was so busy I doubt she'd remember me."

"People at the hospital must have known your mother had a daughter."

Jake pressed her lips together, and Roy wondered how much truth she would tell. When she spoke, truth was evident in her flat tone. "When Mom got sick we went to a clinic for people with no money. The doctor there said she'd ruined her health. He said her care would cost the taxpayers a bundle and wouldn't change anything 'cause she'd be dead in six months."

"A physician said that?" For the first time, Libby seemed sympathetic.

"She didn't go back. I took care of her the last two months."

There was silence as they imagined what Jake had gone through in that time. Libby said in a voice softer than before, "Perhaps they want to make up for their mistakes now, child."

"If you don't mind, I'd rather stay here with you," Jake replied. In her face was the plea she couldn't put into words. Roy guessed she'd take further argument as evidence that they, like the Great Society, the health care system, and even her own mother, had no concern for what she wanted.

Leo apparently agreed with Roy. "Of course you will stay," he told Jake. "Those people don't deserve you, and we need your help to improve our knowledge of the city."

Libby touched Jake's arm in a comforting gesture. "Perhaps your mother deserved her fate, but only God has the right to judge her." Roy sensed a shift, an acceptance of Jake according to a standard Libby alone understood. He smiled to himself, guessing the girl's life would be easier now.

"But what if it's someone connected with last night's murder who's looking for Jake?" he asked.

"We must all stay inside for a time," Leo said.

No one disagreed, and after a moment Libby raised a finger. "If we must, then we shouldn't waste the time. An educated woman should be able to read and discuss, cipher, and present a decent meal." She took the sack of food Roy had foraged. "Come, Jake, we shall begin with tonight's supper."

***

Wary at first, Jake concluded by the end of a week that her new friends were an odd combination of honesty and criminality. Though they lived illegally in the Schmidt, Libby railed at Roy if he "lifted" items they didn't need. They avoided the authorities, but on her third night in Storeroom C they all watched *The Untouchables* on TV, rooting for Eliot Ness. They were strange, but she enjoyed their company, even Libby's once she decided to be nice. Libby had read an incredible number of books, and anyone who read that much couldn't be all bad.

Memnet was sweet, Leo was intelligent and kind, and Roy entertained her with long stories of his clever street scams. Because Libby disapproved, he had to wait until she wasn't around to regale Jake with his exploits.

As she relaxed in their company, Jake revealed things that shocked Libby. "That mother was no mother," Libby fumed one evening after Jake had gone to bed, unaware that she was listening in the doorway. "She spent her time in sordid and largely unsuccessful attempts to attract men."

She couldn't see Leo from her vantage point, but she heard his calm response. "Many women feel incomplete without a man in their lives, Libby."

"To the detriment of her child?" A smack to the chair arm gave dusty evidence of Libby's vehemence. "And Jake's father! She says he was an Arab prince, but I say he was a rat fink." Jake heard Leo chuckle at the idiom, so un-like Libby.

"He went back to his homeland," she went on, "and apparently the mother replaced him with a string of deplorable men. It's unconscionable!"

"Libby," Leo said, "There's a woman named Gloria Steinem who'd enjoy conversing with you."

Jake winced at Libby's unflattering picture of her mother. Was that how she seemed to others?

Libby wasn't finished. "Jake has had little the young people of this day have, not even a telephone."

What they knew of teenagers was what they'd seen on television. Jake guessed she was supposed to wear her hair in a ponytail and have a dad who called her Kitten.

"They moved around a lot," Roy said. "Probably stayin' ahead of the bill collectors."

"I took note of that, though she generally exhibits proper behavior."

"She mimics what you do, Libby" Leo said. "She recognizes quality when she sees it."

"I wonder," Libby said with a glance at Roy, "are we proper guides? None of us knows anything about raising adolescent children." She added ruefully, "We're hardly model citizens."

"I don't suppose we have to be saints," Leo said, "as long as Jake knows she matters to us."

"That's true. It's difficult when you matter to no one." Libby's gaze slid aside as if a memory pulled her into the past. "My father admired intellect, so I learned everything set before me, simply in hopes of making him smile."

Leo nodded. "It was much the same with me. We can often turn the trials of our childhood into strengths, like metal purified in fire. Jake may do the same."

"We must see to her education. She reads, but you must tutor her in the sciences as well."

"I'll help," Roy put in.

Libby snorted an unladylike denial. "What could you teach her that won't get her into trouble with the law?"

Roy opened his mouth to protest, but she raised a finger. "The best thing you can do is be discreet about your whoring and gambling. You're a bad example."

For once Roy had no smart-aleck response, and Jake felt sorry for him. She liked his stories and resented the assumption that hearing them would lead her to a life of crime. Roy was just Roy.

She crept back to bed, pleased in a way she'd never felt before. Four adults were focused on helping her become something good. Four was a lot better than none, even if they were a little weird.

***

The next day the four adults listened with interested as Jake explained the public library and how she'd "borrowed" books on many subjects. Leo declared himself eager to try her method.

Libby wondered if they had cookbooks, though she feared Jakes' method was dishonest. Leo said it wasn't, since she put the books back when she was done.

Reading was a part of every day at the Schmidt. Leo's usual material consisted of textbooks. Libby liked variety and sometimes bought books at second hand stores. Roy often stole novels from newsstands. ("And very dubious educational tools they are," Libby opined) Memnet read no English but enjoyed the pictures in *National Geographic*.

That evening Libby told Leo, "The child has read Shakespeare on her own. I tested her on *Romeo and Juliet* with good results."

He grinned. "She's a bit too tilted to fiction for my taste, but the girl has impressive depth of knowledge in certain areas."

"I loaned her my copy of *The Complete Works* and recommended a few favorites." Libby smiled. "Her response was 'Groovy!' which I understand is good."

In fact Jake had sniffed the leather cover appreciatively. "Where'd you get this?"

"Norman gave it to me when I first came here."

"Who's Norman?"

"The man who brought us to the museum."

"He brought you from England?"

Clattering her utensils into a bowl and setting a batch of scones Roy would insist on calling "biscuits" into the little oven, Libby said, "I am English, yes. Norman was responsible for my coming to America. He made it seem a wonderful place, but all I've seen is Chicago."

"Me too, but I've read about a lot of states I'd like to visit, like Florida, Texas, and Washington."

Libby shrugged. "All Norman showed us was this basement."

"Does he come back when you need stuff?"

Wiping her hands on a scrap of cloth, Libby said tersely, "He is dead."

"I'm sorry."

Libby brushed a strand of hair back into place. "I'm not sure that's appropriate," she said. "At times I could have strangled him myself, but his death was disastrous for us."

"Why are you hiding in this place?"

The question was bound to come up sooner or later, and the companions had decided together what the answer would be.

Looking away to conceal the lie in her eyes Libby said, "We are wanted by the police for something we didn't do. Since we can't prove our innocence, we must hide."

"Can't you split up and lose yourselves in the crowd?"

Libby shook herself delicately. "We feel safer together."

Jake nodded. "It's better to have friends around, people you can trust." Hearing that, Libby felt a warmth in her chest she'd never experienced before. Odd, but quite nice.

"We need to finish this. Tonight is *Candid Camera*, the final episode. I find it ludicrous, but Roy and Leo laugh so hard they can hardly sit upright."

***

Roy insisted Jake should keep the money she had left in her bag.

"If something happens and we're caught, you'll need cash to get out of Chicago."

Jake contended she wouldn't duck out on them like that, so they compromised by agreeing that if the time came when the money was essential, they'd use it.

Memnet became their lifeline to the outside world. She continued to go out on warm afternoons and sing in the El station. The killers in the park had not seen her, she insisted, so it was safe. Each evening she brought home food and other things they needed even more now with five people to feed.

Jake was thrilled at Memnet repertoire of songs, learned from listening to an old radio that worked best late at night. She picked up tunes and lyrics easily and knew most of Petula Clark's songs, old standards like "Stardust," and some of the Beatles' slower pieces, though she often didn't know what the words meant. Jake taught her "You've Got to Hide Your Love Away" and claimed Memnet sounded just like the Silky when she sang it. Memnet assumed that was a compliment.

Each week Memnet hand-washed their clothes, and Jake began helping with the chore. There were two large sinks in the janitors' closet up one flight, and they hauled two boxes of clothes there after the guard's midnight patrol. Memnet showed Jake how to add only a little soap, which was hard to get; rinse thoroughly; and wring the items half-dry. Back downstairs, they hung them on ropes strung across the sleeping quarters. As they worked, Memnet's natural shyness faded and the English words came more easily. That was good, since Jake had a hundred questions.

"How come they don't know you're down here?" she asked. "The guards and the staff, I mean."

"They think Leo is writer from Europe. He says he is friend

to Norman, and he promise them copy of book he is to make."

"Norman, that's the guy who died?"

"Yes."

"Why did he bring you here?"

Memnet shook her head. "I don't know this. I cry every night. I can talk to nobody. Leo help me, Libby and Roy too, but I so scared. Norman scare me. Very mad at me, very angry."

"Why?"

"I don't know." Memnet lowered her face, still ashamed and frightened by the vehemence of Norman's anger. Though she didn't really understand, it had to do with who she was. And who she was not.

***

Libby had accepted Jake, though that didn't always keep the girl safe from her sharp tongue. Only Leo escaped the worst of it. Memnet met Libby's tirades with meek acceptance, Roy with a recalcitrance that infuriated her further. Jake learned to appeal to her pride, which might have been termed vanity.

"You guys are clever to have stayed hidden down here for so long," she said one day when Libby chided her crude attempts to peel potatoes. "How do you do it?"

"Leo has Norman's keys, so he can wander the whole place. Being Leo, he found a typewriter and taught himself how to use it. He took stationery from the curator's desk, and now he composes memos to the staff from time to time."

Jake giggled. "Really? He writes to them?"

Libby smiled. "Above a fine copy of Charlene's signature, he informed the staff that Storeroom C has rats."

"To keep them away."

Libby looked around the room. "We intentionally keep the place drab. When the new curator came, she took one look at Storeroom C and never returned."

"Lucky for you."

"Leo can even make the place smell like rotting eggs."

As they swept the concrete floor the next day, she asked Memnet, "Is Leo a forger?"

Memnet stopped in mid-stroke. "We are suspect of a crime we did not commit—" she began.

"Memnet," Jake interrupted, "If you don't want to tell me the truth, okay, but I don't believe you've spent two years hiding from the world because of a misunderstanding. One of you did something that got all of you in trouble, and you don't know how to get out of it. I'm betting it was Roy, but it could have been Leo."

Memnet went back to sweeping as Jake formed a piece of cardboard into a dustpan. "Someday you'll tell me what you're all scared of, and it'll be okay with me, unless you shot JFK."

Memnet smiled weakly. Jake didn't know if her response indicated relief or discomfort, but she hoped they hadn't done anything really bad. She was becoming attached to them, and besides, they were the only people in the world who cared what happened to her.

Chapter Nine

"It was dark," Roy said for the tenth time. "They only saw shadows."

"Best to be safe," Leo said firmly. "One more day inside."

Roy had become more and more anxious. "I need to know I can leave a place, walk around, and return when I want. Jail does that to a fellow."

Still, Leo was usually right. They'd watched the TV news, and Memnet brought in several days' newspapers, but there was no mention of a murder near the lake. In fact, no death was reported that could have been the man they'd seen shot. The news focused on the death of Che Guevara, killed in South America by soldiers of the Bolivian army. Roy admired his last words, "Shoot, cowards, you're only going to kill a man."

"He sounds like someone I'd have liked," he said, "but to die in Bolivia would be a terrible thing, what with the snakes and the heat and all."

"Really, Roy!" Libby said sharply. "We need to know what became of the corpse we saw *here*."

"I wish we could have arranged their capture," Leo said for the tenth time.

"They were cool customers," Roy said. "At least the one was. Not many men can hit a running target with one shot. Aside from me, of course."

"I hope we never meet him again. It was dark, but we can't take the chance that he could recognize either of us. That murder was meant to be undiscovered."

"It was their bad luck that we were in the park." Libby shivered at the memory.

"Ours as well." Leo's smile was grim. "They must know by now we didn't go to the authorities. What will stop them from killing us?"

"All of us?" Libby asked.

"I doubt such men care how many die to achieve their purpose."

"It's Jake I worry about." Roy glanced toward the room where she slept.

"She's safe as long as she's here, and as long as we don't lead them to her. So we stay in. Memnet can manage alone for one more day."

Roy sighed. "All right. One more day."

***

"It's been a week." Mason was smug. "We scared them pretty bad."

"I hope so," Stoneface replied. "We were lucky to away."

"No chance that riffraff would call the cops. It's a shame the government lets them clog up our cities!" With a smirk he added, "The big guy messed up your face pretty good though."

There was a cold pause. "Do your job, Mason. Find them."

"I've looked, but they ain't around. Must have gone underground."

"Twice that kid has seen me in places where people ended up dead. I need to know she's not going to point a finger at me later, when this all comes down."

"Nobody downtown's seen her. She probably went home."

"I want her farther away than that," Stoneface said in closing. "Like the next world."

***

As in more traditional homes, six was news time in Storeroom C. Tonight's local edition quoted Mayor Daley, who claimed there'd never be riots in Chicago such as Detroit had last summer. There was still no report of a corpse in or near Lake Michigan.

"Are there so many bodies every day that they don't even report them anymore?" Jake asked. They'd added a fifth chair to the circle, a horsehair remnant of the 1940s that dwarfed her. Memnet had covered its torn seat with an old curtain.

"Perhaps drug overdoses are no longer newsworthy," Leo mused, "but if the police knew two men in suits had shot a third man, also in a suit, that would be news."

Local coverage included plans for an exploding scoreboard for Comiskey Park, which Libby thought dangerous, and analysis from Cubs manager Leo "the Lip" Durocher on why they'd had a losing season.

The final piece of news concerned Thurgood Marshall, recently named to the Supreme Court and sworn in October 2nd as the United States' first black justice. The report revealed Marshall would be visiting Chicago in the early part of 1968. The mayor said of the event: "We are delighted to have such an eminent figure visit our city. Local police are already working with federal agents to assure this great American's safety."

National news was next. "I'm Chet Huntley—"

"—and I'm David Brinkley, and this is the *NBC Evening News*." They sat quietly through reports on the war in Vietnam.

Libby, who'd looked it up in an atlas, had learned it was a nation south of China.

The Arabs and the Israelis were furious with each other, as usual. It saddened Memnet to see such turmoil in her homeland.

One feature covered civil rights and the strife that had accompanied each step forward. Reports of huge gun sales indicated people of all races were afraid of the future, expecting that further social change would come with violence.

The final story was lighter, as usual, and centered on Jake's favorite subject, the Beatles. Two of them had gone to study with a famous spiritual guide who offered enlightenment in thirty minutes a day. The yogi planned to take a vow of silence, and the Englishmen had rushed in to become "transformed" before he was forever lost to them. Both claimed they were now more energetic and totally off drugs.

"How nice for them," Libby sneered. In deference to Jake's feelings, the rest remained silent.

"Goodnight, Chet."

"Goodnight, David, and goodnight from *NBC News*."

Chapter Ten

Two weeks after her arrival at Storeroom C, Jake watched Leo shape a chunk of wood into a replacement chair leg. "Leo, you're Italian, right?"

The rhythmic scrape of the chisel paused briefly. "By birth, yes. I was living in France when Norman found me."

"Did you see the Eiffel Tower?"

"No, I never did. I was in the south."

"What were you doing there?"

"Earning a living." He was adept at answers that revealed nothing.

"And what did you do?"

"At that time I was arranging a production, a play."

"So you were a director?"

"Sometimes." He smiled, raising his hands. "I am what they call a jack of all trades."

"Master of none?" she teased.

"Perhaps." Setting the chisel aside, he blew on the wood to clear the dust. "Would you like to visit the museum tonight on a private tour?"

"Go upstairs?"

"We don't do it often, but it is rather like a vacation when we've spent too much time together."

Jake's interest was piqued, and she abandoned her questions, which she suspected was part of the reason Leo had proposed the adventure.

"How can we go up there? There's a guard and alarms."

"We avoid the guard." Roy looked up from his book with a grin that revealed enthusiasm. "And alarms are designed to keep outsiders from getting in. We're already here."

Jake felt a thrill of excitement. "Sounds great."

"Then it's settled," Leo declared. "The Fearless Five will storm the bastions of the Schmidt." He made them sound like a comic book team, Jake thought. Like they belonged together.

Anticipation was enhanced for the adults by the prospect of showing Jake around. "You've been there before," Roy said, "but it's different without permission. More fun, I think."

Like cautious deer, with ears alert and heads raised to sense danger, they crept up the stairs after the guard's midnight round. Roy eased the latch of the door open with the tiniest click and looked out. "It's Stosh's mealtime," he said softly. "He'll nap afterwards until at least two." Leading the way, he traversed the corridor and opened the second door. Five stealthy figures entered the display area.

The museum, with its circle of partitioned rooms radiating off a central court, reminded Jake of a giant game of *Clue*. Each segment could be entered from the main hall, but there were also archways between rooms, like the game board. In the center were cased displays, and they spent a few minutes perusing them and pointing out favorite items. Leo told Jake it was safe to speak if they kept their voices low, since two walls with closed doors separated them from Stosh's limited hearing.

With street lamps shining in the windows, glowing EXIT

signs, and scattered pale pink wall sconces, it was light enough to see quite well. After Roy answered all Jake's questions about Colt and Gatling guns, they began a stroll through the smaller rooms, set up to display home life in various cultures and times.

"The idea is clever," Leo said, taking on the role of guide.

"Then it obviously wasn't Norman's concept." Libby's tone was acidic.

Leo ignored her. "Each display is separate unto itself, creating an aura of the period."

"That's what I like about it," Jake said. "You feel like you're there."

Leo agreed. "I have many favorites, among them the palazzo, of course, but the Mongolian yurt is also quite remarkable. To think that people made themselves so comfortable in a movable dwelling amazes me. I have never been in a modern trailer home, but I wonder if an Airstream can compete."

"I like how they even add scents," Jake added, sniffing the lingering remains of the incense from the India room. "Makes it more real."

They spent an hour moving through the displays, sitting on chairs, rugs, or divans and chatting about those who'd occupied such places in real life. Memnet said they didn't have the details of the Egyptian household altar right, but Libby said nobody ever understood the Egyptian gods, even the Egyptians themselves. Memnet, who never argued with Libby, went silent.

The African kraal brought on a discussion of sexual roles. "If females did the planting, growing, harvesting, child-raising, and housekeeping," Jake asked, "What did the men do?"

"Smoked and discussed the state of the world, as is proper."

Roy received a punch on the arm from Libby for that.

"Good thing I wasn't there," Jake declared. "I'd be leading an equal rights movement in a heartbeat."

"A woman must have twice the determination of a man to lead anything," Libby observed. "I doubt most women are up to the challenge."

"Then someone's got to convince them," Jake insisted. "When some guy doesn't stick around, a woman shouldn't spend her life feeling sorry for herself." Everyone except Jake realized she meant her own mother, but there was no way to agree without criticizing. Stepping to the partition doorway Leo announced, "Let us consider the glories of ancient Greece."

After they'd seen the home displays, Leo led the way to the upper floor, which held a reading area, conference rooms, staff offices, and small collections of interest to sociologists. Here their weight caused the old wood floors to creak in protest, but Leo assured Jake that Stosh never came to investigate.

Using Norman's passkey, Leo opened the reading room. Passing their one flashlight from one to another, they each sought a book for later reading. Memnet looked at several but found nothing of interest to her. Roy returned to a favorite, *The Outlaw Trail*. Jake wanted a dozen, but Libby ordered, "One. A few are less likely to be missed." Jake chose *Cannibal Land* by Martin Johnson.

When they descended to the main level again Roy asked, "Shall we show Jake the wardrobe room?" The others approved, though Libby warned they'd have to watch the time.

"Here the mannequins are dressed," Leo explained. "They keep clothing, wigs, and hats of all kinds."

With a slight jingle of metal against metal, he found the proper key and unlocked a door. Once they were inside, he closed the door and turned on the lights. "No windows," he told Jake. "We can have all the light we want."

Jake's reaction to the room brought smiles to the adults' faces. She gasped at the rows of clothing, shelves of hats and shoes, wigs of many styles and colors, and boxes filled with other paraphernalia used to outfit the dummies. Every available option was employed to maximize the space, so the walls and even the ceiling were almost completely hidden.

Wooden boxes lining the shelves each had a handhold cut into the front so they could be slid out and tilted down for ease of access. Neatly printed cardboard labels taped onto each revealed someone's passion for order in limited space. *Gloves* said one, while another said, *Hats, soft.* The room smelled of mothballs, old leather, and dust. Jake was delighted.

Childhood often returns when costumes are at hand, and the little group spent a half hour laughing at each other as they tried on hats, wigs, and coats. Libby often hissed at them to be quiet, but it was difficult to contain their mirth. "We're at the other end of the building from Stosh." Roy assured her. "Anyhow, I doubt he'd hear a truck coming through the wall."

When Libby donned an elaborate wig of auburn curls with cascading pearls, Jake clapped her hands. "You look beautiful, like a picture I saw in a book. Somebody important, I think."

Libby set the piece back on its stand. "I have worn wigs form time to time," she said in a light tone.

"When my mom went on a date she'd wear one too, or a fall. She had this short black dress with sequins, and in her wig, she looked like Marilyn Monroe in *Gentlemen Prefer Blondes.*"

"We don't know it," Leo told her.

"It sounds like one I should put on my list," Roy drawled.

"Your mother, she was pretty?" Memnet asked softly.

"Oh yeah! Petite with blond hair and blue eyes. Nothing like me." She attempted lightness, but pain showed in her eyes.

Despite his inability to grasp women's rights issues, Roy knew when a gentleman's judgment was required. Taking Jake's small chin in his hand, he said, "Little lady, there's nothing more beautiful in this world than those eyes of yours, and the rest of you just adds to the effect."

***

Jake had a hard time getting to sleep. *This has been the best night of my life.* Exploring the museum had been an adventure. They'd felt like a family—a sneaky one, but that added to the thrill. The feel of fluffy feather boas, rich velvet capes and stiff brocade had mingled with a sense of happiness.

Leo knew all kinds of stuff, which he'd explained like a college professor grandpa. Libby had been relaxed for Libby, letting them put wigs and hats on her for fun. Because of the passkey that once belonged to Norman What's-his-name, Jake had seen places the patrons weren't allowed into. And at the last, Roy had said she was beautiful, right out in front of the rest, and nobody had snickered or anything.

Men, even King Arthur, preferred their women soft, fair, and pink. Jake looked foreign, dark, and surly. One of the guys Lorna brought home had said it. "Where'd you get a kid like that, and why's she got that surly look on her face?" Mom said later to forget it, but she hadn't. *I look surly. And different.*

At school Jake was different too, not black, but not white

either. She heard whispered comments and sensed animosity. Miss Karsten had explained where Arabs come from and sketched their long, distinguished history, but it didn't help. Miss Karsten herself had honey-colored hair and green eyes, the opposite of Jake.

As a result Jake had stayed inside the covers of a book: at recess, at home, even during class when she could get away with it. She knew about literature, but not much about being a kid.

Dying, Lorna had clung to her daughter as she never had in life, and Jake recalled her mother's hands growing ever whiter against her own dark ones. Lorna had often cursed Jake's father, who'd married her then returned to Syria, leaving them on their own. Jake knew her looks reminded her mother every day of the mistakes she'd made. She looked different, and different was bad.

So when Roy said she was beautiful, Jake had held her breath, waiting for Libby to snort or Leo to gasp or Memnet to look away. But none of that happened. They'd smiled, and she sensed their agreement. Maybe I'm not so ugly. Not as pretty as Memnet, but not terrible. Roy had done the nicest thing ever. She hoped someday she could pay him back and help him find a little happiness, the way he'd helped her tonight.

Chapter Eleven

Leo and Roy began foraging again the next day. They were out of many items, and Memnet and Libby were hard-pressed to keep them supplied. Libby remarked, "The child eats a surprising amount for her size," but she said it in an approving tone, not as a complaint.

Reluctantly, Roy left his western jacket behind, shaved his sideburns, and cultivated a mustache. "It makes me look like a wanted poster," he complained.

Memnet returned from the second-hand store with an apologetic look and a sweatshirt that said *Peace Now*. Eyeing it with distaste, Roy sighed. "I hope those two got clean away, because I can't wait to return to my personal style."

That evening he contributed a whole sausage, wrapped in butcher paper and hidden inside the baggy shirt. "Oktoberfest in Germantown," he said with a grin. "They won't miss a chunk."

"You should have brought sauerkraut to make the dish complete," Leo joked.

"Couldn't do it," Roy replied with a mock-solemn expression. "The police would have followed the smell and found us, and this little escapade would be over."

Leo had returned to the mission, where he'd endured questions from staff, who assumed he'd been on a drunk. He feigned shame, promised to do better, and brought home rolls, meatloaf, and boiled potatoes. Memnet refused the latter, being unable to acquire a taste for them.

Libby had found a cherry pie at a day-old bakery, so overall they dined well. "Though we are never full, we're seldom hungry," she declared at the end of the meal. "Our spare diet keeps Leo from getting fat, as southern Europeans tend to do in their middle age."

"And you never gain an ounce," Roy commented. "How is that?"

"My mother's people were thin, my father's red-haired," she told him. "I got the best of each."

"I'll be bald at forty," Roy confided. "All my uncles were." He turned to tease Memnet. "Will you get fat when you're old?"

She gave serious thought to his query. "I never know my family so I don't know how I look old."

Roy recognized belatedly that he'd erred. "I wouldn't worry about it," he mumbled. "You'll always be beautiful." Memnet blushed and looked at her plate, and Libby, with all the skill of a practiced diplomat, changed the subject to tomorrow's laundry.

***

The closeness that developed between Jake and Memnet resulted in great improvement of the latter's English. Practice was part of it, and the girl's patience did the rest.

"My dad was from Syria," Jake said one night as they sat cross-legged on their respective pillow-beds. "Is that where you come from?"

"No, Egypt." Memnet's voice softened. "I play in the Nile as a little girl."

"Played," Jake corrected. "Aren't there crocodiles?"

"Oh, yes. Children must be careful always."

"I wouldn't want to live there!"

Memnet tilted her head. "Is bears in America?"

"Are there bears. And, yes, there are."

"There, now you are afraid of them? No! We fear new things and accept these around us. I bet more peoples die of cold here every year than of crocodiles in Egypt."

"You're right." Jake tilted her head. "Why did you come here? You don't seem happy."

Memnet sniffed. "Who want to be in cold, with concrete everywhere and smoky to breathe?"

"Then why did you come?"

"Norman bri—brought us to Chicago."

"Why?"

She shrugged. "My English is not so good then. Norman want us...be famous, Libby say."

"Famous how?"

"We are not sure what he think—what he thinking," she corrected as Jake caught her eye. "He brought us then he die, leave us afraid we never go free if anybody know. This is why we hide."

***

October, 1965

As curator of the Schmidt Museum, Norman Bohn had chosen Storeroom C as his personal, secret retreat. One of three large storage areas in the museum, C was the least convenient for the staff, two stories below street level and without elevator access. Storerooms A and B, both larger, sat opposite each other on the next level. Along with its distance from daily operation, C's insufficient lighting cast gloomy shadows in its corners. Deep in the earth, the floor sometimes produced puddles, creating mold and odor problems. As a result, though it was part of the museum, C was apart from it, never cleaned or rearranged, seldom even visited.

Having nowhere else to go and terrified of discovery, the undisclosed tenants had stayed on in Storeroom C after Norman's death. "Among things like us," Libby phrased it, "that belong nowhere."

Discovery of Norman's corpse had closed the museum for almost two months. A search for a new curator was begun, and responsibility for the planned renovation of the main display floor fell to Norman's assistant. The unsettling sound of hammers and electrical saws threatened the sanity of Norman's "guests," but as repairs went on upstairs, Leo realized the general confusion provided the opportunity to do their own renovations.

At night, using material pilfered from the building project, Roy and Leo constructed a false wall across Storeroom C. Running the width of the room, the new wall created a narrow space they divided into two chambers to serve as sleeping quarters and hiding places when anyone came downstairs.

"They'll see the room is smaller," Roy objected when Leo proposed the project. "It'll look new."

"They won't notice a few feet missing from a room this size," Libby replied. "We will paint the wall to match the others, and Leo will use *trompe l'oeil* to age it."

Unwilling to ask what that was, Roy went on to his next objection. "What about the doors? Any fool will see there are holes in the wall that weren't there before."

Impatient with impertinence from one with no right to an opinion, Libby turned to Leo and switched to Italian. After a rapid exchange she told Roy, "He says the doors will be three feet off the floor and just large enough to step through. We will hang pictures to conceal them."

Roy obligingly stole a large canvas tarpaulin and odds and ends of paint from the workspace above. Though Leo shook his head at the selection available, he cut two pieces from the tarp and used the paint to create garish roses in red, blue, orange, and turquoise. Roy pronounced it ugly, but Libby explained, "We don't want anyone to like them and haul them upstairs."

They framed the painted tarps and fastened them on the miniature doors. Over the rest of the wall Roy hung other paintings salvaged from the storeroom's corners, making it look as if they'd been hung there to preserve space. Once the project was finished, they no longer had to hide under furniture when someone came downstairs. Instead, they entered their retreat and closed themselves inside.

"They require agility, these doors," Leo remarked. "We must never become too large."

"Not much danger of that on our present diet," Libby answered. Roy, used to their conversing without translating for him, ignored them. He liked the idea of a secret hideout, though he wondered why a robust man like Leo had chosen to paint roses. Libby seemed to think it was a tribute to her.

***

It became too cold for Memnet to sing in the El station. The sky was an unremitting gray, and tiny flakes of snow drifted onto the dirty streets, turning dingy as they wet the pavement. Hurrying from one warm place to another, people no longer stopped to listen.

She had never known winter until coming to Chicago, and

she considered it the earth's greatest curse. Egypt had cold nights, but nothing like the bone-deep chill that assaulted her from State Street to the bus station or down Lake Shore Drive. Her first venture outside had been in November, and she'd thought it couldn't get any colder. December and January had taught her otherwise.

Memnet's winter wardrobe suited her dislike of the season. At a second-hand store she'd found a shabby, fur-lined man's overcoat so long it brushed the ground, which she considered a plus. Under it she wore two sweaters, corduroy pants, and boots with heavy wool socks, scratchy but warm. Her hat, decidedly unfashionable, brought to mind sled dogs, but its earflaps could be folded down and snapped under her chin. Since it was still October, Memnet had not gotten the hat out yet, but the air smelt of winter and the wind nipped at them. Its time was close.

She was thinking of the hat as she and Roy made their way down Dearborn Street. They carried three shopping bags full of dented canned goods they'd found behind a grocery. The bags were fragile, but they'd feared if they went home for something sturdier, their bonanza would be gone when they returned. Memnet had to use both hands to carry her bag, which left her ears exposed to the wind. In her longing for the hat, she didn't notice for a moment that Roy had stopped.

"What?" He stared at a man who'd come out of a building and stopped to light a cigarette, scratching the match on the wall. "Roy, what?"

"I think that's the guy."

She looked closer. The man, who shook out the match and crushed it between his fingers, had two damaged eyes. They'd probably been quite black, but the bruises had faded to green and yellow. One eye still had a red blotch on the white, and now that she noticed, the nose looked crooked as well. Someone had hit him many times, perhaps a week earlier on the shore of Lake Michigan.

He was about Roy's size, with broad shoulders that filled the jacket he wore. His suit was gray, his shoes black and highly polished, his hat a dignified fedora. He might have been posing for a cigarette ad as he leaned against the building, an ordinary guy taking a break.

Pulling smoke deep into his lungs, he looked up and noticed the two on the sidewalk below him. Immediately he took a pair of aviator sunglasses from his jacket, put them on, and turned away. After a moment he turned back and stared straight at them. Setting her bag down, Memnet pulled Roy to face her, pretending to button his jacket. When she looked again, the man was no longer on the steps, and a taxi was pulling away.

They looked at each other. "Are you sure it is him?"

"Pretty sure. Do you think he recognized me?"

"I don't know."

"He came from there." Roy squinted at the nameplate over the door.

"What is this place?"

"The Federal Building," he replied. "Among other things, it's the main office of Chicago's Federal Bureau of Investigation."

***

In her own mind Jake called her friends the Little Mob, since she was sure they were connected. Her theory was they'd done something to anger the Big Mob and gone into hiding from them and the police as well. They had to be careful: three foreigners

96

and a cowboy didn't fit into most crowds.

It was hard to see Libby's place in the Mob, but with all her lists, she might have kept some don's books. Leo could have forged money or documents which Roy, probably an enforcer, passed and got caught. No matter what the others had done, Memnet was an ignorant though *not* stupid pawn, like Judy Holliday in *Born Yesterday*. Roy had probably done whatever he'd done to impress her, or maybe to buy her something nice.

Watching them together, Jake tried to decide exactly how Roy and Memnet felt about each other. They didn't seem like lovers. There were no "public displays of affection," to quote her junior high handbook. But there was tension between them, like they were holding themselves back. They never looked directly at each other. Though she often patted Leo's arm or gave Jake a hug, Memnet never touched Roy. There had to be something from so much nothing. Even if she didn't know much about lasting relationships, Jake had eyes.

Chapter Twelve

As boredom set in, Jake began sneaking upstairs during the day and blending in with the museum's patrons. Libby fussed about it, but Leo said the guards had seen her before so it shouldn't be a problem. She chose times when the place was busy, often joining a group of school kids or trailing behind a family with children. No one noticed. Since nothing had happened there for a long time, the staff went through their duties half asleep.

In the reading room she found a pamphlet titled Schmidt Museum: History and Purpose. It was cheaply produced, with typos and a greasy plastic cover, but she settled into a carrel and read every word.

The Schmidt Museum was founded in the late 1940s to complement Chicago's other museums. The first curator, Mr. Schmidt's daughter Ellen, was the creative genius behind the unique set-up. She'd been in control until 1953, when Norman Bohn was hired.

Norman was curator from 1959 to 1965. His credentials included bachelor's degrees in anthropology and science from the University of Chicago and advanced degrees in nuclear physics and astronomy. He'd worked for the government during World War II, doing classified work.

"Dissatisfied with laboratory procedures," the booklet said, "Mr. Bohn returned to his first love, anthropology." He'd served briefly as an assistant to the curator of the Field Museum then held a job at the Royal Ontario Museum in Toronto for less than a year. Following that was a span of time unaccounted for. Then he'd come to the Schmidt for his final job.

The word used to describe Norman's tenure was *solid*, which Jake took to mean nothing changed much while he was in charge. It was a great tragedy for the Schmidt, the pamphlet noted, when Mr. Bohn died in an accident. There was no further explanation, but Bohn's dedication to the job was stressed. He'd apparently spent an unusual amount of time at the museum, maintaining the Schmidt's high standards.

"Yeah, except he sneaked in a few friends into the basement," Jake mumbled. Still, they never spoke of Norman as a friend. What had Libby said? "Sometimes I could have killed him myself."

The present curator was Charlene L. Dobbs, a 1954 graduate of Singler University. She looked to be about forty when the picture provided in the pamphlet was taken. A snooty expression betrayed no sense of humor, and Jake thought it would be bad if Charlene ever caught on to Leo's practice of writing memos in her name. The list of her interests, committee roles, and memberships on boards of directors was long, which accounted for the fact she didn't dig much into what was going on at her workplace.

Efforts for change were under way, however. Miss Dobbs, it said (Jake bet she preferred Ms.), was determined to continue modernizing the museum. "The renovation of the main area was a start," she was quoted as saying. "Now we will improve facilities on the second-floor to make the Schmidt accommodating for meetings, study, and research."

"Probably wants air-conditioning in her office," Jake groused. *She* liked the building exactly as it was.

Putting the pamphlet back, Jake wandered downstairs. Stosh was on duty, his eyes slightly red. Roy claimed he kept a bottle in the main floor men's bathroom and took a hit every hour or so.

Of all the guards at the Schmidt, Stosh was the easiest to work around. He had no curiosity about anything, and he'd answer any question she asked and never wonder why.

He stood near the Japanese display, where a sliding frame covered with paper made a traditional entry. His uniform was grubby and smelled of cigarettes, and his stomach sat under his clothes like an ostrich egg. His eyes focused on the wall about eight feet up as if something interesting might happen there any second. In her best schoolgirl manner, Jake pitched her voice high and said brightly, "Excuse me, sir. I have a question."

She hated it when people said that. If you had a question; why not just ask it? "I love your museum."

"Um?" was all the answer she got.

"Are you in charge?"

"That would be the curator. Ours is a woman." The word was an insult.

"Gee," Jake gushed, "a lady curator? Is she the first one?"

"I dunno. Before her was Norman." A smile came and went. "Never had a boss like Norman, before or since."

"I'll bet he was really smart."

She'd hit on a subject Stosh liked. "I'll say! Knew about everything, atoms, stars, history, all that. Once he spent a year living in his car out west, New Mexico, I think. Then he went to Australia or Austria, whichever one's by Germany, and studied with some guy there. He had stories, believe me."

"Cool." She waited, and Stosh did a little stroll down memory lane.

"He'd come to our room after hours and talk, not like some that's too good to mix with the help. He talked about stuff that would curl your hair."

"Like what?"

He wiped his wet mouth with the back of a meaty hand. "Just stuff."

"Where's Norman now?"

"Fell down the steps and broke his neck. Died right away, the docs said."

She made a sympathetic noise. "Wow. Maybe I'll become a curator when I grow up."

Jake moved off. She'd killed two birds with one stone. Since she'd claimed interest in being curator, Stosh had even less reason to question her presence. If he noticed. And she'd figured out where Norman had met Roy. In New Mexico.

***

After the incident in front of the Federal Building, Roy agreed a permanent change to his looks was required. His beloved fringed leather jacket, it attracted notice, so it had to go.

Roy had many friends among the street people. He found them interesting, at least when they were straight and sober, and besides, they seldom asked questions about the past.

Pig—that was what he called himself—told long, rambling stories about his experiences in Vietnam. From what Roy gathered, there was fighting between "gooks" and "Arvins." Pig, a light-skinned man of mixed race, had fought for the Arvins and lost an eye from getting "fragged." Pig added layers as the weather cooled, but on top was always a green army jacket.

"Why you do that?" Pig asked when Roy offered to trade coats.

"I've been admirin' that jacket for a long time."

Pig looked down at the olive-drab, government-issue jacket with the I.D. band that read "Hoag." His single eye regarded Roy incredulously. "This?"

"Yeah. It's cool."

Pig touched the soft leather of Roy's sleeve reverently. "That coat is outa sight, man. You don't want to be tradin' for no O.D. green piece of—"

"I tell you, I've been wantin' one like yours. Memnet will sew it up and make it like new."

Pig looked sly. "Yeah, Memnet. Now there's a lady!" Everyone on the street assumed Memnet and Roy were a couple, and he never denied it.

Before Pig could wax eloquent on Memnet's charms, he asked, "Trade?"

"Hell yes, man. You want to give up a coat like that, I'll trade you."

They made the exchange, though Roy carried Pig's coat rather than putting it on. Since hygiene figured low on Pig's list of concerns, he'd have Memnet wash it as soon as possible.

Two days later Roy went out for supplies, avoiding the Federal Building on Dearborn Street. On Ohio, he heard a shrill "Yoo-hoo!" and turned to see Molly, dressed in a once-bright orange kaftan topped with a fun-fur coat that had seen better times. The seventy-something woman, who made her living telling fortunes on the street, knew everyone and kept Roy informed about local events, when he could understand her.

"Greetings, Lover," Molly chirped. Today her hat, the only piece of her costume that changed, was a man's porkpie. "How's my favorite leading Paul New-man?"

"Good enough," Roy answered. "Been up to the theater?"

"Yeah, but it was all teenyboppers, there for *A Hard Day's Night.*" She made a disgusted sound. "All giggles; no money-that's-what-I-want. How'm I supposed to get to Tampa?"

Molly considered herself a Chicagoan, living here and there around the city until the weather turned cold. Then she hitch-hiked to Florida, where she wintered. "It's what retired people do," she claimed, and Molly considered herself retired. *Retired from reality,* Roy thought, *but always entertaining.*

He sympathized with her. "Cash is hard to come by."

Molly shook her head, and cheap gold earrings hanging almost to her shoulders moved wildly. "I'll be okay when Foghorn Leghorn gives my investments back."

It was her familiar refrain: back in Wisconsin her son, in collusion for some unknown reason with J. C. Penney, retail magnate, had stolen her money. The son, who apparently resembled a rooster, had tried to put her in a home full of what Molly termed "crazy jaybirds." Escaping in her nightgown, she'd come to Chicago and taken to living on the streets where people "live and let loon," as one smart aleck put it.

Noting his missing leather jacket, Molly dropped her tone to a confidential level. "No coat-of-many-cowhides, I see. Need a loan, Lover?"

Memnet had refused to even touch the filthy fatigue jacket, and Libby had sided with her. Faced with two determined women, Roy now wore a plain pea coat they'd found at a consignment shop. The price had been more than they could afford, so Roy tossed it out a window in the back and retrieved it from the alley later.

"We're okay. I just wanted somethin' new."

Molly's eyes twinkled. "Even now you've taken in the girl from Ulysses S. Park?" Roy nodded, wondering how Molly knew. "Seemed like a nice kid."

"She's something," Roy agreed. "I gave my coat to Pig—"

"Pig!" she interrupted. "He met up with a double-0 7 yesterday."

Roy paused to translate. "Killed? In a fight?" Pig had a notorious temper when he drank.

Molly shrugged. "In between. The banshees came screeching through, and I peeked before they took him away. Scaramonga did it."

Pig had been found in an alley, killed by a gun, and taken away by ambulance.

Molly took up her bags. Roy heard the clink of bottles, and an alligator back-scratcher stuck out of one. Adjusting the weight, she said, "I thought at first it was you, Lover, 'cause of the jacket."

***

Roy approached a police officer as he left the diner where he'd had lunch.

"Hey, Officer Calucchi, how's it goin'?"

"Can't complain, Cowboy." Calucchi shifted his heavy leather belt. "What's happening?"

"Just waitin' for that million dollars to drop out of the sky."

"You and everybody else," the cop replied with a grin.

"I heard you had some excitement on 10th. Pig, huh?"

The cop's face narrowed. "He was wearing your jacket. Why's that?"

"We traded. The leather one was tight across the shoulders."

The cop nodded as his partner joined him, picking up his last words. "That's what Pig told people. Otherwise, we'd have some questions for you."

Roy grinned, but it was an effort. Instinct screamed this was no random incident. Had exchanging coats with Pig caused the man's death? "You fellows know I'm harmless."

Calucchi rubbed his expanding forehead then set his hat into place again. "I've seen worse done for a coat. We guessed you wouldn't have put holes in it if you wanted it back though."

"So who killed Pig?"

"That's a mystery. I guess the deluded bastard went off at the wrong guy one time too many."

"Goin' into an alley to fight a guy with a gun? Even Pig wasn't that crazy."

Calucchi's partner rubbed his hands to warm them. "Tell ya what I think. Pig saw something he shouldn't have, and somebody made sure he never told."

Shocked and sickened, Roy started for home. Unusually fearful, he turned to look whenever footsteps sounded behind him. He agreed with the second cop's analysis of why, but knowing what he knew, his guilt-stricken mind said the victim was supposed to be him, not poor old Pig.

Chapter Thirteen

Leo didn't share his plan for Monday with the others. Pocketing an apple for lunch, he left the museum early. It was his intention to find out how Norman Bohn had done what he'd done to them.

Jake had shown him the pamphlet on the Schmidt Museum that revealed Norman's past, and the mention of Argonne National Laboratory struck a chord in his memory. In the 1940s and '50s, Argonne had been controversial due to research projects conducted there. A 1500-acre site in a wooded area twenty miles west of them, it had connections to the now-famous Manhattan Project, nuclear submarines, and other secret biological, chemical, and atomic studies. Since Norman had worked there for some time, Leo wanted a look at the place.

Combining train and bus transport, he reached the laboratory just after ten-thirty. The main building was understated, with the lackluster style of places not meant for public visits. Inside, a large lobby contained only a reception desk. Behind it were closed doors from which people came and went with businesslike efficiency. A metal staircase led up to more doors, also closed.

Leo introduced himself as a high school chemistry teacher hoping to bring his students to tour the lab. The uniformed guard at the entry made a call, and a charming young woman who said she was a University of Chicago intern appeared. Her name was Chris, and they chatted pleasantly about teaching, his supposed career and her future one. She showed Leo the areas open to visitors, explaining possibilities his class might enjoy, depending on when they visited.

When they'd seen what Chris was allowed to show him, Leo

put the next part of his plan into effect. Clutching his left arm, he rubbed his chest. "I have a bit of angina from time to time. Might I sit down for a moment?"

The young woman led Leo to the commissary, where she insisted on fetching a cup of tea for him. While she went off to get it, he looked around for a way to take the next step.

Across the room a man sat at a table alone, wearing the manner of one who spends his life peering into microscopes and writing arcane notations. Leo wasted no time but approached him and asked, "May I join you?"

The face that turned up at him resembled a turtle peering out from its shell. His eyes were milky brown, and white eyebrows hung low as if to hide them. Reluctantly he made a rude grunt that indicated Leo might sit.

"I am Doctor Leo DiMucci, from Milan. Perhaps you heard I was coming?" Jake had once said DiMucci was the best Italian name ever, though Leo had no idea why.

The man shook his head, and before he could speak Leo said, "I am touring your facility thanks to Dr. Duffield, but he was called away."

"Name's Walter Mesick," the man said. "They do what they want around here without my say-so." Leo smiled at learning he'd chosen wisely. Mesick was obviously misanthropic to the core, which meant he probably paid little attention to what his co-workers and supervisors did.

"It was suggested I speak to you, since you know the facility so well."

Flattered, Mesick sat straighter in his chair. *Just in time,* Leo thought. Chris was on her way with a steaming cup of tea.

Rising, he stepped forward to meet the young woman, stopping far enough away that Mesick couldn't hear what was said. "I'm sorry to be such a bother," he told her, accepting the tea. "I took my medicine, and this will certainly help. You've been very kind."

"Are you sure you're all right?"

He waved a hand. "These spells never last long." Glancing over his shoulder he added, "Oddly enough, I met an old friend who has asked me to spend the afternoon with him."

Chris looked doubtful, whether because of policy, Leo's health, or Walter's hostile tendencies, he couldn't say. He held his breath, hoping she'd take his word for it. She didn't, but his luck held. Approaching Walter, she asked, "Dr. Mesick, are you taking responsibility for this gentleman?"

Mesick grunted once before finding his voice. "I'll see he's taken care of." He wasn't gracious by any means, but his comment satisfied Chris. Making Leo promise to take it easy, she left him with Walter and returned to her own work.

Leo insisted Mesick finish his lunch, a bowl of soup and a Kaiser roll. The man hunched over the plastic tray like a wary hound, his head almost at the level of his food. Leo had noticed many older people had backbones that shrank and began to curve like a drawn bow, pulling their heads downward. Someone should study the problem, he thought abstractly.

Chatting with determined cheerfulness, he ignored the surly replies he got from Mesick. Leo inserted subtle flattery into the conversation, and the older man began to answer more willingly. Like most, he enjoyed talking about himself. In a voice raspy from disuse, he explained what he did at Argonne.

Walter's project was something called a *computer*, a machine he said could store tremendous quantities of data and perform miracles with it. It sounded farfetched to Leo, and he asked about other projects Walter had worked on since the lab's establishment in 1946.

The man shrugged. "The research I did back then I can't discuss. We're pretty cautious here, though it's not a place of evil doings, like some reporters like to claim."

"I've heard they're determined to learn Argonne's secrets."

For the first time, the old man's face formed what might have been a smile. "Yeah. Some young reporter name of Harvey—" He paused to remember. "—Paul Harvey, that's it—got caught trying to sneak onto the grounds. Got a ride in a cop car for sticking his nose where it didn't belong!"

Leo chuckled at the story, hoping he'd warmed the man sufficiently to get an answer to his main question. "Do you remember a man named Norman Bohn? He worked here."

"Bohn." His mouth snapped shut, again reminding Leo of a turtle. "Don't recall that name."

"Norman was an acquaintance of mine. He's dead now, but—"

"Lots of 'em dead. I'm still working." Mesick sounded as if being alive made him somehow superior.

"Norman was employed here in the forties and early fifties, perhaps in nuclear research."

"My sector and nuclear don't mix much."

"I'm trying to find someone who knows what he was working on."

"They wouldn't tell you if they knew. Everything was secret

back then."

Leo had been optimistic upon meeting Walter, but he'd learned nothing. "Norman wanted to tell me something, but he died in an accident before we could meet. I feel I've missed something important."

The old man gave one of his quick upward glances, and Leo met his eyes, trying not to look desperate. Never in his life had he wanted anything so much as the knowledge Norman Bohn took to his grave.

Mesick stood, which took a great deal of effort. Spreading both hands on the table, he gave a sort of groan and pushed his protesting body upright. "Come with me."

They followed corridors until Leo was sure he'd never find the way back to the exit. Walter moved like a turtle, putting one foot in front of the other with dignified precision.

Finally he stopped at a door marked *Personnel,* knocked twice, and opened it. "Maddie can help you," he said. "If she doesn't know, nobody does." Without further word to Leo or the invisible Maddie, he shuffled on, leaving his unofficial guest deep inside the lab. So much for building security.

Stepping into the office, Leo saw no one, but a cheerful voice said, "I'll be right with you."

Peering behind the door, he saw a woman of at least seventy dragging large volumes off a shelf in the corner. Taking them from her, Leo set them on the desk. A nameplate on its cluttered top said, *Madeline Vandermele, Staffing Coordinator.* She thanked him for the help and sat, indicating Leo should do the same. Her chair made a soft hiss as the padding adjusted. Tall and straight-backed despite her age, Maddie had large bones, white hair cropped mannishly short, and a plain face with character but no trace of femininity. Leo thought she'd make a great subject for a painting.

"Mrs. Vandermele—"

"Miss," she corrected, but she smiled as she said it. Not a bitter old maid. "Maddie will do."

"My name is Leo DiMucci. I met Walter Mesick in the commissary, and I mentioned a friend who once worked here. He said you might give me some information on him."

She looked doubtful. "Our records are private."

"I understand that. This friend had asked me to collaborate on a project, but he died."

"I'm sorry to hear that," she told him. "Was it recently?"

"Two years ago, but since I'm visiting Chicago now, I thought I'd try to find out what he wanted."

She frowned. "I don't see how I can help. As I said, information is private, even if he's gone."

"I only wondered which section he worked in when employed here."

"Oh," she said. "That's not classified." She turned to a filing cabinet. "What's the name?"

"Norman Bohn."

She stopped, turning toward Leo. "Norman?"

"You remember him?"

She gave a small sigh. "Yes, I knew Norman."

"Do you know what he was working on?"

"I couldn't tell you."

"Meaning you don't know or you aren't supposed to tell?"

She gave a tiny smile but no answer. "Who are you?"

"As I said, Norman told me he'd made a great discovery. He died before I was able to discuss it with him in any depth." It wasn't a lie, merely an inventive phrasing of the truth.

Maddie took her hand off the drawer handle. "I'd like to help, but I simply don't know what he meant."

"But you can tell me what sector of this facility Norman worked in, yes?"

Maddie's expression turned ironic. "Norman worked in several sectors while he was here, which is how I got to know him. He was always either asking for a transfer or being transferred." She gave Leo a look. "He was not well liked."

"And why was that?"

She sighed. "Norman didn't care about people much. He was far ahead of most scientists in some ways, but he was always going off on his own."

"You say he worked in several areas?"

She sighed. "He'd work in a sector for a few months. Then there'd be some kind of brouhaha, and he'd go somewhere else." She shook her head. "I got the impression he was here to soak up everything he could learn from the brilliant minds here." Pursing her lips she added, "Norman could have been one of them, but he had no interest in other people's projects."

"What *was* he interested in?" Leo leaned forward as he waited for her answer.

"He talked about history a lot." Leo waited, his whole body still. This was what he sought: someone with first-hand knowledge of the workings of Norman's mind.

Maddie sat back, resting blue-veined hands on the chair's arms. "He'd come in here, sent by an irate section head who wanted to throttle him. He'd rant—they were all idiots. Then he'd come out of the blue with some goofy question." She frowned at the wall behind Leo as if Norman stood there.

"What kind of question?"

"Nothing that made any sense. He could never concentrate on the present. Norman was either years behind or years ahead of everyone else."

"Why did they keep him on if he was so disruptive?"

A smile and a shrug. "He was exceptionally bright. Some of the scientists saw that and tried to help him become what he could have been. He was Michael Millen's protégée until Miss Hap. That was the last straw."

"Excuse me. Mishap?"

She laughed, a short gust. "Our little pun. One of the rhesus monkeys used for biological research somehow got pregnant. The baby was named Miss Hap, and she became quite a pet." She raised a brow, adding, "It wouldn't have done to become attached to the others."

Leo nodded. "Experimentation requires certain sacrifices."

"Anyway, that crazy Norman was caught red-handed trying to smuggle the monkey off the facility. When they caught him, he said he needed her for a research project." Maddie waved both hands at Norman's obstinate behavior. "That was it. Biological was about his last chance, and he bollixed it up in just a few months. He was let go."

"He never said what his research project was?"

She shook her head. "He was more upset at losing the monkey than his job. He claimed she'd have become the most famous primate of all time."

"I suppose he used some other creature," Leo mused. "A dog, maybe."

"What?"

Catching himself, he waved her question away. "Might Norman have continued experimental work on his own?"

"Not likely." Maddie spoke distinctly, making her point so Leo couldn't miss it. "Norman Bohn was mentally ill. Delusions of grandeur, I think they call it. He insisted he was going to come up with something revolutionary that we'd all hear about someday. But after his shenanigans here, he couldn't get another job in the scientific community."

"No," Leo agreed. "He took employment at a museum."

She grimaced. "I heard. After he was gone they found out he'd stolen some equipment too."

Leo's pulse quickened. "What sort of equipment?"

"I don't recall." She moved in her chair. "I'm afraid I've said more than I should as it is."

"I have no intention of making trouble for anyone." Leo rose. "Thank you for your help. I've done what I could to fulfill my promise, but it seems my old friend lost touch with reality toward the end."

"I'm sorry he died, but Norman was one of those brilliant dreamers who never accomplish anything in the real world."

Leo could have told her differently, but that wasn't what he'd come for. "Thank you, Maddie." He shook her hand, though the gesture between a man and a woman always felt odd to him. She escorted him to the east entrance, and he left Argonne, having gained more information but no answers.

Chapter Fourteen

Jake continued to question her friends about their past. "She does not believe what we say," Memnet told Leo, "and she ask me all the time."

"She's a clever girl," Leo replied, "and our story isn't a very good one."

One night as the five of them sat companionably in their chairs, Roy sharpened the blades on a pair of ice skates. The file he'd borrowed from the janitors' closet rasped against the steel as he made a proposal in an informal session that had become their usual method for making decisions. "It should be okay for Jake to go outside. We got her new clothes."

"I suppose she can't stay here forever," Libby admitted.

"Good. Her first outing will be to the ice rink." Roy set the file aside and tested the edge with his thumb.

"I've never ice skated," Jake said, "but I'd love to try it."

"I will make a blanket into a cape," Memnet volunteered. "It is much fashionable this year."

"That would be great, Memnet. Thanks."

"Skating's not hard," Roy told her as he rubbed grease into the old, crazed leather. "When I was a kid, my uncle had a pond, and I used to skate backwards, do spins, and everything."

"Where did you grow up?" Jake asked casually.

With a quick glance at Leo he replied, "Utah. My folks were Mormons."

"Did your dad have six wives?" Libby pulled in a quick gasp of air, but Roy laughed.

"Only the one, but she could preach hellfire and damnation, my momma. She always said I'd amount to nothing 'cause I hated school so bad."

"Did you ditch it?"

"I did, but I'm sorry now, 'cause I'm not smart like Leo and Libby." It was a transparent attempt to be an encouraging adult, and Leo smiled, perhaps thinking Jake's presence would encourage their lawless friend to become a more upright citizen.

"I like learning things from Libby and Leo," Jake said. "They make it fun to learn."

"Ad interim," Leo murmured, and Libby nodded agreement.

The skating suggestion was a success. With Roy's help, Jake took her first tentative steps on ice and soon wobbled along by herself. She fell of course, but the two pairs of pants she'd worn for warmth also provided padding. After an hour she was skating confidently, if a little stiffly. Roy thought they looked like a family, Libby and Leo the grandparents, he and Memnet the parents of this budding beauty whose cheeks turned rosy and whose dark eyes sparkled with delight as they cheered her on.

***

Libby rolled her eyes when Jake positioned herself with her rear in the chair's seat backward, her legs propped full length up its back, and her hair hanging over the seat edge. When Libby commented it looked like torture, Jake insisted she was comfortable.

Eyes closed, Jake savored her memories of the day. Skating was fun, and she hadn't done badly for her first time. People

117

assumed Roy was her dad from the way he beamed when she finally took off on her own. The other three had cheered and clapped until she'd blushed. Maybe that's how family was supposed to be, supportive and embarrassing all at once.

When Jake tired of circling the small rink, they'd walked around the downtown, looking in shop windows and choosing what they would buy if they were millionaires. Libby stopped to gaze at a dress in the window of Saks that Jake considered awful. Fashionable gowns of the season were simple, with empire waists and fitted sleeves. This dress, made of stiff taffeta with beaded trim, had a full skirt gathered onto a waistband that came to a sharp V at the center front. The others waited, stomping the cold from their feet as Libby gazed at it for a long time, fingers pressed against the glass.

In a faraway voice she said, "I had one even grander, with pearls sewn all over it and yards and yards of fabric in the skirt."

"Libby," Leo said gently, but it was a warning.

Shaking herself, she laughed. "At least I dreamed I did."

That led Jake to a new theory. They were international jewel thieves who'd been forced into hiding when things got too hot. Leo was the mastermind and Roy the cat burglar who actually took the loot. Libby was the fence, since no one would suspect such a proper old lady. Jake still saw Memnet as an innocent, on the run only by association.

She liked the new theory better. The Mob was mean and never gave up, but if her friends were jewel thieves, they could someday get new identities. Why would the American police care about something that happened in Europe more than two years ago? She made a note to look up the statute of limitations on theft.

***

118

The next day was Saturday. They had a breakfast of toast topped with each person's chosen spread: orange marmalade for Libby, grape jam for Memnet and strawberry for Roy, apple butter for Leo, and peanut butter for Jake, all courtesy of Smuckers and a local diner. As they cleared the meal, Libby announced they were all going to church. Jake looked surprised, Roy reluctant, Leo agreeable, and Memnet radiant.

"Our beliefs are quite dissimilar," Libby told Jake. "By accident we discovered Baha'i, a faith that encompasses all the religions of the world. It is a good, if unorthodox, answer to our diverse modes of worship."

"The temple is some distance away, so we don't often attend," Leo said.

"Which is all right with me," Roy added, but Libby glared him to silence.

Libby enjoyed religious services and cared little what type they were. Though she had no patience for fanaticism or need of a particular creed to cling to, attending church helped her refocus on the good in life and things she wanted to achieve. Memnet too enjoyed reflective time, and Leo was amenable to their needs. Roy went only because the others wanted him to. It helped that the Baha'i service was only fifteen minutes long.

"The House of Worship in Wilmette is known for its beauty," Libby told Jake. "I believe Leo spends his time there admiring the architecture rather than pondering his sins, but that's his choice."

"Did your mother take you to services?" Memnet asked.

"Only on Christmas and Easter. I'm Catholic, but sometimes I went to a Bible school they had at the projects that was for all religions."

"All Christians, not all religions," Memnet corrected.

"I read the Quran a little, because of my dad. It seemed a lot like the Bible to me."

Libby nodded. "At the temple they read from that and several other books of scripture. There is a short service every day of the week."

"I don't believe in most of it," Roy said. Libby looked shocked, as did Memnet, but he added stubbornly, "I think for myself."

"One priest we had said everybody who isn't a Catholic is going to hell," Jake declared. "I don't believe that, so I guess I think for myself too."

"I also am a Catholic, but a bit of a freethinker," Leo said.

"I am not a Catholic." Libby chuckled as if amused by the thought. "I've been called a freethinker and worse."

They took the train, which made Roy grumpy. "Hate the damned things," he muttered. At Libby's glare he added, "Well I do!"

The car was almost empty, its green interior marred with graffiti, its corners cluttered with smelly brown bags and discarded candy wrappers. The rattle and sway was hypnotic, but drafts as the doors hissed open and shut kept them awake.

Traveling on the Howard Line to the end, they took transfers to Wilmette and rode to the last stop. From there it was two blocks to the temple. Libby seemed pleased when Jake expressed wonder at the structure. With an hour until the 12:15 start of devotions, the others followed as she explored.

The building sat amid nine gardens, not at their best in November. Still, the temple was impressive, its circular base made of steps leading to entrances set into nine facets. The second tier was similar to but smaller than the first, with huge, delicately-made windows in each facet. These were topped by a third tier, dome-shaped, with nine ribs rising to meet at the top.

Leo pointed all this out to Jake, ending with, "It's more Greek than St. Paul's, more rounded than St. Sophia's, and more delicate than St. Peter's. It is a combination of styles that makes a harmonious whole." He added with a chuckle, "Where else could a Mormon, two Catholics, an Anglican, and a pagan worship together?"

After the service they went back outside, quieting their footsteps in reverence. When Libby asked Jake what she thought of the experience she answered, "It was beautiful, and interesting too. I liked it."

Libby nodded, satisfied. "I find it good that people seek to believe, as long as they don't start killing each other because of it." Looking into the distance for a moment she finished, "As always, I said a prayer for my mother's soul and one for my father as well, though I fear for his chance at Heaven."

Chapter Fifteen

Memnet caused her friends a great deal of trouble, for which she suffered terrible guilt afterward. The day began with attending a religious service together, which pleased her. They seemed like a family, sitting respectfully together, and she found herself imagining what it would be like if Roy and she were Jake's parents. She'd had to stop herself from taking his arm as they left the temple. Perhaps it was her preoccupation with such thoughts that led to the mistake.

The adults knew from the first that Libby had more than one purpose in mind when she'd proposed the trip. While it was true they enjoyed their trips to the temple, it was also practical to travel some distance from home for their more extensive thievery. From necessity they'd formed a set of rules for foraging. They didn't steal much from any one business, didn't take non-essential items, and avoided returning to the same store whenever possible. It lessened the harm they did, which was a concern for three of them at least, and it also lessened the chance they'd be caught.

To find new opportunities, they traveled from time to time to outlying areas with a list of items Libby made as needs arose. Roy had whispered in Memnet's ear, "We must really need supplies if Libby's willing to pay train fare for all five of us."

After the service Libby gave the "shopping" list to Leo. Her part in the scheme was to take Jake to do some "sight-seeing" so the girl didn't realize what was going on. Roy commented privately to Memnet, "Even if she was willing, Libby's got no knack for thievery, so we're better off without her." Memnet wished she didn't have to participate, having no appetite for theft herself, but she was determined to do her part.

As Roy went off to find socks and underwear, Leo and Memnet looked at winter clothing for Jake, whose tattered Keds and jeans jacket weren't much protection for winter. In a Kresge's store they located the children's section at the back, a small extension of the main room that smelled of Johnson's shampoo and talcum powder. Leo pointed out a pair of side-zip boots that Memnet judged acceptable. With a quick look around to see that no one was watching, they went into action.

On such excursions, Leo kept a shapeless cloth sack stuffed in his inside coat pocket until they found the items they needed. At that point the sack became Memnet's purse, with the smaller one she carried into the store concealed inside it. Leo blocked Memnet from sight while she stashed the boots in the bag. He stood back as she hung it on her shoulder, nodding to indicate that it didn't bulge noticeably.

Memnet hated everything about stealing, but the worst part was leaving the store afterward. Judging from his grim expression, Leo disliked it too. As Memnet followed him toward the front, she noticed a door with a sign that said *EXIT*. That was one of the few written words of English she recognized. With some relief she thought that if they left by this door, they'd avoid passing the checkout counter and the sharp-eyed clerks who might stop them.

"Leo, here!" she whispered. Moving quickly in her desire to be done, Memnet pushed the door open. A loud blare sounded, repeating itself a second later, and again, and again. Panic gripped her, and she saw fear in Leo's face as he pushed her through the doorway into the street. Because of the awful din, she couldn't hear him, but his lips formed the word "Run!" as he closed the door on her. Heart thudding, Memnet ran.

***

At least Memnet had escaped, Leo consoled himself as two clerks converged on him. He saw what she hadn't been able to read, smaller letters that said, *Exit in Emergency Only—Alarm Will Sound.* Why hadn't he insisted she learn to read English?

Still, she had the stolen goods. He'd be all right if he presented himself as a tipsy old man who'd stumbled against the wrong door.

Leo couldn't have predicted he'd run afoul of a small man with a power fixation. He knew the type, having met such men before: Harold Muldoon was a petty man with a petty job who exercised the tiny bit of authority he had to its fullest extent. Bad luck had brought Leo into his limited sphere of influence.

Head clerk and therefore in charge of store security, Muldoon escorted Leo to his closet of an office with barely suppressed zeal. Locking the door behind them, he sat down at a large desk and looked at Leo as if he were lunch.

No more than five feet four, Harold had a skinny neck stretched almost to bursting by a protruding Adam's apple. He was immaculately groomed except for his fingernails, which looked as if he'd been sorting through bits of broken glass. Jake would have recognized the scent that accompanied him as English Leather. In abundance.

Following his plan, Leo acted a bit addled by drink, tipsy but not disgusting enough to be hauled to a cell to sleep it off. The questions began.

"What are you doing so far north of the city, Mr. Bohn?" Leo had produced Norman Bohn's I.D. card from the museum, which usually allayed doubts about his identity. In American society, any person with a job was respectable on some level.

"I went to services at the Temple." He saw too late that mentioning Baha'i was a mistake.

"One of those, huh?" The pipsqueak's tone indicated distrust of odd religions. "What were you doing in the children's department?"

"I was looking for a bathroom."

Harold pressed thin lips together, unsatisfied. Leo's heart sank as he pulled a phone book from the desk drawer, looked up the number of the Schmidt, and dialed it. Checking the clock, Leo saw it was getting late. Perhaps no one would answer.

Someone did. The pipsqueak's voice was high-pitched but clear, and he looked distastefully at Leo as he said, "I'm calling from up in Wilmette. We have a man here who claims he works at your museum, a Norman Bohn?" The question in his voice was answered, and his eyes hardened. "I see. Since when?...That long, huh? And who is this?...Could I speak to the present curator?" A long pause, and Muldoon focused a glare on his prisoner. Aware the game was up, Leo tried to appear calm. Muldoon kept staring until Charlene was located.

"This is Harold Muldoon, up at Kresge's in Wilmette. We have a gentleman who claims to be Norman Bohn, but I understand he died....Well, I'll be turning him over to the local police, ma'am. From the large, hidden pockets in the coat he was wearing, we suspect he intended some shoplifting." He nodded. "I'll keep you informed, and yes, I'll be happy to send the identification card back to you."

Muldoon had begun to enjoy himself. Leo could imagine his retelling of the incident at dinner, highlighting his service to the head of a downtown museum. He ended the call with obsequious offers of "…anything further I can ever do to help, Ms. Dobbs."

Looking at Leo with a smirk, he pushed the cut-off button. The next call was to the local police, as Leo already expected it would be.

***

When Memnet located Roy she lapsed into her native tongue, which meant it took a while for him to grasp the situation. Once she calmed enough to use English he listened carefully then said, "Find Libby and Jake and take the next train home. Stay there and wait for us." If they were in trouble, and Roy guessed they were, he wanted the women to be safe.

Roy went to Kresge's and hung around until his worst fears were confirmed. Lingering at a candy counter laden with aromas of licorice, peppermint, and heavily-waxed chocolate, he saw Leo led out in handcuffs by two uniformed locals and a bantam rooster type in a bad suit. The guy seemed proud of himself, and hearing him say something about "foreigners" and "citizenship" made Leo's would-be rescuer feel even worse.

If they'd checked Leo's ID card, he couldn't play the confused sot anymore. They needed a better story, and that was Roy's responsibility. He was pretty good at alibis.

When he entered the police station an hour later, Roy wore a cream-colored Nehru jacket, burgundy pants with flared bottoms, and the most pointy-toed shoes a man ever forced onto his feet. He'd added love beads and a peace symbol on a pendant, all courtesy of a man about his size he'd seen leaving an apartment building. The space where the man's car sat identified the unit he'd come from, and after confirming the place was empty, Roy had jimmied a window and assembled an outfit for himself from the man's closet.

The police station's reception area was totally pressure-hose-

126

able: plastic furniture, asbestos floor tile, and a gun-metal gray counter with file storage below. Sounds echoed off the hard surfaces, making each step of Roy's too-tight boots a statement.

Adopting a worried attitude he approached the desk, where a cop who looked like he belonged in junior high sat filling in a form. "I'm looking for my uncle. He's about so high with long, gray hair. Wears a black overcoat." As the officer stared blankly Roy added, "He might seem, um, a little off, you know?"

Harried-nephew-rescues-crazy-relative might explain the situation, especially if the nephew was willing to pay. If it cost every cent they had, he needed to get Leo away from the police.

The guy checked his log as if he booked hundreds of prisoners a day. "We have a gentleman matching that description. Have a seat, and you can talk to him in a while."

"Can I at least see if he's all right?" He touched his chest meaningfully. "He's not as healthy as he looks."

Baby-face was polite but uncooperative. "Have a seat. I'll let you know."

The cop scooted his chair along a plastic mat, clicked a sheet of paper around the typewriter platen with a practiced hand, and hit the return lever until the bell sounded. The conversation was at an end, his actions said.

Roy had no idea what story Leo had told, and Leo had no way of knowing Roy was out there. In the movies, suspects were allowed a phone call, but that wouldn't help, since there was no one to call.

He tried once more. "Look, I know Uncle Larry didn't mean to do anything illegal, but if he did, I'll cover the cost and throw in a little extra for time and inconvenience." No response. "It upsets my wife when he gets into these scrapes. She'll start nagging we should put him in a home." He leaned over the counter to catch the man's eye. "He's my only living relative, you know?"

The cop glanced significantly at the bench in the waiting area and went back to work. Roy sat, trying to appear more impatient than worried.

For over an hour he sat there. The Boy Scout behind the desk answered the phone and filled out reports, using the typewriter faster than anyone Roy had ever seen. Still, the novelty wore off, and he was reminded how hard a wood-slat bench becomes, no matter how many times the sitter readjusts his buttocks. Every fifteen minutes he asked if he could see his uncle. The infant was polite, neither bothered nor amused.

It was after six when the door to the Chief's office opened and an eager-looking man hurried out. Stepping past Roy, he opened the door, apparently having seen a car arrive out front. His voice carried from the entryway: "Sorry you had to come all the way up here on a Saturday, Agent Blackburn."

"That's what I get for being the new guy," said a voice from the foyer.

"This guy had a fake ID, and he's got a heavy Italian accent. I thought you'd want to know."

The inner door bumped open, and two men entered the room. The newcomer gave Roy his second shock of the day. He'd seen him twice before: once outside the Federal Building downtown, and before that, on the dark shores of Lake Michigan, where he'd watched Agent Blackburn kill another man in cold blood.

Chapter Sixteen

It took Jake a while to figure out what was going on. They'd planned to meet at Fourth and Linden at 5:00 p.m. Memnet was there when she and Libby arrived, but she looked like the Bomb was about to be dropped on Illinois. With trembling lips she told Jake, "Libby and I must talk."

They moved away, but with Jake's excellent hearing and Libby's sharp exclamations, she got most of it. Leo had been arrested, and Roy had gone to his rescue.

In her eight weeks with these people, Jake had figured out that the little bit of money they got from Memnet's singing didn't go far toward feeding and clothing five people. Though Libby often tried to shut Roy up, Jake knew he stole things when the chance arose and wasn't bothered in the least by guilt. Leo didn't like what he called foraging, but he did it too. They seemed to think she didn't know where her meals came from, and they must have hoped she wouldn't realize they were going to steal things today.

It was time to work together. No more secrets.

Approaching the worried women she ordered, "Tell me what's happening." When neither replied, Jake said, "Look. You need someone who knows how the legal system works."

Memnet looked to Libby, who told Jake in a few sentences what had occurred.

"Okay." Jake took a deep breath. "First we need to call the police station. I think they have to tell us if he'll be held, and where."

They decided Libby should make the call. Memnet still had trouble with English under stress, and Jake sounded like the kid she was. Extremely nervous, Libby made Jake lead her through the scenario several times before she twisted her shoulders to relax them and declared herself ready.

"Geez, Libby, it's just a phone call," Jake commented.

"Dial the number," she ordered. "I must concentrate on what to say."

Once on the line she did pretty well, using her most commanding tone and speaking directly, if a bit too loudly, into the phone. As she listened, her face fell.

Jake pulled on her arm. "What is it, Libby? What?"

"They're being taken into custody by the FBI."

Jake's eyes widened. The FBI? Theories of jewel thieves and Mafiosi didn't seem so wild now.

Libby almost ended the call, but Jake said, "Find out where they are and if they'll be moved."

After a large gulp, Libby asked the question. She listened carefully, thanked the speaker, and replaced the phone. As the coin rattled into the bowels of the machine, she held onto the receiver as if loath to cut their remaining tie to the men. "They'll be allowed their phone calls soon. Then they will be taken to the Federal Building downtown for further questioning."

"I am so stupid to open that door!" Memnet moaned. "I should follow Leo." She rubbed her forehead. "Roy sayed we should go back to the museum."

"That was before he knew he'd be arrested too," Libby replied. "We can't leave them there."

Jake could almost see the older woman pulling courage around her like a shield. "I agree," she said. "Let's find the police station. Memnet, maybe you should go home." Jake didn't want to hurt her friend's feelings, but she could see she was close to breaking down completely.

Both women disagreed. "We might need Memnet's help," Libby said, and her eyes told Jake not to argue. She got it. Memnet would feel even worse if they sent her away now.

"Okay. Let's hope it's not too far from here."

It wasn't far for people used to walking everywhere, but once there, they were unsure what to do. Libby said, "I could go in posing as a relative."

Jake stomped her feet, trying to warm them. "If they figured out who Leo and Roy are, won't they be looking for you two?"

Libby's brows lifted. "Whyever should they?"

"What if your picture's on the wall?"

Despite the desperate situation, Libby laughed aloud. "My dear child, if the police have our pictures on their wall, I'd be amazed. There is no one looking for us. In fact, no on in law enforcement has any idea we exist."

***

Roy had to give the FBI guy credit. He hardly flinched when he saw him sitting on the bench in the squad room. He followed the police chief down a hall, where he was allowed a peek into a room where Roy glimpsed the toes of Leo's shoes. When the newcomer nodded, the chief shut the door again and went on to his office.

It was time to go. Rising, Roy said to the desk officer, "I'd better call my wife and let her know I'll be a while."

As he spoke, the phone on the desk buzzed shrilly. The officer answered, listened, looked at Roy, and said, "Yes, he is." Roy turned toward the door, but two more officers were just coming in. He was trapped.

The kid replaced the phone and rose, one hand on his sidearm. "Agent Blackburn would like a word with you." Seeing no other option, Leo's failed rescuer went quietly.

They put Roy in a room with a table, three chairs, and the strong smell of coffee and cigarettes. The only sound he heard for the next half hour was the buzz of a bad ballast in the fluorescent light above him. When the agent finally entered the room alone, he smiled, but the effect wasn't warming.

Nothing about Blackburn said "murderer," unless you'd actually seen him shoot a man in the back. He was ordinary looking, not handsome, not homely, with wide shoulders and muscular arms. Closing the door, he leaned against it. "I owe you something, Cowboy, and I intend to pay you back."

"I want to talk to the chief," Roy demanded.

His enemy laughed. "Do you think he'll interfere in an official FBI investigation? He thinks he's caught a team of hit men, and he expects a citation." Blackburn's lips twitched. "I've relieved him of the responsibility for you two desperadoes, for which he is grateful, since I told him how ruthless and clever you are. I assume the guy in the next room was with you on the shore that night."

"That old guy? I saw him get arrested for shoplifting and thought maybe I could help him get out of it."

"I don't think so. Now these guys saw an Italian with false papers and thought Mob, but I doubt that. Guys who are connected would have stayed out of my business that night."

132

Blackburn ran his tongue over his teeth. "It's the kid, right? She your daughter?"

Roy chose silence, and the agent said matter-of-factly, "It doesn't matter. She'll come out once you're not there to steal for her. And I got a look at your woman at the Federal Building. That'll help."

The stale smell of the room and deepening dread turned Roy's stomach, and he thought he might be sick. This guy would murder him and Leo and dump their bodies, as he'd done to the man in the park. Then he'd go looking for Memnet and Jake. And what could Roy do about it? Helpless rage filled his chest: pretty little Jake and sweet, lovely Memnet needed protection. He wanted to be around to provide it.

There was a knock on the door, and the Chief stuck his head in. "Sorry to interrupt, Agent Blackburn, but do you want us to fingerprint these guys? We can do it here and save some of your Saturday evening."

Roy rose. "Sir, I need to talk to you alone."

The chief pointed an admonishing finger. "Listen, you. The agent here gave me your history, and my officer told me your yarn about poor old Uncle Larry. Don't even try it."

"He killed a man!" Roy said. "Leo and I saw him do it!"

He'd never been so honest with an officer of the law before, and it got him nowhere. The chief turned to Blackburn. "The fingerprints?"

"We'd just have to do it again downtown," the agent answered. "I want them in federal custody as soon as possible. I thank you, and I'm sure you have paperwork for me to sign."

Papers were produced, signatures were affixed, and Roy and

Leo were handcuffed together, officially prisoners of the person most dangerous to their health and safety. With repeated thanks and congratulations on two of the three sides, they parted company with the Wilmette police, ushered by two cops into the back seat of Agent Blackburn's sedan.

***

A person standing on a certain street corner in Wilmette, Illinois, on that November evening would have witnessed an interesting little drama. Three females stood outside the police station as a man exited a black sedan and entered the building. Seeing him, one of the women became agitated. The others calmed her, listening to what she had to say.

There followed a spirited discussion full of pantomime, after which the three women walked two blocks, to the corner of 3rd and Mirre, where a sign said *U.S.-41 South—Left*. There they vanished into the shadows, each in a different direction.

It was close to 9:00 p.m., and the flow of traffic had slowed. The wet pavement shone, reflecting streetlights above it. The women waited, each in her spot, but for what?

It took a while, but several men came out of the building: two uniformed officers, two men handcuffed together, and the man who'd arrived in the sedan. The prisoners were put into the back seat. After handshakes, the uniformed men returned to the building. The man now in charge of the prisoners got into the car and drove off.

As he turned left at the corner, the driver didn't see the woman under the street lamp signal to someone farther down. He'd hardly had time to accelerate when a hunched figure appeared directly in front of him. He braked hard, but the woman hit the front fender with a thump and fell onto the pavement,

134

According to the men in the back seat, the driver at this point said some very bad words. He considered driving on, but the old lady had disappeared under the front of the car. Behind him, a voice called, "Oh, my god! She's hurt!" Someone had witnessed the accident.

Smacking the steering wheel, the man pushed open the car door, got out, and strode to the front. At that moment, the smallest of the women approached the car from the back, got into the driver's seat, and opened the passenger door in one agile movement. The second woman got in just as the car's owner realized what was happening. He hurried back to the driver's side, but both doors slammed shut, and the locks clicked.

As the vehicle jerked ahead, the former driver grabbed the door handle. The car's movement spun him around, and he staggered backward, forced to let go. Exhibiting admirable reflexes, the man pulled a gun from his coat, but he was disoriented. The two shots he fired at the wildly weaving car did nothing to stop it. Glaring at its retreating shape, he apparently remembered the reason he'd stopped. He looked angrily around, but the woman his car had struck was nowhere to be seen.

Chapter Seventeen

Libby waited at the corner a block down and one over. With a screech of tires Jake braked for her and then started again almost before the older woman was inside the car. Out of breath but proud of her derring-do, Libby accepted commendations from all directions for undertaking the dangerous stunt. "It was Jake's idea," she admitted. "She says children in the projects do it for fun. I was the logical victim, since Mr. X had never seen me."

"His name is Charles Blackburn," Roy put in.

"Memnet said he's the one you saw at the Federal Building. We knew we had to do something."

"It's good you did," Roy said. "He planned to kill Leo and me then go looking for Jake."

Jake had a terrible time keeping the car on the road, and she hit several curbs before she got the knack of cornering. No one suggested taking over for her. "I had imagined American teenagers were born with an instinct for managing an automobile," Libby commented, holding on with both hands, "but I now see the error of that theory."

Using the insides of Blackburn's pen, Roy released himself and Leo from the handcuffs as they left Wilmette behind. "There's the turnoff to Wrigley Field," Leo said. "We can leave the car there."

Jake made the turn into the parking lot and stopped the car. "Should we wipe off our fingerprints?"

"Ours are not on record," Leo replied. "Unless you yourself have run afoul of the law so early in life, Jake, we are safe."

***

At the end of each week, Blackburn called the head of an unpublicized but well-funded organization to report events that might influence their plans. Unfortunately, his employer was already aware of the fiasco in Wilmette when Blackburn phoned on Friday.

"Since they're without resources, how do these people continue to escape you?"

Blackburn gritted his teeth. "I won't underestimate them again."

"I would hope not." The old man dropped that subject. "Have you found someone within the Bureau suitable for our purposes?"

"I have." Blackburn was relieved to be able to offer something positive. "There's a young agent who fits what we have in mind perfectly. I've assigned him to the detail."

"Good. We'll proceed as we discussed. In addition, I've found someone with access to a building perfect for our base of operations."

"Is he a member of our organization?"

"She, and no, she's not, but she's eager to be seen as important and therefore easy to manipulate."

"Things are coming together."

"I'd be happier if that band of worthless gypsies didn't keep stumbling into your affairs. Get rid of them." The caller remembered something before ending the call. "The agent we'll be using as scapegoat. We need to connect him to the cause."

"His name is Danner. Clay Danner."

"Danner. Arrange something social so the news people have

something to speculate on."

"Yes, sir. I'll see to it."

***

Caution reigned again. Storeroom C's non-paying tenants had many worries: Agent Blackburn, the police, and even Charlene Dobbs. Though Leo thought it unlikely she would guess the man with Norman's identity card was living in the basement, Memnet and Libby fretted anyway. Too many things had gone wrong, and their peaceful time in the museum seemed at an end.

Two days after their encounter with Blackburn, the little warning bell tinkled softly. Rising quickly, Roy and Memnet pushed the chairs into the corner. Leo and Libby moved the dresser in front of the TV. Jake emptied the refrigerator and tossed their personal items into the secret rooms. By the time the door opened, they were huddled in the men's quarters in total darkness.

Voices sounded, one woman and two men. "There's not a thing in here we'll ever use," the woman said. "Clear it, and we'll store the new Christmas decorations when we're done with them."

"That'll work," said a man whose voice sounded like he had a sore throat. "Long as we put pallets down so they don't soak up the damp."

"I didn't even know this room was here." The second man had a higher voice.

"Used to be the furnace room," the older man replied. "There was this old coal burner we took out in pieces. Once it was gone, we started keeping the really junky stuff down here."

"The holiday light display will be up until after New Year's, so you men have that long to get this mess cleared out." The woman's sharp footsteps retreated then echoed on the stairs.

"You men better obey my every command, or I'll have your jobs!" The older man said. "Damned women's libber!"

"She ain't even polite about it." They resented their boss' faults in silence for a while. "You wanna start now?"

The rasp-voiced one huffed in disgust. "We can't just haul it out and toss it. We have to get someone on staff to check it off the inventory. It's gonna be a big job."

"I might take this chair," High Voice said. "My old lady could recover it. She's pretty clever—Hey, look, there's a book in the cushion: *Cannibal Land.*"

Jake made a tiny squeak, but Leo silenced her with a touch. "Looks like it belongs in the library upstairs," Low Voice commented. "Wonder how it got down here?"

"Maybe Stosh sneaks down here at night and reads." High Voice tittered at his own joke.

"He wouldn't do that," the other said with a chuckle. "Stosh can't read."

"You got that right. I'll take it to Ms. Dobbs."

They left, but it wasn't long before the bell rang again. Just out of hiding, the friends quickly retreated a second time. This time there was no talking, only the click of high-heeled shoes across the floor. When the woman finally left, she went up the stairs slowly, as if heavy thought weighted her steps.

***

The next morning Jake and Memnet visited the public library, the post office, and the hall of records, returning with several blank documents and a copy of Jake's birth certificate.

That evening, Jake made Roy and Memnet watch *The Patty Duke Show* to get an idea of their roles. As the set warmed up, she sang a few bars of the theme song for them, obviously pleased she'd won her argument at last.

As the young couple studied middle class mannerisms, Libby and Leo went upstairs, taking Norman's keys. Libby returned with paper, pens, and an assortment of other items. Leo followed more slowly, carrying a typewriter.

All night Leo worked at forging papers to create identities for Roy and Memnet Parker, husband and wife from Waukegan, Illinois. Seals had seemed impossible, but Libby found an embossing press in Charlene's desk. Its imprint was for the Schmidt Museum, but Leo found when he applied the seal over a gold circle of candy wrapping foil, it made a convincing fake.

The museum had a machine called a laminator that sealed things in plastic. Libby fretted about the smell of plastic that emanated as it heated, but Leo opened a window and turned on a small desk fan to dispel the odor.

When they were done, Roy thumbed through the tidy stack of documents that established his authenticity. He was now a married contractor from Waukegan who'd served honorably in the United States Marine Corps. "You made an honest man of me, Leo," he drawled. "Dishonestly, but you did it."

***

After a great deal of discussion, they had agreed to implement Jake's original idea. Memnet would pose as her aunt so Jake could get her mother's insurance money. To achieve her goal she had defeated three arguments. When Libby scoffed that Memnet was not confident enough of her English, Jake suggested Roy could come along, posing as her husband.

Roy was willing. "I can look upstanding," he insisted. "I really can."

Leo worried the three of them might be exposed and possibly arrested, but Jake answered that staying at the museum was equally dangerous. "And where can we go without money?"

No one had an answer to that.

Memnet's argument centered on Jake. "It is your money, Jake. We should not use your inheritance for ourselves."

She turned assertive, pounding her fist on the table. "You guys are my family now. If my money gets us a place to live together, I'll be happy."

"She's right," Roy said. "It's the only way unless—"

Knowing the bank robbery idea loomed, Jake stepped in. "Then we agree. We get my money and use it to everyone's benefit. It's what I want. Besides, you guys need me, or you'll end up on Alcatraz." Roy was the only one who got her joke, but he didn't seem to think it was funny.

They located a store near the Loop that sold high-end castoff clothing. The prices were steep, even for second hand, but Roy didn't plan on paying. He selected a well-cut suit in brown, his best color, a white shirt, and a thin tie. Jake insisted the suit required dark socks and wing-tips, and he reluctantly agreed. Once Memnet had trimmed his hair and mustache Jake pronounced him "pretty dreamy for an old guy."

Memnet chose a Mary Quant A-line dress with blocks of color separated by black piping, last year's style but still "mod," according to Jake. They matched it with black patterned hose and a white fake-fur coat with a matching hat. She looked stunning.

While Roy stuffed the items out a window in the back room, Jake stood lookout and vowed they'd pay the store back when she got her money.

Chapter Eighteen

Dressed in what she described as a "dorky-looking" plaid dress and matching headband, Jake entered the offices of the Merit Insurance Corporation, ("We Care About Your Life") accompanied by her new aunt and uncle.

"Good afternoon," Roy said to the woman at the reception desk. "This is Jerilyn Kay Marks. I think you people might be lookin' for her." He was cool as could be, while Memnet's dark skin looked ashy. As for Jake, she felt like she had the word *LIAR* embroidered on her headband in big block letters.

The waiting room was tastefully decorated with potted plants, classic artwork, and heavy wooden chairs with burgundy velvet seats and bronze-studded armrests that called to mind Sherlock Holmes. Deep-pile carpeting muffled the tapping of the receptionist's electric typewriter. Jake hoped they hadn't spent her money on upgrading the decor.

The polite woman made some calls and discovered that the agent assigned to Jake's policy, Mrs. Bilman, had a client at the moment. She asked if they would please wait. It was nerve-wracking for Jake to sit calmly, hiding her turmoil. If these people didn't believe their story, then what? Roy and Memnet might be arrested, Jake would be sent to a juvenile facility, and they'd never see each other again. Somehow it hadn't seemed real before, but she suddenly felt the urge to tell her friends how much she liked them. She also wanted to tell Roy and Memnet to stop pretending they weren't attracted to each other. She considered running back to the safety of the museum, but that safety was a feeling, not a fact. There was more danger of discovery any day.

"Jerilyn?" Jake looked up to see a middle-aged lady with glasses that sat halfway down her nose. She was smiling, a good sign.

She stood. "Hi. This is my Aunt Memnet and Uncle Roy." She stuttered so much she was afraid the woman could tell what a liar she was. Mrs. Bilman smiled even wider.

"So nice to meet you. Please come back."

They followed her down a hallway. Mrs. Bilman was almost as tall as Roy and strongly built. Jake guessed she had a weekly appointment at a salon, where a beautician arranged her hair then sprayed it rock hard so it stayed that way until next time. Her mom had done that, sleeping on a satin pillowcase and wrapping her hair in toilet paper to protect her "look."

The office was wood-paneled and tidy. The smell of lemon oil remained from last night's cleaning. The desk was piled with folders, each color-coded with a small tag that identified its origin. Rows of filing cabinets had similar tags tucked into small metal brackets. There was a goldfish bowl on the desk, and two angel fish swam to and fro among plastic greenery. Jake had never liked seeing fish stuck in a bowl with nowhere to go they weren't on display. To her it didn't seem like much of a life.

After fetching a third guest chair from an office next door, Mrs. Bilman stepped behind her desk and indicated they should sit. Jake sat between Memnet and Roy. Memnet's hands shook, but she folded them in her lap.

"Miz Bilman," Roy began, "let me start by apologizin' for taking so long to contact you. When my wife's sister-in-law died, Jerilyn here was very upset. She went to our home in Waukegan, knowin' we would take her in, and of course we would have been glad to." He smiled at Jake, one eyelid closing in a wink the woman couldn't see.

"Unfortunately, we'd gone overseas for several months to visit my wife's family." He leaned toward Mrs. Bilman, resting his outstretched hands on the smooth, polished surface of her desk. "We had no idea that Ja--Jerilyn's mother was so ill. The last time I spoke to her, she didn't say a word about it."

Jake went into her act. "Mom didn't want you to cancel your trip to Syria on her account, Uncle Roy. She thought she'd make it until you came back."

"Your momma was a brave woman." Roy shook his head sadly. Memnet looked down.

Mrs. Bilman seemed impressed. "I'm sure you had no way of knowing."

"But Jerilyn has been alone all this time. It was lucky she knew where we keep the key, so she could let herself into the house." Roy put a hand on Jake's shoulder. "I would hate to imagine what might have happened if she hadn't been able to get in."

"What a terrible experience for a young girl!" Turning in her chair, Mrs. Bilman pulled on a file drawer that opened quietly on well-maintained roller tracks. Pulling a red-tagged folder and placing it in front of her, she perused its contents. "Well, Mr. uh..."

"Parker, Roy Parker."

"Mr. Parker, the policy was written by Jerilyn's grandfather, Arnold Banks. The beneficiary is Miss Jerilyn Kay Banks." Here she frowned. "Banks?"

"My mother took her name back when Dad died," Jake explained.

Memnet looked down in supposed grief over her brother's death, and Roy said, "We can take care of Jerilyn's needs. Any money due her here will be saved for her college education."

"That was Mr. Banks' intent."

Roy nodded. "It was good of him to provide for Jerilyn, since I know he never approved of the marriage." He smiled ruefully. "My wife's family was almost as upset when she married me as Mr. Banks was with Lorna, but we worked things out." He took Memnet's hand and patted it. "We have no children, and we're more than willin' to give our niece a home."

Mrs. Bilman breathed a sigh that was half relief at solving an overdue claim and half admiration for the handsome Mr. Parker. Jake smiled to herself. They had her.

Of course documents had to be shown. First they established everyone's identity. Then Roy showed a court order to prove the Parkers were granted custody of their niece.

Leo had done a wonderful job, aging some of the papers with folds and stains, while the "court" document showed white and new against the rest. As Libby always said, he was an artist. According to the papers, Jake's aunt was authorized to safeguard her finances until she was eighteen.

Jake's euphoria was stilled when the agent decided she should speak to the court before finalizing the transfer of funds. "I don't doubt you, but twenty thousand dollars is a lot of money."

Jake gasped, having never heard the exact amount. Even Roy seemed nervous at the prospect of that much money, and a sheen of sweat appeared on his brow. It was a surprise to them both when Memnet, in a voice both confident and clear, said, "I have the name of the man who handle the matter." Rummaging in her bag, she took out a business card and handed it to Mrs. Bilman.

"He is Mr. Leo DiMucci."

***

Leo and Libby sat nervously in the back of Trader Vic's as the bustle of breakfast died down and the restaurant emptied. Seated in the booth nearest the pay phone, they wondered how long they could nurse their tea and pretend to converse. When the waiter returned a third time, Leo admitted they were waiting for a call. He retreated without comment, though his expression said if they were truly upstanding citizens they'd have their own telephone. A few minutes later the call came, and Libby hurried to answer before anyone else could.

"Judge Brennan's office, how may I help you?" Her clipped British pronunciation was impressive for an imaginary legal office. She listened, nodded to Leo, and spoke again. "That would be Leo DiMucci, officer for children's court. One moment, I'll connect you."

Leo stared at the receiver until Libby nudged him and mouthed, "Talk!"

"Yes, hello. This is DiMucci." Leo had practiced a Midwest twang. Libby, who had a flair for languages, advised keeping his jaw tight and letting the sound come out his nose.

"This is Genevieve Bilman at Merit Insurance. I have here Jerilyn Banks and Mr. and Mrs. Roy Parker, concerning a policy we hold for Miss Banks. Since she was missing, the policy was never paid, but now she seems to be settled with her aunt and uncle."

Leo paused as if recalling. "Yes, I handled that case. She ran off to their house when her mother died, but they were in Africa or somewhere."

147

"Syria."

"That's right. The aunt is Arabic. Pretty thing."

"So Jerilyn is now in their custody?"

"Yes. The judge signed the order last week. There's insurance, you say?"

"Yes. A good amount, that's why I'm checking."

"Well, I don't think the Parkers need it. He made plenty helping the Arabs find their oil, and now he runs a small company up north somewhere."

"Uh, Waukegan."

Leo smiled. Bilman was perusing the papers he'd created. "That's it. I was glad the girl has family to take her in. We simply don't have places for them all."

"Thank you for your time, Mr. DiMucci."

"Certainly. Anything I can do to help."

As Leo hung up the telephone, Libby surprised him with a quick hug. "You were magnificent, Leo. Jake will have her money, and no matter what happens to us, she'll be well."

They were so relieved to have pulled off their part of the plan that Libby tipped the waiter, something Leo had never seen her do before. It was only a nickel, but still.

***

Once outside the insurance offices, the Parker family collapsed in fits of hysteria that made some passers-by frown and others smile. "Memnet, Memnet, Memnet!" Roy gasped between waves of laughter. "Who'd have imagined you could be such a smooth liar?"

"Leo guess they will want proof. He waits by a telephone with Libby, who plays the secretary."

"And you didn't tell us?" Jake asked.

Her face turned devilish, a difficult feat for one so angelic. "Roy is sure his plan will fool them. I think, maybe I wait and see if my help is needed. If not, it is good. If so I am, what do you say? Cool?"

"Cool, far out, groovy and out-a-sight, that's what you are." Jake succumbed to laughter again, but when she recovered, she had a suggestion. "Mrs. Bilman said we can return in three days to pick up the check, and I think we need a bank account by then. Want to do it at the State Bank right there on the corner?"

"No," Memnet ordered. "We go north, to Merchant's Bank. Libby say those who do business there get a free electric can opener, and this we will need for our new home."

Chapter Nineteen

Leo needed pictures of each of them in order to make the documents modern life required. Roy's initial one had come from a photo booth at the drug store, but the quality was poor. When Leo said they needed a good camera, Jake claimed Marshall Field's carried anything a person could want.

Marshall Field's was the premier department store of the city. Its window displays were imaginative, its personnel well-trained, and its reputation stellar. With money in her purse and Memnet half a step behind, Libby felt almost like her old self as she entered the revolving doors.

The Christmas season was over a month away, but signs of the holiday had begun to appear. A placard with changeable numbers indicated thirty-six shopping days remained. Displays suggested yuletide themes. Soon fresh-cut cedar and pine would arrive, filling the store with clean scents, and signs would suggest gifts for the man/woman/child who has everything.

Holidays meant gifts, and Libby had once loved receiving them. Now she saw items she coveted for the others: gloves for Leo, who had a touch of arthritis in his hands; scent for Memnet who loved it so; boots for Roy, whose own were cracking from the wet streets; and for Jake, books and more books.

Though they wouldn't spend Jake's windfall on non-essential items, they looked at everything. Money made things possible: They really could buy the electric mixer in bright red if they decided it was necessary.

The frightening part of their excursion came when Libby asked a floorwalker where to find cameras. Pointing, he said,

"Take the escalator to the second floor."

Libby looked fearfully at Memnet. The dapper little man didn't know he'd suggested feat of daring, but neither of them had ever attempted navigating one of the frightening machines. Staring at the monster Libby asked, "What if one's clothing were to become caught in the works?"

"It's perfectly safe." The man gestured toward what he saw as an innocent modern convenience.

The moment was pivotal. For two years they'd held themselves apart from the world. Now their lives were changing, and they tacitly agreed they must accept the challenge. Libby had used a telephone; Memnet had worn nylon stockings and a garter belt. They would conquer the escalator.

Memnet approached the metallic beast, waited a bit to get its rhythm, and made an unusual but dignified jump, landing with both feet on the rising step. Grabbing the handrail (which also moved!) she steadied herself, and her ascent began. Looking back at Libby, who looked as if she feared she'd never see her again, Memnet gestured for her to follow. Libby remained still, as if her legs had turned to stone.

At that moment the floorwalker stepped forward. "See, madam? Nothing to fear."

Mentioning fear to Libby was like waving a red flag before a bull. Raising her chin, she put her foot on the first step. As it rose under her, Libby's whole body stiffened, but she grasped the handrail, brought her other foot up, and remained balanced. Just barely.

By this time Memnet was near the top. She stared down at her feet, jumping a second time when the step below her melted into the floor. Once she was safe she turned to help Libby, whose jaw tightened as she approached the top. Unwilling to hop, she remained on the step until it disappeared beneath her feet, sending her stumbling forward. Memnet was there to catch her, and they held each other upright until the shaky feeling subsided.

"Well," Libby said briskly. "I imagine after the first time, it's much easier." Ignoring the amusement of the man below, they went to make their purchase, refusing for the moment to think about the ride back down.

***

Jake and her friends knew their time in the museum was short. Men stomped down the stairs every day to remove items from the stacks. Things they'd considered theirs were taken away with the rest. Jake's lumpy chair disappeared with scrapes and a curse for its heaviness. The cabinet where they'd kept their larder was broken down to make it easier to carry out. Stacks got smaller as items were given away, sent upstairs, or consigned to the trash. When they emerged in the evening, they never knew what would be gone.

Everything that might betray their presence was moved to the sleeping quarters, which crowded them and underscored the need to move on. Anytime they left the Schmidt they risked running into Agent Blackburn, so most of their days were spent slouched among the cushions. They read, they napped, and Libby made list after list of future needs and possibilities.

At night they trooped like silent elves up to the library to work on their new lives. Roy pored over maps of greater Chicago, seeking a place for them to live. Leo worked to make them all appear to be legitimate citizens: Social Security cards, a better driver's license for Roy (though he didn't know how to drive), naturalization papers for himself, Libby and Memnet, and various other documents that would prove helpful. He even did a portrait of Jake as a toddler with Memnet, Bassim, and Lorna, using a picture Jake had of her parents. When he finished, it appeared that husband, wife, baby daughter, and sister had posed together.

The site of their relocation caused considerable discussion. They agreed it was unwise to go anywhere near Wilmette again. Jake warned against the crime and decay in her old neighborhood. Roy argued for staying near the lake. "If we ever have to run, we can steal a boat and travel up the Michigan shoreline all the way to Canada. The bootleggers used to do it, so we could too."

"I remember you spoke of it before," Libby said. "You seemed like Francis Drake, advocating a trip into the unknown."

***

October, 1965

"But what are we to do here?" Libby asked Norman the last time they spoke with him. He'd brought hamburgers wrapped in greasy waxed paper, fried potatoes, and something called cola that burned their throats. Memnet turned away from the smell of fried meat, sickened. Seeing her thinness, Libby wondered if she would survive this place.

"Everyone will want to meet you, and they'll pay," Norman boasted. "You'll be famous."

"I've been famous," Roy's voice was a growl. "It ain't all it's cracked up to be." Of all of them he was least offended by the food Norman provided, and he bit off a mouthful and chewed, turning away from Norman's rose-colored predictions for the future.

When Norman had gone back upstairs Roy told Libby, "I'm heading to Canada. There has to be a train that goes north."

Her eyes widened. "What about us?"

"They're not goin' to make it," he said flatly. The older man paged through a book with a perplexed frown, and the girl sat in the corner, staring dully into space. "You should get out while you can."

Libby licked her lips. "Stay one more day. Tomorrow I will speak again to the madman."

He considered it, acknowledging for the first time in his life that he was uncomfortable with being alone. "One day," he told Libby, "then I'm gone. I want no part of Bohn's plans."

"Nor do I," Libby said, "but I cannot leave them here. Who knows what he will do with them?"

Roy turned away, disturbed. He wasn't one to take on other people's problems, but the redhead was right. The old man wasn't a bad sort, and the girl... Well, he'd never seen anything like her. He found himself wanting to touch that perfect cheek, to move into her delicate aura and comfort her, though comfort was in short supply.

When she'd arrived, naked and beautiful, the fragrance of flowers he'd never seen, would never see, accompanied her. Part of him wanted to flee because of her. She was doomed. He could do nothing to help, and besides, she was nothing to him. Still, he agreed to stay. Maybe they'd get out of this mess somehow if they stuck together.

***

1967

Jake's curiosity about her family grew even greater as she watched them in action. Leo, clever enough to make money from his talents, seemed content to remain poor and unknown. Libby, who spoke at least three languages, was afraid of the telephone. Roy, a thief, worked to find a house where they could lead honest lives. And Memnet, lost in the world, insisted on doing her share and more.

What had brought them together: an Italian, an Englishwoman, an Egyptian, and a cowboy from Utah? None of her theories fit. She needed a whole new explanation.

Chapter Twenty

Roy contacted realtors, asking about properties that were available right away, located near the transit system, and roomy enough for five people. One night they heard him on the stairs, heedless of the noise he made. Libby clucked her tongue in disgust as he burst in, his hair wet with snow. The delicate lace shapes faded almost immediately to drops of water.

"I found a house," he said triumphantly. "Decent neighborhood, fifteen rooms on two floors and a full basement. They want to deal, but I said I was lookin'. After a day or two I'll offer low dollar."

"What's wrong with it?" Libby wanted to know.

"Somebody died there. Nobody wants a ghost house, but we're not afraid of haints, are we?"

They all shook their heads, though Jake noticed Memnet looked less than enthusiastic. "We can move right in, and we'll each have our own room." He sounded like an agent picturing his commission. "There's room for all of us and space for our businesses too."

Since they'd need to earn money once Jake's inheritance was gone, they each planned to open a home business. Memnet had listed various craft items she could make, and Libby wanted to expand her blossoming baking skills. Leo thought he might fix things that were broken.

"It sounds good," Libby admitted. "But I don't see why a death in a house would make it hard to sell."

Roy shrugged. "We got lucky, I guess."

"Where is it located?" Leo asked.

"On East 100th." Roy glanced at Jake with something like warning in his eyes. The address rang a bell, but she didn't ask if her memory was correct. She didn't want to know for certain if the former tenants had left this world at the hand of a murderer. Maybe some other homeowner in the area had decided to move after that awful night in July of 1966 when a deranged drifter named Richard Speck bound and strangled eight young student nurses in their house on East 100th.

***

Later that night, Leo continued work on the forged documents that would make them plausible citizens of the great state of Illinois. Libby checked to be sure his syntax was correct. "I taught Leo English when we first met," she told Jake as she scanned his handwritten originals. "Memnet too, of course, but Leo was an amazingly quick study."

"It's cool that you speak so many languages."

Libby's voice softened. "It pleased my father, who was himself very well-educated." She touched Jake's arm. "Memnet's English has improved since you came. From time to time she even speaks without being asked a direct question."

Once they'd finished for the night, Roy carried the typewriter back to the secretary's desk while Libby returned the smaller things to their proper places. She was alone, then, when her disagreeable experience began.

Using Norman's keys, she let herself into Charlene's office. She put everything away neatly, so the curator would never notice anything amiss unless she counted her paper clips. Since the day she came to Storeroom C twice, Charlene hadn't been back. They hoped she'd forgotten about it.

Once she'd replaced the office items, Libby went to the library to return their most recent books. As she pushed the door closed, a nasal voice sounded at her side. "Putting back what you stole?"

The woman sat in the corner, the glow of a cigarette betraying her presence. Why hadn't she smelled the smoke?

Libby forced her startled brain to function. "Sorry. I can come back and clean this room later."

"Don't!" The tone was a warning. "What are you doing in my museum?"

Libby sighed. Charlene Dobbs. Now what? Roy always said to stick to the truth as much as possible if caught.

"I've been staying here on cold nights. I don't steal anything. I borrow books to read, that's all." It was true for her. She wasn't responsible for Roy.

"Turn on the light," the woman ordered.

Obediently Libby pushed the switch, the old-fashioned, two-button kind. The lights came on, illuminating a room trimmed with oak and with 1930s pressed-metal ceilings overhead. A nice place—except for the presence of Charlene.

Looking like a satisfied, rather plump cat, the curator took a drag from her cigarette. Libby didn't approve of cigarettes, though she'd been known to smoke an occasional cigar. Cigarette odor was different, objectionable.

Charlene had one of those faces in which there's nothing wrong but nothing attractive either. She wore a short dress in black and white hound's-tooth print with a black silk bow at the center of the rounded neckline. Her legs were encased to the knee in black, shiny boots that zipped up the inside. She wore rings on several fingers, and her hair was held back from her full-moon face by a band of the same fabric as the dress. She might have been attractive but for three things. She was too old for the outfit by twenty years, her nasty expression ruined the effect of her careful toilette, and she'd laid a sword across her lap, whether for defense or offense, Libby couldn't say.

Stubbing the cigarette out in a glass ashtray she said, "Before I have you arrested, I want to know how you got in, how long you've been here, and who you are." Her voice revealed that Charlene was angry, though she tried to appear calm. *Angry people make mistakes.*

"I stay in the basement when it's cold."

"How do you get in?"

"I slip in when it's busy up front."

"This place is never what I'd call busy," Charlene's tone hinted her talents were wasted in this less-than-grand enterprise. No doubt her rightful place was head of the Field or the Adler.

Libby tried a question. "How did you know I was here?"

"Now that's interesting. My mousy little assistant kept saying books were missing one week and back the next. I ignored her, she's always on about something, but then Gary found a book in the basement and brought it to me. Things started adding up: that old drunk Stosh saying he hears ghosts at night, someone insisting I'd sent out a memo when I hadn't. Weird stuff."

She paused, but Libby could think of nothing to say. They'd become too relaxed, assuming that because Charlene was less than dedicated to her job she was also stupid.

"Then the police called and said some guy they arrested up in Wilmette had Norman's identity card. Now, that card should have been with Norman when he died, and I began to wonder if he smuggled someone in. I thought I'd hang around tonight and see what I could see, and here you are. I can't admire your taste in men, but I give you credit for going undetected this long."

She thinks I was Norman's paramour! Even now, the strongest impression she recalled of Norman was foul breath and the spittle that clung to the corners of his mouth.

Still, Charlene's assumption might allow the others to escape. Assuming a defeated expression she said, "I'll leave, and you'll never see me again."

Charlene gave her a nasty smile. "No, you won't. You'll go directly to jail, without passing Go, and you'll explain why a guy in Wilmette had Norm's ID."

"I-I had no use for it, so I sold it to a man who wanted to come in when it's cold."

Eyes too small for her round face narrowed in suspicion. "You're pretty free with answers."

Libby smiled weakly. "You caught me. What can I do?"

"You can show me where you sleep, for one thing."

That made her shiver with dread. "I move around."

The little eyes got even littler, and Charlene chuckled. "I don't think so. I think old Norm made you a secret spot where you and he could play."

"No. No, he didn't."

Taking a drag, Charlene flicked ashes onto the floor. "He was crazy, but he was a genius, kicked out of more top secret projects than you and I will ever know about. He went over the edge when he ended up in this dump."

"Oh?" No one knew better than she how over the edge Bohn had been.

"The board fought him all the time. He spent his days in the basement and his nights boozing with the guards. I had to do a lot of catch-up when I came."

"You've done well."

Picking up the weapon Libby recognized as a reproduction of a Roman stabbing sword, she pointed it at Libby's stomach. "Let's go." Besides being armed, Charlene was taller than she and sixty pounds heavier. Libby obeyed.

The upstairs rooms lined a curved balcony with stairs to the main hall at either end. Below were dark cases, soft lights, and no hope. The hall was silent, empty. Her friends were three floors down. When they reached the main floor, she thought of the warning bell. It would warn the others, and there'd be nothing for Charlene to see. She was caught, but there was no reason they had to be. "I stay downstairs. I'll show you where."

"Not without backup. I think Carl is on duty tonight."

The sword-point touched Libby's back menacingly, and she started forward again. They passed suits of armor, a case of various bows, and a display of handguns. Just as Charlene poked Libby again to hurry her along, there was a gasp and a muffled cry. The sword fell onto the rubber floor mat with a metallic clunk. Turning, Libby saw Roy's teeth flash white in the semi-darkness. "This way!"

He had Charlene in his powerful grip, one arm twisted behind her back and his hand over her mouth. Stooping to pick up the sword, Libby followed as he dragged the curator toward the stairway door. When a sound came from above, he changed course, ducking into the women's bathroom.

It wasn't long before they heard Carl coming to investigate the noise. A flashlight beam showed briefly under the door as he checked the area around the stairs. He opened the bathroom door a crack, but they huddled in the corner behind it and Carl didn't enter. As his steps retreated Libby wondered if he'd notice the missing sword, but he kept walking, down the center court, around the cases, and up the stairs. Finally they heard a door close above them. Carl had closed himself back inside the guard's room.

After waiting a few more minutes to be sure Carl was gone, Roy propelled his prisoner to the staircase. Stopping him, Libby tore a piece from her skirt and blindfolded Charlene before they descended the stairs.

In Storeroom C, the others hurried forward, surprised and alarmed. Libby told her story, ending with, "She's seen me, but she can't identify the rest of you."

"I was sure surprised when you came through," Roy said. "After I put the typewriter back, I sat down in my favorite spot. I noticed one piece was missing, and that made me think. I guess my luck was working for us again."

"I was never so glad to see you," Libby replied.

"Now what do we do?" Jake's eyes were wide.

"We could throw her in the Lake," Roy offered. He was kidding, but Charlene didn't take it well.

"Please!" she sobbed. "I won't tell anyone! Just let me go!"

"Madam," Leo replied, "we have stayed too long under your roof, and it's time we go. However you must be prevented from reporting us until we finish our preparations."

Charlene slumped in Roy's arms, fearing the worst, but

Libby understood. "Miss Dobbs, you're going to see my hiding place, as you demanded. You will be able to examine it as closely as you wish for at least a day or two."

Chapter Twenty-one

It was one thing to say they'd go, but the question was where. They hadn't closed on the house, though they agreed under the circumstances to take it no matter what its condition. Roy would handle the purchase, with Memnet once again acting the part of his wife. He'd been assured there was no difficulty with immediate occupancy, since the owner was eager to sell.

With no possibility they could move into their new home at 3:00 a.m. on a Tuesday, the question was where they would go. They put Charlene in the ladies' sleeping quarters, tied her with several of Memnet's scarves, and held a council. It was decided that Leo, Libby, and Jake would stay in the museum for two days, guarding Charlene and packing their things. "On Thursday, we have to let her go," Jake said. "After forty-eight hours she'll be considered a missing person."

"We must split up then," Leo said. "I will stay at the Mission, much as I dislike the babble. Libby, might you and Jake find a hiding place at the Planetarium?"

"Excellent idea," Libby answered. "She can study the solar system."

That left Memnet and Roy. "Call the agent," Jake suggested. "Say you want to stay in the area so you can do some work on the house before you move in. If they're eager to sell they'll come up with something."

They'd opened a bank account and collected the insurance check, in both Jake and Memnet's names. "That was the worst nervous I've ever been," Roy had told Libby and Leo, "sittin' there waitin' for all that money to be handed over, um, voluntarily. But Jake made a nice little speech, and Memnet smiled like she got that much every month from her Arab daddy. I got out of there as quick as possible after tellin' Mrs. Bilman we'd keep in touch. Not that we will."

Sure enough, when Roy called the realtor to discuss the purchase, the man was willing to help. The firm owned an apartment, he said, that was presently untenanted. They'd put Mr. and Mrs. Parker up there for a few days for a very modest fee. Would a studio do? Roy thought of Memnet as he agreed it would. She wouldn't like it, but they'd manage.

The next day Roy and Memnet set off in their "respectable outfits" as Jake termed them, with a cashier's check for the down payment tucked into Memnet's purse. Using a series of crowded public conveyances, they located the real estate agent, James ("Call me Jim") Thompson.

Mr. Thompson was a professionally friendly man whose life's work was making it easy for people like Roy, those with a big down payment, to buy a home. Roy guessed he had no interest in them as people, which was good. He gave Memnet a long look, but men did that.

The layout of the house was nearly perfect. "Libby will gripe about the tiny back yard, the garden, she'll call it," Roy told Memnet, "but there's plenty of room, and Leo can have the whole basement for his projects. What do you think?"

She stood in the large entry, looking around in wonder. "I never dreamed we would have such a place for our own," she said, ignoring the scarred woodwork and flaking wallpaper. "It is so full of light, so welcoming!" Her reaction made Roy happy for reasons he didn't want to examine.

They returned to Thompson's office to sign the papers. Roy

insisted they take possession right away, and Jim agreed with a casual gesture. "I'll get a permission letter from the owner," he assured them. "When we finalize, it'll simply be a matter of signing more papers."

Thompson drove them to the apartment in his Buick LeSabre. It was situated over a defunct Chinese restaurant and smelled faintly of soy sauce, but it was clean, furnished, and within walking distance of the house that would soon be theirs. As Thompson had warned, it was one big room with a bed in one corner and a tiny kitchen in another. Memnet's eyes widened when she saw only one bed, but she said nothing. Roy thanked Jim and promised to return the key on Monday.

As he walked him back to his car, Roy asked about nearby second hand stores. As Thompson wrote down some addresses, Roy explained they'd lost everything in a fire up in Wilmette.

"Tough break," he commiserated. "So you decided to relocate?"

"My wife is a city girl," Roy answered, feeling an odd satisfaction in the word *wife*. Why did it sound so right? He was not the marrying kind, not at all.

When he returned to the apartment, Memnet had already hung blankets across one corner of the room, opposite the bed where he surmised he'd be sleeping. She was busily collecting pillows to serve as her mattress. Roy smiled ruefully: Saying "my wife" and actually having one were two different things.

They spent the next few days visiting the dusty, musty places on the agent's list to find furniture for the house. The place had nothing except a round-topped refrigerator and a gas stove in an awful green, but Memnet thought they were wonderful. She played with the burners or opened the door to see the light come on every time she walked through the kitchen. The rest of the furnishings were up to them, and they spent Jake's money carefully, not knowing how long it would be until the businesses they each planned began paying.

Since Jake had explained zoning laws, Roy didn't mention their plan to work from home to Thompson. "People do it," Jake said. "Unless someone complains, we'll be okay."

Starting businesses would require seed money, and Jake was all for using her inheritance. "When we get rich selling Egyptian baskets and English scones, you can all pay me back."

As a shopper, Memnet once again surprised Roy. She was a shrewd bargainer with an eye for classic pieces, and he deferred to her judgment on what to buy. Items many would have bypassed because of obvious damage, she saw as objects of potential beauty. He wondered if her time in the museum had contributed to her ability or if she'd always had the eye for it.

Memnet chose tables, chairs, and beds, bargaining for free delivery due to the amount of business they brought to a store. She'd gained confidence since Jake came, and Roy couldn't fail to notice. Once too timid to cope, she now seemed able to face whatever she had to in order to survive. She'd helped to defeat Agent Blackburn, played the role of Jake's aunt, and now dealt with furniture shops, utility workers, and even curious neighbors with poise and grace. Memnet had become a confident woman, and Roy was no longer sure she wasn't his type. Ironically, she seemed less friendly toward him, retreating into distant coolness. By Saturday, it had almost made him crazy.

***

It had been a hard week for Memnet, though wonderful in some ways. She loved getting the house ready for the others, and shopping with Roy was pleasant. He didn't mind puttering through second-hand stores, climbing over junk to see if a piece she glimpsed at the back was worth salvaging. Good-naturedly, he fought back sneezes as he maneuvered the couch she'd chosen into a truck. The cushions were ruined, but she already had in mind how she'd repair them with a few yards of fabric.

Being close to him was hard. The size of the apartment meant they kept bumping into each other, and they didn't have the others around to serve as chaperones. Memnet told herself her attraction to Roy was due to circumstance. He'd been a hero at the beginning, serving as their lifeline. Now as they set up a home together, the intimacy the experience made it seem as if they could, perhaps should, be a couple.

Libby often urged Memnet to let Roy know she was attracted to him, but even Libby didn't know how complicated things were. In the first place, he could have almost any woman he wanted. In a series of light affairs with Chicago women, he'd never formed an attachment.

In addition to that, Memnet was not allowed to give herself to any man. As a young girl, she had dedicated herself to the temple in which she'd been raised, to a sect that demanded lifelong virginity. The priestesses had taken her in, and she'd gladly made the vows required to remain with them. The question she faced was difficult. What did that vow mean today?

When Roy was near, and even when he was not, Memnet thought of him, wondered what his touch would feel like on her skin. At those times she forced herself to remember that if she gave herself to him, he would within a month or two move on, as he'd always done before. Because of all this, she had remained distant. Still, it was difficult, when they laughed together, worked together, and relaxed together.

They had to walk everywhere, but the stores were decorated for Christmas, and though she didn't understand the holiday, Memnet enjoyed the lights and tinsel. The mechanical devices in store windows fascinated Roy, bubbles that traveled through imitation glass candles and Santas that waved at passers-by.

Back at the apartment each evening, Memnet fixed a simple meal after which they retired to their corners to read. That was the case until Saturday, their last day alone together. Leo, Libby, and Jake would take the train Sunday morning and they would rise early to be there to meet them.

They were both exhausted, having made every effort to make the house as attractive as possible for their friends. The utilities were on, and they could have stayed there, but they didn't want to move in without the others. Having begun together, they would enter into new lives the same way.

Roy sat on the small sofa, checking through his list one more time to be sure everything was ready, while Memnet fried ham and potatoes for supper. She fixed a plate and brought it, setting it on the coffee table. He didn't look up, but when she turned to go, he took her hand in his. Startled, she pulled back, but he did not release her. Raising his eyes to hers, he pulled gently until she sat beside him, her face close to his. Without a word, he cupped her face with a hand and kissed her tenderly.

Unaware of anything but his touch, Memnet moved into the embrace. When the kiss was finished, he stroked her hair. "So beautiful." This time it was she who began the kiss.

A moment later, however, something sliced through the emotions she felt. Pushing herself to her feet, she stepped away, leaving Roy at first surprised and then hurt.

"This can't be," she told him firmly.

"Why?" he protested. "You like me, don't you, Memnet?"

"I can never be yours, no matter what I feel." She felt miserable, cheated out of what half her heart wanted by what the other half said she couldn't have. "It is a vow I made, and it cannot be broken."

He reached a hand toward her. "What used to be isn't ours anymore. If you promised yourself to someone, he's gone."

"It is not a man. It's...more than that."

"But that's gone now, and we'd be good together."

Memnet took note of Roy's words. Being "good together" sounded temporary, something a man said to sway a woman's judgment. Did one break a holy vow for fleeting pleasure? Perhaps some women did. She could not.

"Your food is getting cold," she said in an even tone. Returning to the stove, she retrieved her own plate. Roy's eyes followed, and he seemed to want to say more. In the end he did not, and they ate their meal in silence. Memnet had never liked potatoes but these, tinged with regret, tasted even worse than usual.

Chapter Twenty-two

Jake wished she'd gone with Memnet and Roy. *If you're interested in three days of H-E-double hockey sticks, spend them with Charlene Dobbs.*

The first day Charlene cried, not tears of fear, but irritating, whiny bawling. Libby's insistence she'd be set free unharmed in a few days made no difference. She kept crying. And crying.

What a pain!

They kept her in the women's room, shoving a large cabinet against the door to keep her there. When the workers came downstairs, Libby sat on her to keep her quiet. Libby had to deal with her, since Charlene had already seen her. Roy and Memnet went off to ready the house, glad to escape the curator's distress. That left Leo and Jake to clear their belongings out of Storeroom C, which they did late at night.

Tuesday and Wednesday they sorted and packed things into knapsacks, pillowcases, and whatever else was available. They disposed of what couldn't be carried with them to 100th Street. When they told the museum staff where Charlene was on Thursday at closing time, they planned to be long gone, with no trace left behind.

It was surprising how much they'd accumulated. Leo and Jake stored some bags in lockers at the train station to be retrieved later, keeping only what was essential for the last day. Items they'd no longer need were shoved into various trashcans around the city.

Libby fretted, as usual. "We should have had Roy call the

pay phone down the block so we know how they are progressing on the house."

Jake figured it didn't matter. "Whatever's there, we'll make it work, just like here." She did hope for a real bed, with a mattress in place of lumpy, shifting pillows.

On Wednesday evening, Leo sat on the floor, making entries in his journal, a homemade book in which he kept notes and drawings of things important to him. He seemed unaware she was watching. She'd formed a new theory, researched at the public library B.C. (before Charlene). The answer was so simple she should have seen it right away. Her friends were aliens.

Everything fit once she got past the idea that only crazy people and movie directors believe in life from outer space. Extraterrestrials have no past, which they pretty much admitted: no fingerprints on file, no recorded documents, nothing. Also interesting was their discomfort with modern machines. They all hated the telephone; Roy distrusted anything with a motor; Memnet was afraid of the machine at the drugstore that made malts; and Libby was appalled if Jake suggested they hop into an elevator to get to the top floor of a building.

She guessed their spaceship had crashed, and Norman found them in the New Mexican desert. At school she'd heard about an alien landing that was hushed up. Norman sounded crazy enough to have stolen the government's aliens, and he couldn't have known he'd die and leave them alone in a strange world. The accents didn't fit, but she was working on that.

"Leo?" He raised his head and stopped writing, as he always did when she spoke. "Have you ever been to Roswell, New Mexico?"

He didn't react, though she was watching for any sign of

172

discomfort. "No, Jake, I haven't. Is it nice there?"

"I guess." She returned to her book, but as he began writing again, she watched from the corner of her eye. Was he a pod person like in *Invasion of the Body Snatchers*? Did he wear a disguise, or did his type of alien look exactly like humans? Leo didn't seem unworldly. He often smelled like sweat. She couldn't see any alien behavior, but something did catch her attention. He wrote with his left hand, moving right to left.

Yawning and stretching, Jake rose and circled behind him. He was writing backward, a trick she'd heard of somewhere. She'd never known anyone who could do it. Still, it was human writing, not Venusian markings, so she was no farther along with her theory than before.

***

Leo left the museum for the last time on Thursday afternoon. Soon afterward, Libby and Jake left as well, heading for the Planetarium, where Libby had located an unused office. She was determinedly cheerful, extolling the virtues of the Adler, but they were both a little sad to leave the place that had sheltered them through some of the worst days of their lives. She closed the false door securely as they left. It was doubtful anyone would discover it, and it was uniquely theirs.

Once he was a few blocks away from the Schmidt, Leo called the reception desk from a pay phone and said, "Charlene is in the basement." He repeated it to be sure the astonished woman got it then hung up. Once the staff got to Storeroom C, Charlene's crying would lead them to her.

He spent three nights at the clamorous Randolph Street Mission, aware it was the last time he'd see that place as well. The staff demonstrated the best religion has to offer: care for one's fellow men, and he couldn't help but compare them to the "hawks" in Congress who believed more bombs could somehow bring peace to the world. Despite that, he was more than ready to leave on Sunday. He intended to ask Memnet to check his hair for lice at the first opportunity.

The expedition to their new home began as soon as the trains started running. Carrying a soft duffel bag, Leo waited at the station until Libby and Jake arrived. Despite her dislike of "girly" clothing, Jake wore a wrap skirt and a button-up blouse under a new-to-her wool coat. Her hair was neatly arranged. She looked like a young lady, Leo said as he bowed over her hand.

Some sort of coloring had turned Libby's red hair quite black. They'd used an equally dark make-up on her eyebrows and lashes, which made her appear quite fierce. She'd changed from her usual navy blue skirt and white blouse to a wildly printed skirt of soft fabric that swirled around her ankles and a dark, high-necked red shirt set off with gold jewelry. The outfit was topped with a cape of red wool with black frogs at the neck.

"My dear, you look like a gypsy," Leo teased.

"It's temporary, a rinse," Libby said, touching her transformed hair.

"She tried to pinch me when she saw the color," Jake complained.

Libby looked down at her skirt. "The clothes are Memnet's, but they'll fool anyone looking for a faded redhead in plain garments."

"Not faded, and never plain," Leo said gallantly. "You are lovely either way." That made her smile a little. "Come, let's find the correct train."

Roy and Memnet met them at the station. Leo thought Memnet looked tired, but they were both eager to show them the house. It was only six blocks from the Torrance Avenue Station, and the day was gray but not too cold. After a walk slowed somewhat by bundles, bags, and boxes, they arrived.

It was quite a moment. This was home if they could manage to keep it. Here they'd become the people their papers said they were. Here they would mingle with neighbors, tradesmen, and customers. It was exciting and frightening at once.

"It's seen better days," Libby said, "but it's no worse than other places I've stayed, so I won't complain."

"Oh, she probably will," Jake muttered to Roy.

"The lines are good, and it seems solid," Leo said, kicking a porch post to test its soundness. With a grin and a bow, Roy opened the oval-windowed wooden door, which badly needed paint. "Folks, please enter your home away from museum."

They entered to the smell of Pine-Sol and bleach. A large, high-ceilinged room, painted creamy white, stretched before them. Its few pieces of furniture were dwarfed by its size, but that didn't matter. They broke into a babble of congratulation.

"It's so big!"

"The couch is great, Memnet."

"Where did you find all this?"

Memnet, who'd been holding her breath, gave Roy a quick glance of relief. He smiled broadly, as if he'd known it all along.

Libby admired the "great room," as she termed it, and was delighted with the spacious kitchen. Though Jake had moved many times, she'd never lived in a house. "It's got a front yard *and* a back yard," she exclaimed, peering out the windows.

Leo congratulated Roy on his find. He didn't share with the others his suspicion that several awful murders had occurred there. *The place will soon become ours, and then, like us, it will have no past.*

***

For the first dinner in their new home, Jake bought Colonel Sanders' Kentucky Fried Chicken for everyone. She'd noticed the place a few blocks back, and while the rest settled in, each in his or her own room for the first time in two years, she slipped out and returned lugging a large brown paper bag full of irresistible aromas.

Though a little worried about how much money they'd spent, Jake figured from now on things would cost less. Besides, escape from the museum was something to celebrate. She'd purchased the biggest bucket, mashed potatoes, and coleslaw, with root beer for Roy and Cokes for everyone else. They sat at their new table, which rocked a little until Roy put a matchbook under his side to steady it.

Everyone declared the meal wonderful. Even Memnet had a drumstick, though she ate little meat, and Roy praised the biscuits to the skies. Afterward they settled in the great room, Leo and Jake on the sofa, which Memnet had covered with a bright blanket. Comically Roy described the trouble he and the deliverymen had had getting it through the front door.

The others sat on a mismatched collection of chairs no worse than those at the museum. What's more, these chairs belonged to them. They had no television yet; it was far down the list of necessities. Instead, they talked about what had happened in the last week. Leo made them laugh with an imitation of what Charlene must have said when her rescuers found her. They spoke of what might be done to earn money, but not in any depth. That worry could wait until tomorrow.

A silence fell, neither unusual nor unpleasant. Jake felt tension build in her chest, and her palms became moist with sweat. For her, an important moment had come.

She didn't know when the first hint had entered her mind, but it had. No Mafia, no jewel theft ring, no aliens. Information she gleaned over time had settled to certainty somewhere in the middle of last night. She knew the secret, and it was time to say so. Into the quiet Jake dropped her bombshell.

"Don't you all think it's time you told me the truth?"

Four faces turned grave, but she hurried on before her courage failed. "I'm sitting here in our home, which we got by working as a team, with four people I know pretty well. I think *you* think…" She paused, looking at each one as she spoke. "Leo, you think you're Leonardo da Vinci; Libby, you're Queen Elizabeth the First; Roy, you're Butch Cassidy; and you, Memnet, are an Egyptian princess I can't identify."

Their shocked silence didn't last long. "I told you she was smart," Roy said with a raised eyebrow. "It was only a matter of time."

Chapter Twenty-three

"You pegged every one of us," Roy told Jake, "except Memnet, and she's impossible."

The slight girl who'd walked into their lives and hearts now had to be answered honestly. He glanced at Leo, who seemed more impressed by Jake's deductive powers than dismayed at the result. Memnet stroked the rough petit-point upholstery of her chair as if assuring herself she was real.

"I know that's what you think," Jake said, "but those people are dead."

"Nope," Roy declared. "We're here in your livin' room, like you said."

Leo leaned forward, resting his elbows on his knees. "How did you discover the truth?"

"Little things came together." Jake toyed with the oversized safety pin that held her wrap-around skirt together. "I kept putting what I knew together different ways, making up theories. Roy told me where he came from. Your real name is Robert Leroy Parker, right?"

"Pleased to meet you." He made a comical little bow.

"You said you were from Utah. One day I looked at that book you like so much, *The Outlaw Trail*. Beaver, Utah, is the birthplace of Butch Cassidy."

He nodded. "My parents lived in the godly state of Utah."

"Mormons, you said."

"I didn't want to blacken their name, so when I started riding with Mike Cassidy, I took his."

"And you worked as a butcher for a while, so Butch Cassidy." She frowned. "That was a hundred years ago. How can you be here?"

"It was Norman Bohn's doing!" Libby slapped the arm of her chair. "He performed some terrible experiment and then left us to fend for ourselves. The man had no honor!"

Looking from one to another Jake asked again, "How?"

Leo's expressive hands tensed. "We don't know for certain. Somehow Norman put his knowledge of the different sciences together to create a device that brought us to the present time."

"But you all lived and died in your own times."

"I would give much to learn how both those things can be true," Leo responded. "I spoke no English when I arrived here, but since then I've read everything available on the matter. I will tell you what I know."

An air of expectation fell over the room. Though he didn't much care how Norman had plucked them across the years, since it was a done deal and there was no sense fretting on it, Roy listened, trying for once to understand.

"Norman was fascinated with moving things across what is called time. He claimed great changes will come in the study of time in the next century." Leo held his hand out, palm down. "Time is not a straight line, but a series of parallel lines. In theory, with the right knowledge, or possibly even by accident, the lines can cross. When they do, universes intersect." He stopped at their blank stares. "I'm sorry. I have only a glimmer of understanding."

Roy smiled. "If you only have a glimmer, what chance do the rest of us have?"

"He tried to help me understand it," Libby said, massaging her forehead as if encouraging the memory. "He said time is like a striped blanket, and there's one of me living in each stripe. But the blanket isn't flat. It's crumpled, so a red stripe might lie on top of a blue one. He said he'd reached across the stripes and moved a Libby from one world—one stripe—into another."

"But how?" Jake said again. "What did he do?"

"He claimed it was simple once he figured out the process," she replied. "Inside a device he made, he placed an article belonging to the person he wanted to locate. He'd stolen the items, of course. Something about one's personal belongings pinpointed the search through time."

"A homing device," Jake said. "I've only heard of them in movies, but it sounds right."

Libby nodded. "He started with old dog collars. At first only dead animals came through, but he made adjustments and in the end the animals arrived intact."

"Poor things," Memnet whispered.

"His ultimate goal was to bring people from the past. He spent years working on it in secret."

Roy wondered how many failures Bohn had before succeeding with Libby. He imagined Norman's exhilaration, no doubt quickly followed by consternation when Libby turned on him like a bothered bee.

"I think he tried to convince the government to fund his research," Jake said. "The museum pamphlet mentioned he was mad at bureaucrats."

Libby nodded as another memory arose. "He scoffed at the government for spending money on psychic research, 'voodoo studies,' he called it, yet refusing to believe time was conquerable." Her shoulders rose and dropped. "I had no idea then what he meant. I only wanted to know if he could reverse what he'd done."

"And could he?"

"No." The word was almost bitten off. "He might have learned how, but he didn't want to." There was a moment's silence as they contemplated the selfishness of Norman Bohn.

Jake finally said, "He must have been really smart, inventing time travel all by himself."

"Intelligent but heartless!" Libby's voice trembled. "He took us from our lives, our very selves!"

"He began with Libby because of her many languages," Leo explained. "That allowed him to bring me along. He hoped I could help with the project." His expression turned wry. "I would have taken great interest in reversing his experiments, I can tell you."

"But Norman kept going."

"Yes." Leo rose, accompanied by a groan of ancient couch springs, and placed a hand on Roy's shoulder. "Roy was a whimsical choice, since Norman loved stories of the American west. For us, it was a blessing to have someone acquainted with America and a time much closer to the present than ours."

Jake turned to Memnet. "And you?"

She bowed her head. "I was a mistake."

"But a wonderful one," Leo said quickly. He turned to Jake. "Norman intended to find Cleopatra."

"He claimed we'd have much to say to each other," Libby added dryly. "And I could polish up my Greek and Latin skills."

"An item he stole from the Royal Ontario Museum was attributed to the queen." Leo's tone turned sardonic. "But even museums make mistakes. Norman was furious."

Imagining the frustration and anger someone like Bohn would have shown when his plans went awry, Jake felt a stab of pity for the unwanted Memnet.

"When I woke up here, I was very frightened," Memnet said. "I cry and cry, every day."

"The crossing is quite unpleasant," Libby put in. "One feels sick, as if she's being pulled apart, which of course is true. There's a terrible, howling wind, tremendous pressure as things whiz by, bright things that blind one, and a feeling of falling far and fast. I lost consciousness, and when I awoke, I was on the floor of Storeroom C."

"Stark naked," Roy put in with a grin.

"The child doesn't need every detail," Libby admonished.

"Well, we were," he insisted. "His awful machine ain't natural."

Jake bit her lip. "If I hadn't come up with this idea on my own, I don't think I'd believe it now."

Roy punched her shoulder playfully. "You pinned us down pretty good, Miss Jerilyn."

"Jake," she corrected. "I don't rob trains, but I like my nickname, like you did, Butch!"

Roy raised his hands in mock surrender. "You caught me! I'll go along quietly."

Turning to Leo, Jake asked, "Your mirror writing was another big clue. Who but the great da Vinci can do that?"

"It helps to keep my mind sharp," Leo said tapping his forehead with a finger. "The concentration, you know."

"I suppose I was easy enough once you'd got the other two," Libby ventured.

"Yes." Jake counted the clues on her fingers. "I thought of a queen when I saw you in the red wig that night in the wardrobe room, then again when you admired the dress in the store window. When you tried to pinch me yesterday, I remembered reading Queen Elizabeth used to pinch servants who upset her."

Libby's expression turned rueful. "If I could go back, I'd be a lamb to all my poor ladies!"

"Once I teased Roy about being Mormon and asked if his father had six wives. You almost choked." Jake grimaced. "Sorry if I brought up bad memories."

"I have come to terms with my father's weaknesses." Libby looked around at the group. "I defy anyone to say that he was not a great king."

"History bears out your opinion, and you did him proud as his successor." Leo managed to convey a bow of obeisance without making one.

Libby gave a royal nod of recognition, and Leo went on, "Might I suggest we leave this for another time? We've all had an emotional day and need rest. I commend Memnet and Roy for their hard work and care on behalf of us all, and I want you to know, Jake, life will be easier now that you are truly a member of our secret society."

They all rose, but Libby surprised Jake by putting her hands on her shoulders. "What we most dreaded, discovery, has occurred, and for my part it brings relief rather than dismay. You have earned our respect, child, and our trust." Starting for the stairs, she added drolly, "I never thought I would say this, but Jake, you read entirely too much."

Chapter Twenty-four

Within a few days, Jake remarked that if it were possible financially, Memnet and Libby would fill the whole house with plants. They both loved growing things and had missed tending them in two years spent below ground. Now that they had places for them, one or the other was always bringing home a new specimen. Leo smiled, but Roy complained the women were turning the place into a greenhouse and spending money uselessly to boot.

"We buy discounted plants," Libby said in their defense.

"Which means a fifty-fifty chance the poor things will survive."

"One day you'll be glad to have fresh basil or chives, or you would if you weren't a culinary philistine!" In return for the insult Roy patted Libby's head, which always made her furious.

Plants continued to appear, adding color and fragrance to almost every room. Leo was bemused by a Christmas cactus, having never seen one before, and Jake loved the amaryllis that seemed to grow a foot a day. She reported on its progress almost hourly. Libby got a book at the library, and they studied unfamiliar flora together. "It reminds me of Hampton Court to have green things around," she told Jake. Though the reference to her favorite home was rueful, it was probably a relief to be able to say such things aloud.

Jake amused them by recounting her earlier theories of their origin. "I never guessed you were from another time, but I did think for a while you were from another planet." Leo especially enjoyed that idea, and he drew whimsical pictures of spaceships in his notebook for Jake's amusement.

The adults were pleased to be able to ask questions about things that had long bothered them. The first morning in their new home, over a breakfast of cocoa and toast, they questioned Jake on social, economic, religious, and political issues until she protested, "I'm a kid! I don't know everything."

They had each read their own histories and knew how their lives played out, at least in the present universe. Libby and Leo were satisfied that people remembered the good they'd done, though Libby vehemently denied she was ever as vain and manipulative as the books claimed.

Jake figured since she wasn't a queen anymore, Libby had learned to compromise, but it was an ongoing process. Her imperial manner would always be her shield until she warmed to a person.

Roy was frustrated with the end of his own story, because there wasn't just one. Some claimed he died in Bolivia, "like that fellow Che Guevara." But other accounts claimed Butch Cassidy lived out his days quietly in his home state of Utah.

"It drives a man crazy not to know how he died," he said ruefully. He showed Jake an account from his sister Lula, who claimed he'd visited his family as late as 1925, long after his supposed death.

"Would your sister lie?" Jake asked bluntly.

"Well, I reckon that would depend on how much money was involved," Roy answered, helping himself to one of Libby's fresh biscuits and burning his fingers in the process. "She was a good Mormon, but I could never resist easy money, so I can't blame Lula if she profited from my outlaw reputation."

He went silent, apparently musing on the outlaw he'd been. Jake thought Butch was slipping away, being replaced by Roy Parker, who wanted to make a home for himself and his friends. He seemed willing to abide by society's rules, at least most of the time, if it made fitting into their surroundings easier. It might have been a natural effect of maturity, but watching him watch Memnet, Jake suspected it also had to do with her.

***

The first few weeks in the new house were busy. Furniture needed repair, and Memnet insisted on beautification as well. Leo was an enthusiastic partner, sanding, scraping and smoothing until damaged wood was ready for a new finish. Over time, many of the old pieces she'd chosen became valuable assets as well as functional furniture.

Surprisingly, Libby deferred to Memnet's taste in home decoration, and she even helped make drapes from an old bedspread. When they finished and hung the finished product above the large front window, she clapped in approval. "There's something to be said for doing one's own work," she said, smoothing the fabric into place.

Each of them had chosen a trade except Jake, who would return to her studies. She'd tried to convince Leo and Libby she didn't have to go to school to become educated, but they couldn't chance neighbors reporting her as truant. They agreed she would stay home until the new semester, which began in less than a month.

In the meantime, Jake helped Memnet and took cooking lessons from Libby, who'd claimed the kitchen for her own. She entered whole-heartedly into the role of teacher.

"There is a great deal of laughter in this kitchen," Leo

observed one day.

Giggling, Jake pointed to a very lopsided cake. "We made a mistake somewhere. I think we used baking soda when it said baking powder."

"That is why you and Roy are valuable to have around," Libby told him. "You are too much a courtier to criticize, and for Roy any dish is laudable as long as it is sweet."

One afternoon while she and Memnet cleaned vegetables for supper, Jake asked, "Why don't you just tell who you are? You all could get rich from interviews and movie rights."

"And never have another free moment," Libby retorted, her back to Jake as she assembled a casserole. "Think of folk who declare they are Jesus or Julius Caesar. They're locked away and given frightful drugs. We have no proof of what we are, Norman is dead, and we don't understand what he did. How would we explain it to others?"

Having read *One Flew Over the Cuckoo's Nest*, Jake knew she wouldn't want to be in a mental institution claiming to be five hundred years old. And Roy? They'd give him a lobotomy first thing.

Memnet took up the argument. "If they believe us, it is almost as bad."

"We'd be freaks. Studied, questioned, and kept in captivity, like the supposed aliens from Area 54 you told us about." Vehemence vibrated in Libby's voice, and she slopped melted butter onto the table. "Disastrous."

Especially for a shy person like Memnet, Jake thought.

"We discussed it at length that first year," Libby went on, "once Leo and Memnet were able to communicate. Accepting there'd be no return, we decided we would live as anonymously as possible."

Memnet rinsed the bowl she'd used. "It was best for us."

"Best for me too." As Jake sliced a carrot with uneven but forceful chops, she saw Libby's eyes meet Memnet's. They smiled at each other, pleased that she understood.

***

Memnet's first money-making enterprise was baskets. She bought materials at a local craft shop and began turning out merchandise while the others were still deciding details for their own projects. Within days a half-dozen finely-woven, practical baskets were strung across the front porch on a rope. Leo made her a sign, *Christmas Baskets.* Jake remarked, "If anyone knew who made the sign, we'd never have to work again."

Proud to again contribute to the family, Memnet felt her confidence growing. She made small decisions without asking Leo or Libby, and she chimed in when household matters were discussed. She'd even stood up to Libby on the question of bath towel color, which caused Roy to comment, "I had no idea such things contributed to the sense of peace in a bathroom."

From the first day, people began stopping to buy the unique baskets. Jake served as clerk, making change and promising there would be more before Christmas. A woman who bought three small baskets to fill with baked goods for her uncles asked in an odd tone if they liked their new house. From her manner Memnet sensed there was some tragedy in its past. Roy said someone had died there, but she decided it didn't matter. Their present happiness shouldn't be tainted with irrelevant events.

One afternoon Memnet went out to tie her latest finished product on the line, hurrying because of the cold, and found a man standing in the yard. A little under medium height for an American male, he was still taller than Memnet. Having grown up among dark people, she noticed first his hair, cut short and almost colorless. He wore no jacket, and his breath made little clouds as he spoke. "That's the one, right there." He pointed at the newest addition. "That will convince my mother I'm her favorite son."

From his smile she concluded it was a joke. "That's good, yes?"

"Very good." He looked at her in a way that might have meant something more than the basket. With a little bow he said, "I'm Clay Danner. I live down the block."

Having seen American women make the gesture, Memnet stepped forward, put out a hand, and shook firmly. "I am Memnet Parker." Turning, she took the basket down and handed it to him for inspection.

"Memnet. That's lovely, and very different."

"I am from Egypt."

"Wow. I haven't been there, but I mean to go someday."

"You will like it, but wait until the...hostility is quieted." She was proud to have recalled the word from newscasts.

"The Six-Day War, yeah. If everyone there were as nice as you, I bet there'd be no problems."

It was time to head off possible misconceptions. "My husband is out at the moment, but my father-in-law is here, if you'd like to come in for coffee."

Her hunch had been right. Danner seemed disappointed. "Thanks," he said, backing away, "some other time." Remembering the basket still in his hand, he asked, "How much do I owe you for this?"

"May I give it to you? Where I come from, we give gifts to new friends."

His smile turned genuine again. "Thanks. I'll find a way to pay you back."

"It's not necessary."

He raised a hand as if making an oath. "But I will."

Just then Jake came outside. Memnet introduced her, feeling proud to be a homeowner, a family member, a part of society. "This is Mr. Danner, our neighbor. Jake, my niece."

"Pleased to meet you, Mr. Danner," Jake said. "You live around here?"

"Four doors down. The place with the green shutters."

"The old mansion." They'd marveled at the place in passing. Surrounded by lesser dwellings and hemmed in by stone walls on three sides, Danner's house was twice the size of theirs with a roomy porch, wings in every direction, and an honest-to-goodness turret. Though somewhat run down, its innate grandeur overcame the neglect it had suffered.

"I'm not home much," Danner said. "I work downtown."

"Are you a salesman?" Jake asked.

"Nope, a G-man."

Memnet saw Jake's face tense, and she said to Danner, "You work at the Federal Building on Dearborn?"

"That's the one. Have you been there?"

"I used to live downtown, so I went by it on my way to school." Glancing at Memnet Jake asked, "Do you like working for the FBI?"

Memnet's heart sank. They'd moved all this way to end up a few doors down from an FBI agent! Where was Roy's famous luck now?

"It's not like you see on *The Untouchables*." He put his hands in his pockets. "Mostly I do paperwork and follow the big guys around, doing what they tell me to." Jake chuckled at his candor, and Memnet relaxed a little.

"So you don't chase bad guys down and arrest them?"

"Sure I do, just not every day. Right now I'm setting up security for Justice Marshall's visit to Chicago next month."

"We heard about that on the news. I'd like to see him."

"You could. He plans to stop at the B.R.I.C.K. center and say a few words."

"Oh, yeah. Across from the Schmidt Museum."

Memnet wasn't interested in going back downtown, but Jake seemed to be. "Maybe I'll go. I really admire him."

"Grandson of a slave and one of the best legal minds of our time." Danner scraped his feet on the sidewalk to warm them. "Old Strom tried to keep him from being confirmed, but he answered all the questions, no matter how trivial they got."

"And you're responsible for his safety when he's in town?"

"I help with the details: routes, how he'll get from place to place, that kind of stuff." Hanging the basket on his arm, Clay stuck his hands in his pockets. "For the next month I'm not actually chasing bad guys. I'm working to prevent them from causing trouble."

"Who's the toughest agent in Chicago?" It was the kind of

question a kid might ask, but Memnet guessed Jake's purpose.

"My section chief," Clay answered without hesitation. "The guy transferred here from Dallas in September."

"What's his name?"

"Blackburn, Charles Blackburn." As Jake and Memnet pictured the man they'd narrowly avoided twice, Danner added, "My boss could scare J. Edgar himself."

Chapter Twenty-five

Roy thought the evening meal deserved more attention. With a real kitchen, Libby had become an excellent cook, and tonight she served Yorkshire pudding, which he'd never had, along with a beef roast, vegetables, and pumpkin pie. Quite a spread.

Though an FBI agent living in the neighborhood was disturbing, Roy managed to do justice to the cooking. "Libby," he said when he finished, "that was a 'specially good meal."

Jake's news had upset her, but Libby never overlooked a compliment. "I checked out a book from the library by a woman called Betty Crocker. She seems very talented."

"Then I plan to buy you that book with my very first pay."

"But what do we do about the FBI man next door?" Memnet asked.

"In the first place," Jake argued, "he's not next door. In the second place, why would he suspect us of being anything but a normal family?" She obviously liked Danner, which meant he was young and nice-looking.

The local news was full of Charlene telling the world about her ordeal with the crazed street people. She claimed there'd been three of them, two men with deep, threatening voices and a small, Ma-Barker-type woman the curator was sure she could identify. She milked the story for all it was worth, and headlines said things like: *Museum Curator Faces Desperate Band of Kidnappers*. A composite of Libby drawn by a police artist looked, Libby said, more like Lucille Ball than her.

"Why should we worry?" Jake said with the confidence of

youth. "Nobody's looking for us."

"Except Agent Blackburn," Leo reminded her.

"And he's downtown. Clay's a junior agent, so he won't be having Blackburn over for Christmas dinner. We're safe."

"I suppose she's right," Leo conceded.

"I don't like the fellow and I haven't even met him," Roy said, helping himself to a second piece of pie. "We will not get friendly with Agent Danner. Neighborly, but not chummy."

***

Saying they'd avoid Danner and doing so were two different things. The next day he arrived at the front of the house in his car, which was "boss," Jake informed them.

"It's a '67 Chevy SS with a 327, and a Muncie 4-speed." He slapped the shifter. "Posi-traction, dual exhaust, and of course, Rally Wheels."

He asked if he could take Jake for a ride, and Memnet said later she couldn't refuse, seeing the girl's face. They roared off at an alarming speed and returned in an hour, having stopped for fries and Cokes at his favorite restaurant, McDonalds. Jake went on about the car for the rest of the day.

"And it's got racing stripes!" she gushed at dinner.

"Showin' off," Roy scoffed. "What does he need with a car like that? Rides the train to work, like everybody else, I bet."

Leo told Libby later, "Jake's interest bothers Roy, I think."

Libby's smile was arch. "I'd say Memnet's possible interest is the real sticking point."

A few days later, things got worse. It was December 24th, and they'd done what they could to make Christmas for Jake.

Each made her a gift, which they put along the fireplace, under the stockings Libby had hung there. She was making candied apples when footsteps sounded on the back porch. Wiping her hands on her apron, she opened the back door to find Clay Danner, grinning, she told Leo later, like Motley's fool.

"I'm Clay." He stepped in without being asked. "C-cold! Is Jake home?"

Hearing sounds coming from inside his coat, Libby looked at him questioningly. He grinned again just as Memnet entered the room.

"Hi," he said. "Can you call Jake?"

Jake half-tumbled down the stairs, face glowing in anticipation. Danner's coat squirmed and squeaked the whole time. When she stopped before him, he opened the jacket to reveal a small kitten, gray except for two white front paws. Green eyes gazed at Jake as its little nose took in her scent. Then it opened its mouth and mewed twice as loudly as seemed possible for its size.

"It's a kitten," she said needlessly.

"It's your kitten," Danner corrected. "That is, if your family says you can have her."

It's an old trick: show a child a pet and dare the parents to deny she can have it. Libby had never minded cats, and Memnet was as entranced as Jake. They both thanked him several times, and at Libby's invitation, Danner sat down at the kitchen table. She gave him one of the apples, and they chatted amiably while Jake bustled around providing for her new pet.

Libby was drawn to the young man, who was friendly and down-to-earth. Roy would later scoff at a federal agent who blabbed FBI business and hung around with kids, but Libby saw someone lonesome for company away from the high-pressure side of his life. She'd known many like him at court.

She thought herself a good judge of character, and she discerned no falsity in Danner, aside from his obvious flattery to her, which young men use to make older women tolerate them. The kitten was a lovely gift for a girl who needed a normal life. It signaled stability. Before he went on his way, Libby had warmed enough to invite Clay to Christmas Eve dinner.

"Won't you be going to see your mother on Christmas?" Memnet asked.

"Mother lives in Miami, and Christmas just means she plays more games of mahjong than usual." His tone was light but there was a tinge of bitterness. "I'd be happy to join you, and I'll bring the relish tray."

Since she didn't know what that was, Libby guessed it wouldn't duplicate what she'd planned. They would have turkey, which was inexpensive and, according to Betty's book, easy to prepare. For Memnet's sake there would be rice with vegetables. Roy had requested Yorkshire pudding again, and she hoped including it would placate him when he learned they'd invited a guest. Leo would taste everything but eat mostly fruit and cheese. Having had great success with her first pie, Libby planned on three for tomorrow: pumpkin, which was her favorite; apple because Roy claimed nothing was better after a turkey dinner; and for Jake, chocolate cream. The child claimed it was "the best," and the recipe looked simple enough. She imagined the cheers as she presented all three to the assembled diners at her table.

***

Queen Elizabeth I, 1587

The crowd cheered as their queen came down the steps on

Cecil's arm and stepped onto her brightly-painted boat. Her gown was velvet, with a jewel-studded collar that rose to her chin. A stiff ruff protruded from its upper edge, framing her face from ear to ear. From the crowd, shouts of "Good Queen Bess!" and "Gloriana!" reached her ears. She leaned out from the sheltering awning to wave as the boat pulled away, the oarsmen maneuvering expertly and making almost no splash in the murky waters of the Thames. These were her loyal subjects, except, of course, for the Papists, criminals, tax evaders, misogynists, and who knew what else among them.

Despite her smiling acknowledgments, the queen felt sick. While she reveled in her royalty, there were days, like this one, when she wanted nothing so much as to flee to a place of solitude. It was February 8, and today Mary, Queen of the Scots, would die. After years of wavering and delay, Elizabeth had agreed to the beheading of her cousin and fellow monarch.

No ruler should have to make such decisions. Why should she, whose mother was beheaded, be forced to order Mary's death a generation later? She looked down at her fine gown and jewels as cheers from the shore faded. The crowd's adulation wasn't enough—not today. She'd trade it all to not be the Responsible One, responsible for life, war, peace, taxes, death. Let someone else take on the yoke. But the thought finished itself: *Who else?*

***

1967

Libby enjoyed her new life. She loved the house, though the grocer had told her a story she didn't share with the others, a tale of a madman who'd turned the place into a slaughter-house. It was their home now, and it would be more of a tragedy to miss having real friends, a kitchen where she could create things to please them, and, she admitted to herself, a child to care for.

In the last few days she'd found herself pitying that other Elizabeth, who'd learned early to show no true emotion and trust no one. History books told of her manipulation, temper tantrums, and falsity, and she had to admit it was largely true. No one could understand unless they'd lived through what she had. Now, as she depended on these people and they on her, she'd become a different person. For the first time in her life, Libby, once known as Elizabeth, was part of a family: an odd one, to be sure, but true as ever was.

***

Christmas Eve dinner was a success, except for Roy's grumpiness. He'd come close to ordering Libby to rescind her invitation, and knowing she would never comply with a direct order was all that held him back.

"We must behave as a normal family, Roy," Libby argued. "People will think it odd if we stay too much to ourselves, and besides, we must have customers to buy from our businesses."

So though he was not happy about it, Roy met Clay Danner. He was an affable fellow, not at all the type one pictured working for the FBI. Before he got down on the floor to play with the kitten, he gave Libby a large box of beautifully wrapped chocolates and produced from under protective tin foil the promised relish tray, which consisted of every kind of vegetable he could find, cut into serving-sized pieces and arranged artistically in the basket Memnet had made.

"I'm keeping it," he told them. "Mother doesn't need it as much as I do."

Seeing Danner smile at Memnet that way, Roy commented that Libby had made so much food they didn't need another thing.

Giving him a warning glance, Libby took the basket from Danner, set it prominently on the table, and ordered everyone to sit.

Conversation was tentative at first but became more festive as meat was sliced from the golden-brown bird and other accompaniments handed around. Jake wanted the kitten on her lap, but Libby firmly refused to have an animal at the table. With good grace, Jake put the fluffy creature down and turned her attention to Clay, whose stories made them chuckle. Roy remained silent to let them know he resented the guest, though his appetite was as good as ever.

"Clay told me Agent Blackburn lost some prisoners once," Jake announced. "If they tease him about it he gets mad."

"Agent Blackburn?" Leo asked innocently.

"He's their toughest agent." Jake's face was carefully blank.

Danner took up the story. "Like Jake says, my boss is really tough, a crack shot, and not very talkative. We'd never have known it happened, but this police chief up in Wilmette called when Blackburn wasn't in and I took the message. The chief said a clerk at the store had remembered there was a dark-haired woman with the man he arrested. I couldn't find a report, so I asked the guy what it was about. He told me how two hit men were caught in Wilmette and handed over to Blackburn."

"Hit men?" Leo asked.

"Men who kill for money," Jake supplied.

"When Blackburn came in, I asked him where the report was on the arrests in Wilmette. He said there wasn't one. Our bureau chief overheard and made Blackburn tell the whole story. He was embarrassed to be caught trying to hide his mistake." Clay helped himself to seconds on turkey, rice, and Yorkshire pudding, drowning it all in Libby's rich gravy.

"So this man lost two suspects from custody?"

"Well, it isn't as bad as it sounds." Clay rested his fork on his plate as he spoke. "The chief up in Wilmette arrested some old guy for shoplifting. He had a foreign accent and a fake ID, so the chief called our office. Blackburn went up there, looked the guy over, and thought he resembled a suspect in a murder in Dallas. Then another guy came along, trying to spring the first one, and he matched the description from Dallas too.

"Blackburn arrested them both and started for downtown. On the way, an old lady walked out in front of him. When he got out to help her, the guys drove off in his car. He chased them, but they got away. When he turned back, the lady was gone too. He was had by a trio of petty crooks."

Clay looked around, no doubt waiting for the laughs the story should have gotten. The Parkers only stared, mesmerized, so he went on. "It turned out the suspects Blackburn thought he had under arrest are in jail in Dallas. The people in Wilmette were just small-time shoplifters. He called around, found his car abandoned in a parking lot, and kept his mouth shut about it."

"Did he get in trouble?" Jake asked.

Clay shrugged. "The big boss didn't appreciate the humor, but he let it go. I have to work for him, but the other guys find ways to remind him he was tricked by two con men and a little old lady." He chuckled, adding, "If he ever catches them, I bet they'll be sorry."

Looking around the table and misinterpreting the silence, Danner hurried to reassure his new friends. "They weren't dangerous, and Wilmette is a long way from here. You don't need to worry."

"I'm sure you're correct," said the little old lady at the head of the table. "Who's ready for pie?"

Chapter Twenty-six

"Blackburn is dangerous," Roy said after Clay Danner had thanked them multiple times, dried the dishes, and finally gone home. "He intended his co-workers would never hear about us."

"At least we know it's not the whole Bureau we have to be afraid of," Jake said.

"But he has at least one accomplice, who might or might not be FBI." Leo looked worried.

"It isn't Clay." Jake petted the kitten who, exhausted from excitement, slept on her lap.

"No," Leo agreed. "The man I fought was as tall or taller than I. But what if Danner mentions us to Blackburn? An odd mix like us can't be common."

"They're looking for street people," Jake argued, "not a family living in their own home."

They'd explained their strange grouping this way: Jake was Roy and Memnet's adopted niece. Libby was Roy's stepmother, and Leo her third husband. They hoped never to have to explain why each of them had his or her own room upstairs.

"Television shows have something they call non-traditional families," Libby maintained, "and we're exactly that."

"Perhaps our affection for each other makes us seem a family despite our differences." Leo had taken up his sketchbook and was drawing Danner's face with deft strokes.

"I don't think Clay likes Blackburn," Jake said, "That makes him a good guy in my book."

"We all know who Danner likes." Roy sounded sulky. "He makes it pretty plain."

Memnet blushed, and Libby said sharply, "We should rest. It's been a long day."

Jake climbed the stairs to her room, wondering what was going on. She'd never seen Roy as rude as he'd been to Clay, but she didn't think Clay had a crush on Memnet. He was too nice a guy to go after a married woman. Roy was acting like a jerk, and it wasn't an isolated incident. Lately he'd been grumpy a lot, and he'd stayed out late several nights, returning with the smell of liquor on him, like some of Lorna's boyfriends.

Jake knocked softly on Memnet's door and asked if she could come in. Memnet agreed, but for once she seemed reluctant. Jake took her usual seat on a pillow in the corner.

Memnet had made her room as much like home as she could get it. There was very little furniture, and the bed was a mattress on the floor with pillows around it. Several small, painted boxes held her things. When time permitted, she drew designs on the walls, and Jake loved to watch as she worked, representing Egyptian gods, kings, and queens in stark black. Her strange writing formed a border at ceiling level. She'd chosen sea green accents, and with the creamy white walls, the effect was stunning. Upon seeing the drawings, Leo had proclaimed Memnet a true artist.

It occurred to Jake that she'd seldom seen Memnet idle. She was always at work to make things better for someone. As they spoke, she sorted her basket-making materials into neat piles.

"Tell me about your life before."

Memnet smiled. "I was raised in a temple, a lovely place with cool rooms and whitewashed walls. At a very young age I dedicated myself to the goddess, promising to serve her all my life. We learned the rituals, how to keep the holy laws and recite stories of the gods, and even to write a little. I was rather a pet, like your kitten, Bastet. Everyone was kind to me, even the queen when she visited."

"You met her? Cleopatra?"

"She is part of our religion and must perform certain rites. I thought her very old, but now I realize she was not. She had to grow up quickly, as Libby did, since her life was dangerous."

"Did you speak to her?" Jake was awed by the fact that she lived with people whose times were not fully understood by anyone else on the earth.

"One day as she stepped onto her barge, her foot slipped on the wet bank. Her headpiece fell into the river, but I jumped in and got it before the current took it away. That is when she gave me the bracelet that brought me here." Her eyes clouded as the happy memories faded.

"I'm sorry. You had a good life, and Norman ruined it."

"It is not so bad since you came to be with us."

"Memnet, why is Roy mad at you?"

The smile turned sad. "I don't know if I can explain."

"Your life is crazy here, I know that, but he likes you and you like him."

Memnet sat down beside her. "You know a little of Egypt, do you not?"

"A little."

"Our beliefs are...complicated. In most temples the women were free to marry, but the group I belonged to was different. We dedicated ourselves to the goddess Maat at puberty, and I vowed to serve her all my life and never know a man."

"Oh." There was a world of understanding in that syllable.

"At first I prayed we'd be returned to our times somehow, and I would serve again, but there is little hope of that. Still, if I break my vow, it would shame the goddess and me as well."

"But no one believes in Egyptian gods anymore, Memnet."

"Except me." She closed the chest with a sharp click.

Jake tried to put herself into Memnet's situation. What if she'd taken the vows of a nun, then been thrown involuntarily into a different life? Would she cling to old rules in a time where her religion had been dead for two thousand years, or would she adapt and forget what she'd promised?

"I don't know what I'd do in your shoes," she admitted.

Memnet understood Jake hadn't meant to be insensitive. "Roy likes me, and I like him too. But what is right for us?"

"Have you talked to Libby about it? She knows a lot about people."

"We talked sometimes at the museum. She says her father's first wife held too long to a religion that could no longer help her. It made everything worse." Jake made a mental note to research the order of Henry's wives, but she guessed that was Catharine of Aragon, the Catholic wife replaced by Libby's mother, Anne Boleyn.

"She says one must feel that a thing is right before she can accept it. She says it takes time." Memnet's expression became even sadder. "But I fear sometimes that since we have real lives in this world now, Roy will meet someone who doesn't cringe at his touch. Then my time to choose will be gone."

***

Memnet, 48 B.C.

Dressed in a pleated white skirt, her hair arranged with care, Memnet waited in a line of girls. Some whispered nervously, while others seemed frozen by the solemnity of the occasion.

The priestess spoke to each girl alone, assuring she freely chose the path before her. "You will belong forever to the goddess. Maat must be honored in all that you do."

"I understand," Memnet said when her turn came. She had no qualms about her promise. The goddess was all she'd ever known.

Every morning, Memnet and her fellow initiates woke Maat, bringing her food and cleansing her image. They spoke to her as if she were alive, for indeed she was, choosing to be metal and stone rather than flesh and blood. At noon they prayed to her, telling her their thoughts and recounting events in the city. At night they once again fed Maat then put her to bed. The rest of their day was spent caring for the temple, the grounds, and the gardens flooded by the Nile, which provided new life to the land each year. Service to Egypt was their reason for living.

Memnet answered the priestesses' questions firmly. She wanted to be dedicated to the goddess. She would serve faithfully. Her request granted, she joined the others as they returned to the temple between two rows of priests in blinding white robes. The temple was cool, exquisitely painted with images of the goddess and her servants. Stones of lapis lazuli, carnelian, and jasper decorated the statues that graced every alcove and corner. It was a beautiful, peaceful place to spend her life.

Common sense whispered, *No other place for an orphan, a pauper, a useless girl-child.* No one but Maat wanted her.

Chapter Twenty-seven

Clay Danner didn't know exactly why he liked the odd bunch down the street. Though he hadn't been thrilled to learn Memnet had a husband, she still was the nicest person he'd met in a long time. And there was the cute niece who was so impressed that he worked at the Bureau. The kid was going to be a looker, like her aunt. When he took her the kitten, he'd met the grandmother, who seemed ornery at first but nice once she decided he meant her girls no harm. It helped that he praised her cooking, but that wasn't hard to do once he'd tasted it.

Clay found himself looking forward to visiting again. It was part loneliness, he admitted, and part disillusionment with his job. He'd thought life as an FBI agent would mean helping others: catching kidnappers, preventing crime, punishing evildoers. There was some of that, but he'd been surprised at how petty much of it was, how focused most were on making the Bureau look good. His colleagues seemed to think everyone outside the agency was either crooked or stupid.

In addition, Clay realized he could never adopt the "Us versus Them mentality required for advancement. He did his job to the best of his ability, but from the first he saw that he didn't fit in. Not gloomy enough and not paranoid enough either.

His boss more than balanced Clay's lack of paranoia. Blackburn trusted no one. It wasn't just his refusal to associate with others in the office or his grim manner. Blackburn was downright weird at times.

One morning Clay had been at his desk, swamped as usual with little jobs no one else wanted to do. Blackburn was in his office when Rhein announced he was meeting an agent from Dallas to discuss guns coming through Mexico into the US. He'd called to Blackburn, "Hey, Charles, the guy says he knows you. I'll bring him around so you get a chance to say hello."

There was no answer. Later in the day, when Rhein ushered his visitor in the guest asked, "Where's Chuck Blackburn? I haven't heard from him since he moved here."

Clay went to fetch Blackburn but found the office locked. At his confused look one of the secretaries said, "He was called away, said he wouldn't be back in until tomorrow."

"That's too bad," the Texan said. "I wanted to get his take on the Super Bowl." He tapped his knuckles on the desk. "Tell him I'll give him ten to one it's Green Bay and Kansas City." Clay promised to relay the message.

The next day when Blackburn came in, Clay said, "Mills says he wants Green Bay and KC."

Blackburn looked at him blankly. "What?"

"Mills from Dallas was here yesterday. He said to tell you hello, and he wants to bet Green Bay is in the Super Bowl against the Chiefs."

Blackburn nodded. "Oh. Green Bay, yeah, but it'll be against the Bears. They're good this year."

Clay wasn't a huge football fan, but he knew those teams were in the same division and couldn't possibly meet in the Super Bowl. At first he'd grinned to himself. Blackburn's football knowledge wasn't so great.

But things bothered him about the incident. Blackburn had told Clay he planned to work in his office all day, but he'd left without a word when told an old friend was due. Clay tried not to read too much into it, recognizing that his dislike of Blackburn made him less than objective. The guy was odd, but rumor had it J. Edgar was a little odd too.

That was the day Clay had seen Memnet Parker as he walked past her house. Now that he'd met his neighbors, his own place seemed empty and cold. The Christmas Eve dinner he'd attended was nice, though Clay got the feeling Memnet's husband didn't approve of him. The others were friendly, and the conversation had been thought-provoking. Though they had differing viewpoints, their disagreements were reasoned and respectful.

The grandfather, Leo, was interested in democracy. Clay gathered there hadn't been much individual freedom where he came from. He and his wife Libby argued the pros and cons of giving the common people power. She was against it, believing they were in general unprepared for the responsibility. It was fascinating to listen to them go at it, and Clay couldn't tell who had the advantage.

The best thing about the Parkers, he thought, was their concern for each other. They were a mismatched group but a real family. In Clay's childhood home discussions had turned to arguments then to screaming matches in no time at all. He'd concluded all households functioned like that, despite *Ozzie and Harriet* on TV Thinking of the Parkers, he felt even less like calling his mother on Christmas. He'd do it because it was expected, but they had little to say to each other and never had.

***

Roy found a TV set at a second hand store and bought it as a gift for the family. It was bigger than the one at the museum and heavier too. He brought it home on a cart Leo fashioned from an old lawnmower.

They all liked television, though for different reasons. Leo, intrigued by the possibility of sending pictures across miles of space, was determined to dismantle one someday and see how it worked. Libby was a student of people, groused at the vapidity of programs like *I Love Lucy* but enjoyed crime dramas and newscasts. Memnet was least interested but wove or sewed as they watched. Jake and Roy liked *Gunsmoke* and knew the history of each character and what he'd do in a given situation.

Their various jobs were beginning to take shape. Below Memnet's sign, Libby had hung a small chalkboard proclaiming *Baked Goods* on which she wrote each day what she had for sale. There were a good many commuters in the neighborhood, and they began stopping to purchase rolls and pies on their way to and from work.

Leo set up a workshop in the basement, and soon pounding and other sharp noises sounded dimly below as he made toys and models and did woodwork and carving. Sometimes he repaired broken gadgets for resale. He spoke of returning to painting, but the others warned he could never sell or even show his work. Roy said they could do a profitable business in forged documents, but Leo discouraged the idea, hoping Roy would someday stop proposing crime as a way of making a living.

On Christmas morning they opened their gifts. Jake said it wasn't fair she got four and they each had one, but everyone assured her it was what they wanted. She'd made them each a soft, warm scarf, working on a small loom Leo made from scrap lumber and nails.

"They're shorter than I wanted," she confessed. "It was tough getting four done." Care was evident in her choice of a color suited to each recipient and the patience with which she'd finished the ends with knotted tassels. As they exclaimed over them, Jake beamed with pride.

Libby gave Jake fudge. Leo had made her a wooden puzzle and found an art book at the dime store. Memnet wove a headband for her hair, which was growing fast, making her look more like a young woman and less like a child. Roy gave her a small bottle of "Evening in Paris," her favorite fragrance. Libby frowned when she saw it.

"I got it honestly," he said before she could object. "It was a boxed set someone dropped all over the store aisle. The cologne bottle broke and the bath powder box got dented. That one's the lucky survivor."

"And I love it," Jake declared, turning the blue bottle in the light. "It smells—"

"Groovy," the others chimed in. She laughed with them then turned to Roy. "I'm glad you got it the right way."

He sighed deeply. "Gotta start bein' an upright citizen."

"You say your parents taught you right from wrong," Jake said, "so how'd you become an outlaw?"

He stared into the fire Leo had lit in celebration of the holiday. "When I was young I was a little wild, but mostly honest," he began. "I worked on a ranch, and one day I rode several miles into town to buy some things. Well, the storekeeper had closed up early and gone somewhere."

He raised his brows. "Locks have never been a problem for me, and I decided to let myself in and get what I needed rather than have to come back. I did that, leavin' the man a note sayin' I'd pay him when I came to town again. Darned if he didn't get the sheriff and have me arrested! The sheriff wasn't very nice about it neither. It made me mad, even though they dropped the charges later."

There was a general sense he'd been wronged. "That made you mad at the legal system?"

"I suppose. It seemed like all my life, Justice assumed I was a criminal, so I ended up actin' like one. Once I told the railroad men I'd give up train robbing if they'd meet with me and talk about things. They didn't even bother to show up." He grinned impishly. "I went and robbed their train again to let 'em know I was upset."

"The law is better these days at catching people than it was a hundred years ago," Jake said earnestly. "You can't ride off to Hole-in-the-Wall and hide until they go away."

"Jake's right," Leo put in. "We need to protect each other now, which means no more petty crimes. If one of us is caught, we're all in danger."

Roy put up a hand. "I already figured that out for myself." He gestured at the blank TV screen. "These riots that are goin' on have people scared, and that gave me an idea for a business. There's that small room off the kitchen we aren't using for anything. The door has a good strong lock and there's no window. It seems to me like a good place for a gun shop."

***

Butch Cassidy, 1896

Crouching behind a rock as the posse passed, the outlaw felt his heart pumping furiously. His breath came in gasps, drying his mouth and throat until he feared a cough would give him away. When hooves no longer sounded on the hard earth, he stepped out and looked around. Nothing for miles. No way home but to walk, since he'd sent his horse on as a decoy.

The heat was stifling, and the confusion and chaos of the day made him wonder why he didn't give it up. At first it had been fun staying a step ahead of the railroad men and posse riders, but there were times lately when he wished he could leave it behind.

The outlaw life wasn't like the dime novels portrayed it. There were moments of excitement, sure, but they were followed by days of insecurity and downright boredom. And he had to admit, the company he kept never got any smarter or more trustworthy. Plodding down the dusty track, Butch Cassidy wondered if he could go back to being Robert Leroy Parker.

***

The others in the family were so relieved to have Roy take up a legitimate occupation that no one objected to firearms in the house. Leo, who'd read everything he could find in the history books, was pleased to learn that Butch Cassidy, train bandit, bank robber, and cattle rustler, had, despite his many crimes, never killed or even wounded a single person.

Chapter Twenty-eight

Memnet liked Christmas, though she didn't understand much of Christianity. She supposed it was no less odd to believe a man died and returned three days later than to believe Isis collected the pieces of her dead husband Osiris and resurrected him. All religions had their mysteries of faith.

Libby, Jake, and Leo decided to go to church to celebrate the day. Libby had found a small, non-denominational chapel that was near enough to walk to. She enjoyed the services once she accepted the idea that church could be positively rowdy.

Their departure left Memnet alone with Roy. For some time he'd avoided her, and he often went out at night. He returned quietly, long after midnight, but she always heard. One morning she'd come in as he and Jake were talking, and the conversation stopped abruptly. She was certain they'd been talking about her.

Though she had intended to stay in her room until the churchgoers returned, Memnet realized she'd left her paint box in the kitchen. Having heard Roy say he planned to work in his gun room, she crept downstairs, hoping to avoid him. As she opened the swinging door, she caught the scent of tobacco smoke.

"It's Christmas day, and a cigar sounded good." He pronounced it cee-gar, which Libby would have corrected had she been there.

"I don't mind. It smells good."

"Actually, they smell better than they taste." He crushed it out in his tin can ashtray.

"I forgot my paint box." She started past, but he put a hand on her arm.

"You don't need to apologize for being in your own kitchen." He sounded angry, but she didn't think he was angry with her. "I'm sorry things have been bad between us, Memnet. You know how I feel about you, but if all I can be is your friend, that's okay."

"No, Roy, I don't."

"Don't what?"

"Know how you feel about me."

He frowned. "You're the most wonderful woman I've ever met. You surprise me every day with something you do or say."

It was not there, the word she waited for. He admires me. He wants me. That's all.

"I am glad to know you approve of me."

"Approve! Memnet..." There was a long pause before he went on. "Jake told me about...things, and I understand. If you don't want me to touch you again, I won't."

Tears rose in her eyes. "When I made that vow, how could I know about you?" She stopped, realizing she'd said too much. Admitting how she felt about him only made things worse.

Roy rose abruptly from his chair. "Damn Norman Bohn," he said vehemently. "Why didn't he think about what he was doing to us? Damn him and his little machine, damn them both to hell!"

Putting his arms around Memnet, he pulled her close. After holding her for a long moment, he kissed her forehead and left the room without another word.

***

Libby found her new church interesting, even fun. At first it felt odd to be the only white people in attendance. The minister shouted about Hell and damnation, reminding her of Puritans she'd heard, but one got the feeling after a time that it was mostly good theater. The choir was outstanding.

Making her way through a brightly-dressed crowd of rustling taffeta, Libby took a seat next to Aletha Jones, a large woman who liked flowers on her dresses as much as Libby liked them in her home. Today her hat, made of blue feathers, made her look like a bright parrot.

Miz Jones, Aletha, as she bade them call her, had welcomed the newcomers from the first. Once she invited Libby to sit in her pew, the others had begun nodding politely and shaking hands after service. Having not spoken to many of African ancestry, Libby had trouble understanding, but they got on.

"Y'all have a nahs krismus?" Aletha asked as Libby sat down beside her.

"Yes, lovely," she replied after a quick mental translation.

"Turkey or ham fo' dinnah?"

"Turkey," Libby replied. "I use Mrs. Crocker's book. I find her a good source."

Aletha frowned. Libby guessed her British accent made understanding her difficult, since she often got that look. "Betty Crocker. Thas a good one."

"Has she written any other books, do you know?"

"No, ah don' know of it," Aletha said. "You from England, you said?"

"Yes. And my husband here is from Italy." Looking slightly lost, Leo nodded but didn't speak. "We live with my stepson on 100th Street."

"Thas real nahs. Y'all need anathin', jest call me up. Ah'm usually home, and ah know where things is aroun' here." Digging into a huge handbag at her side, Aletha found an old cash register slip and a pencil, scribbled a number and an address, and handed it to Libby.

"Why, thank you, Miz Jones. I'll remember that." Libby stored the paper in her own bag, thinking maybe they should look into getting a telephone.

Back at home, Libby reheated food from last night's dinner. Things seemed to have resolved somewhat between Memnet and Roy, and he even teased her about the paint fumes upstairs. They spent the afternoon at various tasks: Leo in the basement, Libby in the kitchen, Memnet and Jake in their rooms. Roy worked to create his gun repair shop, cleaning industriously and drawing diagrams of the setup he wanted for the room. Leo was researching the legalities of such a place and would help him get the necessary permits.

Leo had also begun replacing the forged documents he'd made at the museum with genuine ones. In the courthouse files he found a person named Robert Parker who'd died in infancy twenty-odd years ago. He sent Roy to get a copy of that person's birth certificate as if it were his own. Using the birth record, he could get a Social Security card, and from there, additional documents. Once Roy was legitimate, Leo would start on the others. In time they'd have no more to fear from encounters with authority.

A horn sounded outside, and Jake came down the stairs, three at a time. "Going for a ride with Clay," she called. She was out the door before anyone had time to answer. Jake had become a bit of a problem, since though they were her family in appearance, they had no real claim on her. Roy thought they should restrict her trips with Danner, but how could he make demands of a girl who'd lived alone on the streets for weeks? They had to hope Danner was as harmless as he seemed.

***

Clay Danner was the coolest guy Jake had ever met. He was nice to her, had a great car, and he didn't buy his clothes at Goodwill. He was smart too, and got to work on important stuff like VIP visits. It bothered her that Roy kept saying he'd tell Blackburn about them. Clay didn't even like his boss; he'd said so. It was safe to hang around with him, and the Camaro was too cool to pass up a second ride.

"Where we going, kid? Nothing's open on a holiday."

"Can we drive up Lake Shore? You could open it up a little." Jake's expression was innocent, but it was a challenge.

"They do say it's good for them to blow the carbon out once in a while," Clay said, smiling. On the city streets he drove the speed limit, but when they got out on Lake Shore it was a different story. There wasn't much traffic because of the holiday, and he took it up to ninety, the engine whining as he shifted through the gears. Jake sat back, enjoying the thrill. Being of the bus-riding level of society, she'd never ridden in a car this nice. It smelled new, and the gauges and dials did all kinds of interesting things.

They stopped in a parking lot and looked at the water for a while. The December day looked warm due to bright sunlight, but gray, restless waves told a different story. No one would be tempted to swim in Lake Michigan when it was that color. Thinking of the man whose body had been dumped in those cold waters Jake shivered, though the heater was on full blast.

In an empty parking lot, Clay showed Jake how to shift a four-on-the-floor. Taking it from a full stop, he worked the accelerator and called out "First!" "Second!" "Third!" and "Fourth! Good job!"

"Next summer I'll teach you how to drive," he promised. "You'll be what, fourteen?"

"Fifteen," she corrected.

"That's about right. You need to practice before you take driver's ed."

"How come you're so nice to me?" Jake asked, unable to completely dismiss Roy's suspicions.

"Hey, I like you. I like your family, except your uncle's a little weird."

"He takes a while to warm up to strangers. Can I try the gears again?"

Afterward, Clay turned the car around and headed south. "You're lucky to have a close family. My mom's only interested in two things: getting married and going shopping. My dad left when I was six."

"I wasn't even born when my dad went back to Syria."

"Really?"

"Yeah. He married my mom to get U.S. citizenship, but he got homesick and left. You don't have any brothers or sisters?"

"Nope. Other kids thought I was a dope because I didn't know how to make a lay-up or catch a fly ball. I was good in school, but since when did that ever get a guy noticed?"

"I'm the funny-looking foreigner that reads all the time. I never invited anyone over, 'cause...you're never sure what's going on at home. I kinda stayed by myself."

"I get it." It was like finding out she'd had a brother all along, one who got it.

"So how'd you get into the scary old FBI?"

"They recruit you. I'd done well in college, and they like people without close family ties." Clay rubbed the leather-wrapped steering wheel absently. "I'd planned on going into business but I was kind of floating, and they said I could serve my country. It sounded good, so here I am."

"You and Blackburn, American patriots, huh?"

His handsome face took on a puzzled look. "I'll be working closely with him a lot in the next two weeks, and to tell you the truth, I don't look forward to it."

"The security for Justice Marshall's visit?

"Yeah. I'm doing liaison stuff while he heads things up."

"Will you get to meet the justice?"

His eyes left the road briefly as he gave Jake a grin. "Yeah, if you call following the man around for thirty-six hours 'meeting' him. We pick him up at the airport, escort him to his hotel, and follow him through a series of meetings with local black, union, and city officials. He gives a couple of speeches, has dinner with the governor, and gets back on a plane for D.C. by 6:00 p.m. the second day. After that, I might get to sleep."

Jake could tell he looked forward to it. "It'll be cool, though, to guard such a famous guy."

"I guess. To tell you the truth, I'm surprised Blackburn picked me to be on the team. This event is important to his plans to move up the ladder, so I'd have guessed he'd pick the more experienced agents."

"How come he's in charge of it?"

Clay downshifted with a practiced hand as they turned onto 100th. "The director makes the decision, but from what I heard, Blackburn started maneuvering to get the assignment from his first day in Chicago. I suppose he wants his picture on the evening news, standing behind Justice Marshall and looking like a guy who deserves to take over when Hoover retires."

"He must think you've got possibilities," Jake said.

With a grimace Clay responded, "Or he needs someone he can blame if every little thing doesn't turn out well."

Chapter Twenty-nine

It wasn't lack of understanding, Leo told himself. He simply didn't have access to the knowledge modern scientists had. Once in a while, snippets of intriguing theories appeared on TV or in magazine articles. The ideas were astounding, but Leo was five hundred years behind, struggling alone to catch up to thinkers who inspired each other to greater and greater discoveries. The world had become smaller, and Enrico Fermi could pick up a telephone and speak to his counterpart on the other side of the world. Leo could speak to none of them, though he very much wanted to.

A name from his conversation with the woman at the laboratory stuck in his mind. Norman had been someone's protégée, and that man might shed light on Norman's thinking. Leo intended to locate Michael Millen.

Early on, Leo had learned a valuable lesson in twentieth-century living: libraries were often staffed by people who took a patron's quest for information as a personal challenge. When Leo explained that he was new to the neighborhood and seeking an old friend, the woman behind the desk left her post to assist him. They started with newspaper archives, which mentioned Millen twice: once when he made a presentation at a scientific symposium, and again when he left Argonne in 1963. Neither article mentioned his current place of residence.

Next Leo's new friend tried *Who's Who* and found a brief biography listing Millen's birthplace, parents, background and achievements, but no clue as to his address. They did learn the scientist would be in his late seventies if still living. Since the news article cited ill health as his reason for retirement, the librarian was doubtful.

"The simplest way might be best," she announced, and produced several phone books. Leo professed embarrassment at his thick accent, and the woman suggested he find the numbers while she made inquiries. After a dozen calls, no Michael Millen fit what they knew of the man. "No wife or children listed in his biography," the librarian said. "Perhaps a nursing home?"

"But there are so many possibilities."

"I guess we're out of options." She sighed, and Leo got the feeling she enjoyed his company.

Leo left the library with his mind working on the problem. The Argonne probably knew where Millen was, but they wouldn't tell him. Unless...Reaching into his pocket, Leo pulled out the coins that rested there. Two dimes and a nickel.

At the corner was a pay phone. He looked up the number for the Argonne, dialed it, and dropped a coin in the slot.

"Argonne National Laboratory."

"Hello. I'm calling for Michael Millen. He didn't receive his pension check this month, and we're wondering if there's been a problem."

"One moment, please. I'll transfer you."

Leo almost hung up, fearing Maddy Vandermele would recognize his voice. To his relief, a man answered. "Personnel." Leo repeated his request.

"Are you Mr. Millen?"

"No. He's too ill to use the phone."

There was a pause while the man thought about it, but he

apparently saw no harm in answering the question. "The check was sent on the third of the month, as usual."

"I see. And the address you have is correct? 1244 Locust Avenue, Schaumburg?"

"Well, no. We have his address as the Quiet Woods Nursing Home in Lake Villa."

"I was afraid of that," Leo said smoothly. "I'll send you the correct information right away."

"Okay. Sorry about the mix-up."

"Not your fault." Leo hung up, pleased with himself.

Next he dialed Quiet Woods, but he was told Millen could see no one. "He's gravely ill," a woman said in a tone that brooked no argument.

"Is family allowed?"

"He has no family, and if he did, they wouldn't have an Italian accent." The call ended abruptly, and a dial tone hummed in his ear.

Leo entered the nursing home during the dinner hour, figuring the staff would be busy helping residents. Quiet Woods was not near any woods, and the inside looked very much like a hospital: pale, bare walls, industrial tile floors, and utilitarian lights that cast harsh shadows into the open doors of the cookie-cutter patient rooms. Outside each door was a slot where a card with the patient's name could be placed. From outside, Leo had noted there were three floors. Guessing the least mobile residents were at the top, he started up the stairs.

On the third floor Leo peered into the hallway. A nurse in a white uniform, white shoes, white cap, and white stockings sat at a desk to the right. She was turned away, writing something down. Leo went left. Luck was with him, and on the fourth door down he read *Mike Millen*. He guessed *Mike* had been some young aide's idea, not the eminent PhD occupant in the room.

Opening the heavy door, Leo stepped into the room. On his right was a closed cabinet, a wooden chair with a folded blanket hung over its back, and a pole lamp in the corner. The next wall had a window with a radiator below it. On the third wall was a hospital bed and beside it, a smaller cabinet. To the left was a small bathroom. The room smelled of urine, rubbing alcohol, and impending death.

Millen lay on the bed, so wasted he almost faded into the mattress. The only things left of substance were his nose, which hooked above toothless gums, and his hands, gnarled with arthritis. His lips were dried and cracked. His chest moved slightly, but the rest was deathly still.

Leo stood at the bedside, unsure what to do. What should he say? "I'm here from another time; could you please explain how it happened?"

And what of Millen's mental condition? Even if he could speak and even if by some miracle he believed Leo, was he able in his current state to make sense of Norman's science?

A raspy voice made Leo start. "Who are you?"

Lies came to mind, but Leo knew there was no time for games. "I'm someone who needs to know what you know." He hesitated then added, "About moving through time."

A dry chuckle shook the bony chest. "No time for time. About done for."

"Doctor Millen." Leo chose his words carefully. "I knew Norman Bohn. You and he devised ground-breaking theories about time, ideas that will change the way we think."

Millen's rheumy eyes opened wider. He looked steadily at Leo, gauging his purpose. "We did."

"Norman is dead." There was no change in the man's expression. "I need to learn what he knew about time travel."

"Time travel?" The croak might have signaled humor or dehydration.

"He figured out how to accomplish it."

Millen looked away, digesting the message. Leo waited.

"You've come at the last possible moment. I don't think I could have waited much longer."

Less than a minute later, Leo had closed the door at Millen's request and pulled a chair close to the bed so the old man didn't have to strain to speak. His voice was not much more than a whisper, but Leo heard every word.

"Norman and I met in 1950. I won't bore you with the details, but I saw his genius. Because he was interested in my work, I never saw the crazy side of him others did." He coughed. "With everyone else he was a real pain in the ass. Norman might've had a brilliant career if I hadn't got sick."

Millen's looked around at the dingy room. "Hard to believe I was somebody once, eh? I've had cancer three times now. This time I intend to go quietly." He grimaced, half smile, half sneer. "A quiet death at Quiet Woods."

"Your work?" Leo prompted.

"Right. You aren't here to empathize. You want to conquer time."

"Something like that."

"Good luck with it." One bony hand shifted, signaling derision. "We had the theory, but there's more to it than that."

"In theory a practice should be easy, but in practice it never is."

"You got it."

"Why don't you tell me the theory?" Leo glanced around for a clock, but there was none. Millen had all the time in the world, and none. How long before Leo was discovered and tossed out?

Millen closed his eyes. "Time is like a striped blanket." Leo felt a chill down his spine as the words Norman had used to explain their presence to Libby were repeated. "Each stripe is a universe, each with its own existence—similar but not the same. This time blanket isn't laid out neatly though. It's thrown into a corner we call space, making lumps and wrinkles. A red stripe might abut a blue one at several points. Most of the time they remain separate."

"But not always."

The old man nodded. "We theorized that holes might appear in the blanket from time to time, due to fluctuation in the continuum. We don't see them, but we sometimes sense things about space that aren't quite right. The holes allow glimpses into other universes."

"You saw these holes?"

He shook his head. "I'm sure they exist, but I wasn't lucky enough to see one."

"If a person learned how to find holes in time, what then?"

Millen thought about it. "Norman suggested we might somehow aim the hole at a particular point and connect two universes." His hands fluttered weakly on his chest in a gesture of doubt. "Even if he was right, the connection would be brief and random. One could become marooned in a different universe, in a time that isn't his own. Who would chance that?"

"No one."

Something in Leo's tone gave him away, and a gleam of understanding lit Millen's eyes. The dying man receded, and the scientist he'd once been shone through. "Tell me why you're here." Leo hesitated, and the old man smiled. "Tell me. I won't be around to make trouble for you."

With a bow he said, "Leonardo da Vinci, at your service."

He lay silent for several seconds. "The son of a bitch did it."

"He did."

"Who knows about this?"

"Norman kept it a secret, and it seemed a good idea to continue that."

"You came across well?"

Leo shrugged. "It wasn't pleasant, but we survived."

"We?"

"There are four of us. As far as we know, anyway."

"And Norman?"

"He fell down a flight of stairs. As you predicted, we're trapped here."

"I doubt you could return, even with his help. The holes are random, so there's no way to be sure you'd land in the same place. You might meet yourself face to face or find that you died yesterday." His faded eyes met Leo's. "What would your contemporaries do then? Burn you as a witch, no doubt."

"I see." Leo's face betrayed his disappointment.

"You thought I'd have the secret?"

He shrugged. "Perhaps it's best to know we can't go back." As he spoke, Leo realized he was the only one of them who hadn't fully accepted it. The others had settled into the twentieth century, liking some things, disliking others, but understanding they were here for good. It wasn't so much that he hated the times or longed to go home. He wanted to understand. He'd been called the greatest thinker who ever lived, and it frustrated him to fail to comprehend the science that had changed his existence so completely. At least Millen had helped with that.

"I'm grateful for your honesty, sir."

The voice grew even softer. "How did he do it?"

"He'd obtained objects that belonged to each of us and used them as locators, some sort of homing device."

Millen licked his dry lips. "So the holes can be aimed. But objects? That means he was locating a specific person, not a time or place." Millen's eyes met Leo's. "Have you heard of DNA?"

"I've read a little about it."

"Each person's is unique. I think Bohn used it to find you."

Leo thought of Memnet, receiving Cleopatra's gift and waking up in Chicago two millennia later. Wearing a bit of finery had changed her life, and ruined Norman's plan.

"But how would he locate these holes?"

"Was there a machine? A device of some kind?"

"A small box that made a strange noise. It was a hum, or a combination of hums, some high, some low. They seemed to weave together."

Millen's eyes narrowed. "Sound, then."

"Of course!" Leo massaged his forehead with two fingers. "Norman joked to Libby that I'd given him the inspiration. In my day, I was interested in the power of sound."

Millen picked up on it. "Libby?"

"Queen Elizabeth I."

"Good God. And who else?"

"Robert Parker, also known as Butch Cassidy. His last experiment went wrong. That's when he stopped." He explained the mistake with Memnet.

"Amazing." Millen put out a weak hand, and Leo took it in his. "I'm glad you found me." He closed his eyes. "And I'm sorry you're prisoners here."

"We've adapted."

"And no one knows?"

"No." Leo discounted Jake, knowing Millen meant no one in the scientific community.

Millen smiled. "Then I'm the only one. And like Norman Bohn, I'll take the secret to my grave."

Chapter Thirty

Leo boarded a bus outside Quiet Woods, his mind focused on Millen's revelations. It was some time before he looked up and realized he wasn't retracing the route he'd taken to the facility. When he confessed his mistake to the driver, he advised getting off at 55th and walking east a few blocks to pick up the correct bus at Plainfield.

The day was pleasant for Chicago in winter, meaning the wind wasn't quite as biting as usual. It was worst going eastward, however, and Leo walked with his head lowered to protect his face from the cold. When he stopped to get his bearings, he saw across an intersection a lovely little church with a foreign look to it. Leo liked churches, though Libby was correct in concluding it was mostly their architecture that attracted him. Surveying this one's lines, he decided the bus could wait. *Well, they don't, but there's always another one.*

Climbing the steps Leo tried the door, which opened to admit him into a warm foyer fragrant with scented candles and wood polish. A discreet sign in hammered bronze, *St. Mark's Coptic Church*, piqued his interest, and he again thought of Memnet. Though each of them had lost his time, friends, and family, she had lost ties to her faith. No one in this world shared Memnet's beliefs. Everything she'd been taught was now considered mere superstition.

Leo often felt empathy for her, and he saw in this church a chance to connect her world to the present one. According to tradition, the Coptics were descendants of ancient Egyptians Christianized by St. Mark. Could they be a bridge to help Memnet enter the modern world? Leo never sought to change another's beliefs, but a connection to Egypt might be what his friend needed to come to terms with the here and now.

Candles flickered on the altar, each tiny addition adding warmth and light to the place. A cassocked priest turned from them to see who had entered. Uncertainty must have shown on Leo's face, because the man approached him, asking, "Can I help you, brother?"

"Do you have a moment to answer a few questions?"

"Certainly." Bearded but youthful in appearance, the man seemed used to being asked about his faith.

"I have a friend who was born in Egypt but lives in Chicago now. I'd like to learn about this church so I can tell her about it."

"Is your friend a Coptic Christian?"

"No." Leo struggled to find a way to explain Memnet. "She's been attending Baha'i services."

The priest liked the idea of a potential convert. "The Coptic church originated in Egypt, as you already know. We have a long Christian tradition, blended with Islamic influences as well. Our beliefs inspired the Nicene Creed, and our founders started the first catechetical schools and began the practice of monasticism."

"Interesting," Leo said politely. Would it interest Memnet?

"Today we work for peace and the resolution of differences between the various Christian churches. Each day we pray for Egypt, for peace there and blessings upon it."

"My friend is quite distressed at the recent unrest."

"As are we," the priest agreed. "Our beliefs are similar to the Catholic church. We perform seven sacraments, our congregations are led by priests, and we revere the Virgin Mary, who fled to Egypt with Joseph to escape Herod's soldiers." Mentally Leo connected the Virgin with Maat, the gentle goddess who had called Memnet to a life of purity and service. Might she accept a new version of her old faith?

The priest went on, his dark eyes earnest. "Unlike the Catholic church, our father confessor has no proscribed method for absolving sin. He decides what must be done on a case-by-case basis."

"So one's specific circumstances determine what she must do to find release from, say, a vow she can no longer live by?"

"Yes."

"Are you one who could help with such problems?"

"I am Father Mark. Does your friend have a problem of conscience?"

"She does. But it can be resolved, I think, with the right approach."

***

Clay scrambled to cover every possibility for Marshall's visit: changes of plan, weather delays, protesters, or anything else that might cause a problem. He wasn't thrilled when he got saddled with a reporter doing a story on the Bureau, but his objections faded once he got a look at her.

Sharon O'Hara wrote for a magazine called *The Citizen,* which Clay had never heard of. On the phone, she said her paper was supportive of the government in general and the FBI in particular. Blackburn had referred her to Clay, who was handling the press. They'd set up a meeting for 10:00 a.m., but Clay was neck-deep in work by then. An unaccustomed silence made him look up from his desk, and he watched Miss O'Hara's entrance, along with every other man in the place.

She was gorgeous, with auburn hair, green eyes, and a knock-out figure. Clay saw her stop at the first desk and ask a question. When the man pointed at him, she smiled like she'd been waiting all her life to meet an FBI man exactly like him.

The interview went well. Sharon was smart enough not to ask about classified material. Instead she delved into Clay's background, his reasons for coming to the Bureau, and his view of the job. After about twenty minutes, she closed her notebook. "One more request, Agent Danner. I'd like to get a photographer over here for some shots. Do you ever get time off from scouring the city to keep it safe?" Her smile said no sarcasm was intended.

He wasn't sure what the Bureau's policy on individual publicity was, but he guessed they'd frown on it. Sharon saw his hesitation. "I'll clear it with Agent Blackburn." She rose and held out a hand. "If he says it's okay, meet us at twelve at Styros, the new Greek place, and I'll buy you lunch."

She left, causing Clay's coworkers to take a break from their work to watch the back view. In ten minutes, Blackburn called and suggested Clay meet Miss O'Hara for lunch. "These days it isn't often the Bureau gets positive publicity. Her magazine is read by some very influential people. Besides—" Clay could hardly believe his boss sounded almost human, "—I think she likes you."

Clay met Sharon an hour later outside the restaurant known for great food and rude waiters. The photographer, a dour type who said, "Do this," or "Do that," and nothing more, took several shots of him. It was a little embarrassing with people passing by, but they got through it. When Mr. Gloom shouldered his camera case and left, Clay hoped Sharon had arranged it that way so they could get to know each other better.

Over lunch, they chatted about everything. Sharon was a pleasant companion who, rather surprisingly, knew what glasspacks were. As they left the restaurant, he wondered if he could see her again. A woman as perfect as she was probably attached, but he worked up the courage to ask, "So when you go home, is someone there waiting?"

"Just Daryl," she replied. As his heart sank, she added with a grin, "My poodle is the only man in my life right now." She touched his hand before striding away, her long legs attracting admiring glances all along the street. Clay's heart was a little lighter as he returned to his endless stack of work.

Around two he took some papers in for Blackburn's signature. He tended to let them collect until he had several, minimizing the number of times they interacted. Clay couldn't tell if Blackburn approved of his work or not, but he was pretty sure the man didn't like him. He also got the feeling his boss didn't trust him, but that wasn't a surprise. Blackburn didn't seem to trust anybody.

As he walked into the office, Blackburn was turned away from the door, talking on the phone. Clay heard, "Follow the little creep everywhere he goes for the next twenty-four hours. Once we have an idea of his schedule we'll work from there."

Clay cleared his throat, and the senior agent turned, saw him, and inverted the notepad he'd been writing on. Into the phone he said, "I'll check with you later," then hung up.

"What creep are we watching now?" Clay asked.

"Nothing to do with you. Is that the itinerary?"

Reminding himself that Blackburn wasn't obligated to share everything with him, he handed over the sheet he'd typed up. "Marshall's planned stops, possible routes I've plotted, and agents who'll be on duty."

Blackburn looked it over critically. "This looks good, except I want you on duty here." He pointed at the Sunday, 8:00 a.m.-4:00 p.m. slot. "We'll be the lead team on that shift, with Marks and Van Stee for peripheral. Chicago's finest will be all over the place too."

Unconsciously Clay straightened his tie and raised his chin. It was nice to know the agent-in-charge wanted him on his team.

They went over the itinerary for Marshall's visit: pickup at O'Hare with a brief news conference in a meeting room there, dinner with Mayor Daley, a speech at Northwestern, and return to the Palmer House. The next morning, Clay and Blackburn would relieve Hawking's team at 8:00 a.m. and escort Justice Marshall to the B.R.I.C.K. headquarters downtown. There he would meet the public and say a few words. Clay didn't like the fact that he'd speak outdoors, but Marshall refused to yield to fears of assassination.

"He's right," Blackburn said. "Guy can't live in a bubble because some crazy might shoot him."

When they finished, Clay reached to pick up the itinerary sheet he'd typed and knocked the notepad from Blackburn's desk onto the floor. Embarrassed to be such a klutz, he hurried to pick it up. He got only a glance, but the address of the "creep" Blackburn wanted followed was on 100th, his street.

Chapter Thirty-one

Roy couldn't stand to pay for a newspaper he'd be finished reading in five minutes. Though he could easily have lifted one while passing a newsstand, he'd given up thieving unless it was absolutely necessary. In a stroke of good luck, on his way home from the hardware store he spotted the current *Tribune* in a trash basket near the bus stop. After a casual once-over assured it had no nasty attachments, he removed the paper, re-folded it, and stuck it under his arm. He went on looking like Brian Keith in *Family Affair,* a completely upstanding citizen.

The headlines contained Jeanne Dixon's predictions for the year of 1968 and news that the Israelis had attacked an airport in Beirut and done a great deal of damage, at least according to Arab sources. Another story concerned Christiaan Barnard, the doctor who'd performed the world's first heart transplant twenty-five days before. Louis Washkansky, the guinea pig, was now dead of double pneumonia, but Barnard was a hero.

It might be old-fashioned, Roy thought, *but I could never borrow spare parts from somebody else.* He doubted such things would become common, no matter how excited doctors got about it.

He entered the house to a terrible racket upstairs. "Jake!" he called in a firm tone, and the volume of what she called music decreased. Leo had repaired a phonograph they found in the basement, and Libby had bought a new needle for it. Now Jake spent her money on "forty-fives," plastic discs that made more noise than a cattle drive. The rest of them suffered through it, but Roy insisted on a reasonable volume when he was in the house.

Currently it sounded like someone was saying, "I am a walrus," but that couldn't be right.

In the kitchen Libby was taking a dish that smelled wonderful out of the oven. Her cheeks were pink from the heat, and tendrils of hair hung in spirals around her face. While he was at times bored with life here, Roy had never seen Libby happier. She'd become downright grandmotherly.

For the hundredth time Roy promised himself he'd try to be more pleasant. To begin it he set the table, toting plates, cups, and silverware into the dining room. "It's good of you to help," Libby said. "I'm a bit behind, since I spent the day baking for a sale at church. Miz Jones says they never get enough pies, so I made a half dozen." Libby and a Negro woman had been exchanging recipes after services, Leo reported.

Once he'd done his part, Roy sat down on a stool in the corner. As Libby banged around the kitchen, scraping pans and running water, he browsed the *Tribune*.

In the city news, his glance stopped at a headline. When he made an "uh-oh" noise, Libby put down her spoon and came to read over his shoulder.

FBI Investigates Uninvited Guests

Charlene Dobbs, curator of the Schmidt Museum, informed the Tribune *today that the FBI is looking into her recent kidnapping. After spending three days in the basement of the museum, Dobbs was released unharmed. The kidnappers escaped, but today Dobbs claimed the FBI has taken interest in the case.*

"There is more to my ordeal than the authorities

first thought," Dobbs reports. *"We now believe there is a connection between my capture and some people who recently escaped custody. I hope federal law officers can bring these ruthless criminals to justice, since the Chicago Police Department has no leads whatsoever."*

"I bet she called the FBI herself," Roy muttered.

A pan boiled over and water hissed onto the stove, and Libby went to deal with it. "How did she make the connection?"

Roy read the next passage aloud. *"Ms. Dobbs found a ring of keys in the basement where she was held captive. Serial numbers indicate they belonged to Norman Bohn, a former curator of the museum. One of two men arrested in Wilmette earlier this month was using Bohn's museum identity card. Dobbs believes the men killed Bohn and have been squatting in the museum ever since. 'It gives me the creeps when I think of the times I worked late and was practically alone with crazy people,' Dobbs said."*

Closing the paper Roy rolled his eyes. "Charlene's got quite an imagination. We killed Norman? She worked late?"

"What nonsense!" Libby grumbled. "Norman tripped when he tried to carry too much at once."

"Exaggeration makes good copy," Roy said. "Lord knows I was painted worse than I was by them newspapers in my day."

"Those newspapers," she corrected him absently.

"Yes, ma'am. *Those* newspapers don't mind if somebody like Charlene says ridiculous things. It sells copies, and they can claim they're only quotin' what was said."

Libby leaned a hip against the counter. "The worst thing is

they've connected what happened in Wilmette with our presence at the museum. Charlene can identify me, and Blackburn has seen most of us. If he's described us for the FBI, we have to be even more careful."

"And Danner's nearby. We might have to move."

"That would look suspicious, since we just arrived." Libby took an onion from a bag under the counter. "In addition to that, we put a good bit of Jake's money into this house. We might not be able to sell it again and recoup our investment."

"You're right." Roy recalled how eager the real estate agent had been to make the deal. "Then we'll have to act as much like normal folks as possible and hope Blackburn forgets about us."

Steps sounded on the back porch, the scuffle of feet being cleaned of snow, and Leo entered. When Libby showed him the article, his agile mind focused on the crux of the problem. "What is this Blackburn up to?"

"I surely don't know," Roy replied.

"Clay told Jake that his new boss came to Chicago at about the time we witnessed the murder in the park." Leo raised a finger. "What if he isn't an FBI man at all?"

"What do you mean?"

"Was what we saw something FBI agents would do? Dragging a suspect into the darkness and then shooting him in the back?"

"Perhaps it was a secret operation." Libby began chopping, and the sting of onion juice filled the air.

Leo was leading them in the direction his mind had already gone. "What if those men killed an agent who'd just arrived in Chicago, a man no one at the local bureau had seen before?"

241

"Where'd you come up with that idea?" Roy asked.

"I've been putting together things Clay said, memories Jake told me of her days on the street, and images of our encounter on Lake Michigan that night. If Blackburn's purpose was simply to murder that man, he'd probably have moved on when he realized there were witnesses to the crime. Instead he stayed in Chicago, I think in order to take the dead man's place."

Libby dropped her onions into a hot skillet. "They were determined to hide the crime. They stayed in the park to remove the body even after the police arrived."

"But how would this guy get the papers to make it look like he was legitimate?"

Leo raised his expressive hands. "How did we?"

"He's taking a chance." Libby stirred the onions, which had turned a golden color. "If he meets anyone who knew the real Blackburn, he's in trouble."

"Which means he won't stay a moment longer than he has to. Whatever he's planning will happen soon."

"He might intend to steal something," Roy said, "like gold."

"Or he might aim to do what we've already seen him do," Leo finished. "Kill someone."

***

"Wonder of wonders," Clay said as he spun in his chair, neglecting the stacks of work awaiting him. Miss Sharon O'Hara had called, a little apologetic, to ask him for a date!

He'd recognized her voice as soon as he answered the phone. "Agent Danner?"

"Please, call me Clay."

"Clay, I feel really stupid about this, but I'm invited to a social event tomorrow night, and I don't know many people in the city. I, um, thought we hit it off the other day, and...I realize it's late notice, but I wondered if you'd be my escort."

"You want me to take you to a party?" Clay knew he sounded dense, but it was the kind of surprise that could start a man stuttering.

"It's fine if you can't, but I'd feel better knowing at least one person there."

"Of course." He was beginning to get his breath back. "I'd be pleased to take you. I mean I'd be happy to. Go with you."

"Great. I'll pick you up at six. Wear your dinner jacket."

"You'll pick me up?" He was already thumbing through the phone book for formalwear rentals.

"They're sending a car for me, so I'll come by if you tell me where you live." Her chuckle was warm, even sexy. "I almost forgot to ask."

The evening was interesting. The affair (Clay figured that's what those in attendance would call it) was held at an impressive home in Evanston owned by a man named Anson Ballard. Sharon explained on the way that she'd been invited because of a piece she'd written about him for her magazine. "He donated a half a million to fund a library. Can you imagine having that much money to simply give away?"

The house was situated behind tall iron gates, its driveway longer than the block Clay grew up on. Trees lined the way, so the house couldn't be seen until they rounded the last curve. It was massive, with the feel of solidity and age. Inside, a butler took their invitation and directed them inside, where their coats were taken by a trim black maid.

They entered a room with ceilings much too high for efficient heating. The room was domed, and around the edges danced creatures of Greek myth, beautiful and useless except as decoration. Below them French provincial furniture arched daintily, supporting and framing lovely *objets d'art*. The room whispered wealth and the good taste to let a home decorator decide what it should contain.

Sharon and Clay met their host and hostess at the door. Anson Ballard was white-haired and erect, the sort of man the word *debonair* was coined for. Mrs. Ballard—Clay never learned her first name—had probably once been pretty, but now her face melted into her neck and her torso bulged like tires on a display rack. Though her gown was cut to flatter, some things can't be overcome.

"So nice of you to attend," she said, pressing Clay's hand.

"Yes, we were eager to see Miss O'Hara again." Ballard smiled warmly at Sharon. "She is exactly what this country needs: a journalist willing to defend American values." Ballard eyed Clay with speculation. "Where do your people come from, Mr. Danner?"

"Here, sir. I grew up in the northern suburbs."

Ballard frowned. "I mean your ancestors, man. Your roots."

"Oh." Clay was embarrassed to have misunderstood and slightly put out at the question. "My father is third-generation Polish. My mother's German with Slavic connections."

"So Danner is not your real name."

"It was Danairachek or something like that. They simplified it when they came over."

"I see." Ballard looked like he'd tasted something rancid, but he turned to Sharon, which brought back his smile. "We're so pleased to see you." Dismissing them both, he said. "Be sure to enjoy yourselves."

"Thank you, sir." As their hosts turned to other guests, Clay said to Sharon, "That was fun."

She laughed. "He's nice once you get to know him. Dad admires him."

"Then I assume your dad came over on the *Mayflower*."

"Old money gets a little full of itself sometimes," she admitted, "but Mr. Ballard works to make sure our country remains a land of opportunity for deserving Americans."

The other guests were wealthy types as well, and Clay felt completely out of place. Talk was all of where they'd been or where they were going to escape the cold. San Moritz, Vale, and Bali were places Clay knew only from *National Geographic*. From time to time Sharon caught his eye and gave him a helpless look to indicate she was as ill at ease as he. Mostly they nodded and smiled, listening to the dignified hum of the crowd and pretending they understood.

Somewhere after midnight, the party began to break up. People circled the room saying formal goodnights. Sharon said they should time their exit so they were neither first nor last to leave. In the car they laughed about the whole thing. She said it was deadly dull, and she never wanted to be so rich she didn't enjoy life. "If it weren't for work, I wouldn't have gone."

"How'd you get started at the magazine, *The Citizen*, is it?"

"Yes. My father's the founder and editor."

"Then am I in the company of a publishing heiress?"

Sharon rolled her eyes. "Not even close. We operate on a shoestring."

"That's too bad." Clay had never heard of either Eagle Press or *The Citizen* before meeting Sharon, but her admission revealed why she'd been eager to attend Ballard's party. Someone like him could help a struggling magazine just by noticing it. "He likes the sort of thing you publish?"

"We do material for specific groups, mostly patriotic stuff, and he funds a lot of that."

"That's in addition to articles on heroic FBI agents?"

She nudged him with an elbow, laughing. "I'd never want to miss that!"

They parted at Clay's driveway. Sharon leaned over and gave him a quick kiss, indicating with a tilt of her head at the driver that she was embarrassed to do more. Entertaining the thought she might have wanted to, Clay counted the evening a great success as he waved goodnight and climbed the steps to his house, which seemed extra-empty after Sharon's delightful company.

Chapter Thirty-two

The next day at work, Clay joined the crew at the coffeepot, unable to resist letting them know he'd gone out with Sharon. Helping himself to the near-lethal-strength brew replenished constantly in a pot seldom cleaned, he added five cubes of sugar and casually mentioned his date. The others were suitably impressed, but the mood changed when he told them they'd gone to a party at Anson Ballard's.

"You were invited there?" Marks asked.

Clay shrugged. "I'm not much for gate-crashing."

"Anson Ballard the millionaire?"

"He'd have to be to own that house." A look passed between the other men. "What?"

Belding looked embarrassed. "You might want to watch it, Danner."

Marks leaned in and lowered his voice. "Ballard is rich all right, but he's a little odd."

"He seemed okay to me." The comment recalled his unease at the old man's questions.

"He's not a criminal or anything," Marks said, "but he's ultra-conservative. Doesn't like anybody who's different."

"Like what kind of different?"

Marks spread his hands. "Jews, Mexicans, Asians, blacks. In his view, the white race is pretty much superior to all others. He spends his money trying to convince other white people that the 'inferior races' are a threat to the American Way."

"You're saying he hasn't seen *In the Heat of the Night*?"

The men seemed relieved that Clay took their advice with humor. Sipping the coffee and making a face, he assured them, "I'll never see the guy again, but thanks for the warning."

Returning to his desk, he wondered if Sharon knew the subject of her article was a known racist. He also wondered if his Jewish ancestry would matter to her, as it probably would to Ballard.

It was tough to pick bigots out of a crowd. Clay found himself wondering if some of the guests they'd met last night were members of the Ku Klux Klan. He dismissed the idea, figuring the Klan was probably less black tie, more redneck. Since he'd had a whole evening with Sharon at his side, he didn't care what delusions Anson Ballard and his group operated under. Getting to know her better had been worth it.

***

The newspapers were filled with speculation on who the mystery inhabitants of the Schmidt Museum might be and where they were. Charlene kept coming up with wild explanations, and most reporters seemed willing to print them. She proudly announced she'd ordered the false wall removed and the fake paintings burned.

Wish I could tell her to her face that she just destroyed two da Vinci paintings! Jake imagined Charlene's satisfaction turning to horror upon learning the Schmidt could have become the most famous museum in the world.

Jake didn't miss living in the damp old basement. Here she had her own room and Bastet, who sat like a person, on her backside with front paws resting on her lap—if cats have laps. The kitten ate only what Libby offered. At night she slept with

Jake and by day followed her around like a dog.

Jake would soon return to school, but she'd decided she didn't mind. She liked her family, was pretty sure she loved them, but they were old. Sometimes she wanted to talk to someone who knew what it was like to be a teenager in the '60s—the *nineteen* sixties. They didn't like her music. Even Memnet didn't pay attention now that she didn't sing in the subway anymore. Besides, school would be different at with a normal family at home. She could invite friends over, and Libby would bake them cookies.

Jake had tried to interest Libby in reading *Rosemary's Baby*, but the older woman was horrified by the whole idea of Satan having a child. She said Ira Levin should be boiled in oil, which was creepy since she'd probably ordered that done once or twice when she was queen.

That was another reason Jake liked Clay. He was older, but he hadn't crystallized yet. He'd been busy though, working extra hours to prepare for Justice Marshall's visit. He'd found time to take her skating the Sunday before, even rented a pair of skates for himself and taught her neat tricks like skating backward and stopping on her toes. Memnet and Libby came to watch, and on the way home, they'd had a brief snowball fight, which Memnet didn't like at all. "Snow is cold," she complained. "Why would you throw it at people you like?"

Once home, they feasted on cocoa and peanut butter cookies, Libby's newest effort. "This type of butter is used in many ways," she told them. "I shall try making pie with it next."

As he munched a second cookie, Clay told stories about the people at work. When he mentioned Blackburn, all ears at the Parker home perked up. "Today he told everybody about my

249

excellent scores on the firing range."

"You're a good shot?" Jake asked.

Clay buffed his fingernails comically. "Actually, I am, but I didn't think the boss knew it."

"Does that mean you have a double-O rating?" Jake asked.

"Me and James Bond. Can't you see the women flocking after me?"

Clay had met a girl he liked named Sharon, but she'd gone out with him once and hadn't answered his calls since. While they made dinner, Jake asked Libby why that was.

"For all his twenty-odd years," the older woman said as she sampled her gravy, "Clay is still a boy at heart. Women, at least the sort he's attracted to, understand on some unconscious level that he's a long way from being ready for marriage."

"But he's great with the three of us, and we're women."

"He doesn't relate to us in a romantic way." She touched Jake's nose with a floury finger, leaving a white spot. "I'm too old, you're too young, and Memnet is married, as far as he knows. With us, Clay can be himself and not try to impress."

So Clay thinks I'm just a kid, Jake thought. *Well, wait a few years, Clay Danner, and we'll see.*

New snow had fallen, the crunchy kind that felt like cornstarch underfoot. A little after six, Jake wandered down to Clay's house, bored and looking for company. A thin white carpet on the ground showed a man's footprints going onto the porch. The shoe prints were big, and it flashed through her mind that Clay had big feet for a small guy.

Clay had wrapped the railing with boughs for the holidays

and hadn't yet removed them. Needles littered the floor, and she caught a whiff of pine as she passed. Stepping onto the porch, she approached the door, which had one of those sectioned windows, *mullioned*, Libby called them. Jake could see into the entryway. Typical man: no curtains.

She wasn't really snooping, but something caught her eye. A man was searching the drawers of a desk in the hall. When Jake tapped at the window he looked up, surprised, turned to the back of the house, and disappeared.

"Hey!" Jake hollered, trying the door. It was locked. As she turned to run for help, she almost flattened Clay, who was just stepping onto the porch.

"Hey, Midget," he yelped, grabbing the rail. "What's your hurry?"

"There was a man in there! I think he went out the back."

"Go home, Jake. Tell your uncle to call the police." Clay pulled a gun from his coat as he spoke.

Jake started for home, but she knew they couldn't call anyone. "Roy!" she called as she burst through the door. "Clay's got a burglar in his house."

Roy came out of his shop. "Stay here." Taking a poker from the fireplace, he ran out the door.

***

By the time Roy arrived, Clay was once again on the porch. "He's gone."

"Did you get a look at him?"

"No."

When Roy explained they didn't have a phone yet, Clay

called the police from his own. While they waited, he and Roy searched neighboring yards for signs of the intruder. Footprints led to the walk on the other side of the block. There he'd taken to the street, so there was no further trail.

"I'll bring Jake back here so she can give the police a description." Walking home, Roy realized he was on the other side of the law, helping to find those who broke it. *It doesn't feel bad,* he thought with a grin, *but it sure feels different.*

When the police arrived Jake described the man, but he didn't sound unique: a little above average in height, dark, straight hair, a pale complexion, trench coat, and deep-set eyes. When they'd finished the report and gone, she sat down with Clay, Roy, and Leo, who'd returned with them, at Clay's kitchen table. "I'm sorry my description was bad," Jake said.

"You did great," Clay assured her. "And by the way, you almost knocked me flat. Were you going to chase him down?"

She shivered. "He had no right to go through your stuff."

"He didn't take anything. Must have panicked when he saw you at the door."

"Perhaps," murmured Leo. Jake knew him better than Clay did and knew there were other possibilities on his mind.

When they were back at home Leo asked Jake to describe the man once more. "Close your eyes and picture him. What's the strongest impression you got?"

"He was pale, like I said," Jake responded. "Funny pale, like a worm."

"Right."

"Leo, you think you know who the guy is?"

Roy looked to Leo and nodded some sort of encouragement.

"This burglar who took nothing sounds like the man who was with Blackburn the night of the shooting on Lake Michigan. I remember he looked pale, like someone who's been inside for a long time." He added, "Perhaps in prison."

"Maybe he works nights," Libby suggested, but no one agreed, and even she didn't sound as if she believed it.

"We know Agent Blackburn asked Clay to work a certain shift this week," Leo said. "Whatever he has planned, I believe it is imminent."

"Mormons don't gamble," Roy said soberly, "but I would bet Leo is right. Do we tell Danner to be extra careful?"

"I don't see how we can without explaining things we have no explanation for," Leo replied.

"Then we'll just have to keep an eye on him," Roy said. "The guy has no idea what kind of bad things might happen."

Chapter Thirty-three

On the second day of 1968, Libby learned the change of year came in January in the present century, not March as she was used to. She decreed a celebration, though it was somewhat late.

"We have truly made a new start," Leo agreed. "We lead productive lives, Jake will soon resume her education, and we are together. These are accomplishments."

"I'll get the wine," Roy offered. "No Boone's Farm or Ripple either."

Jake immediately asked if she could have some. Roy looked to Libby, who clasped her hands as she made a decision. "One glass to welcome the year will do no harm."

Memnet offered to get the food, and soon she was on her way with Libby's list. It was four blocks to the little market run by an aging German couple where she did the shopping, but the day was sunny and the sidewalks were clear.

Their new neighborhood felt more open than downtown. Though a bit run down, there was little crime. Memnet enjoyed shopping there, and sometimes Roy came along. They talked about nothing on those trips, but it made her happy. Since he'd gone to the liquor store today, she went alone.

Memnet was learning to use money, something she'd left largely to the others until recently. Coins were easy, but bills confused her, being all the same color and general appearance. She had to study the numbers so as not to be cheated.

Leo had begun teaching her to read English, since she didn't want to ever again be the cause of problems due to ignorance.

Letters were more difficult than picture writing, especially when a letter didn't always indicate the same sound. Still, there were only twenty-six of them, which Leo claimed was an advantage.

To practice, Memnet read the headlines whenever she passed a newspaper rack. Today's paper was accompanied by a picture that struck her as familiar: a woman with blond hair and too much makeup. She stopped, deciphering the message slowly, her lips moving and her interest growing as she read: *Schmidt Museum Curator Disappears 2nd Time.* The picture was of Charlene Dobbs. Memnet took a paper from the stack and added it to her basket. The others would want to see this.

As she started home, Memnet considered the church Leo had described to her: a Christian church Egyptian in origin. He said the priest might understand her situation, but she doubted that. How could she explain that two thousand years ago she'd made a vow she now wanted to break? Leo said it wouldn't hurt to meet the man, and Memnet had agreed.

Deep in thought, she missed the danger until it was too late. She passed two empty storefronts with an alley between. The street was deserted, and a draft swept out of the alley, causing her to hunch her shoulders. Glancing sideways, she saw a man leaning against the side of one building, hat pulled low over his eyes. Though she was startled to see him lurking there, Memnet kept walking.

A tingle at the back of her neck signaled a warning, but before she could react, she felt a hand on her mouth. Another slid around her waist. She was picked up and carried, struggling desperately, into the alley where a car waited, its motor running. The man forced her into the back, closed the door, and got into the front. The car took off with a jerk, pressing Memnet against the seat back. Desperately she reached for the door handle. There was none on either side.

Memnet's attacker turned to look at her, a satisfied grin on his pale face. The driver watched the road, but she recognized his profile: FBI Agent Charles Blackburn.

***

The Parkers became concerned when Memnet didn't come home. Jake and Roy went looking for her and returned looking grim. A grocery bag containing a ham, a newspaper, and the other items on Libby's list had been dropped, not set down, near an alley. Memnet was in trouble.

"We have to call the cops," Jake urged.

"Jake," Libby replied, "you know we can't do that."

"Well, we can't just sit here and do nothing!" Jake fought back tears. Where was Memnet?

The discussion was complicated by the fact that Roy was almost raving, promising death and destruction to whoever had taken her. He paced the kitchen, periodically slamming his fist into whatever unlucky surface was nearest. Leo and Libby tried to calm him, and an hour was wasted in circular argument.

After they'd talked themselves out with no decision made, Leo noticed the newspaper headline. Scanning the article, he summarized. "Charlene was abducted on her way to work yesterday morning. A neighbor happened to glance out the window and saw her forced into a black sedan by two men."

"Charlene was kidnapped too?" Libby was shocked.

"It says the police fear the same gang is behind her disappearance, since she can identify at least one of them."

"Memnet's abduction must be related to this," Leo declared.

"We have to do something." Roy smacked the door casing, sending Libby over the edge of composure. Grabbing him by the shirtsleeve like a schoolmarm with an unruly student, she pushed him into a chair and leaned into his face.

"What would you have us do," Libby demanded, "go knocking on every door in Chicago asking if anyone's seen a young Egyptian woman? Think, Roy!" Cowed, Roy controlled his temper, at least for a while.

***

Clay rubbed his forehead. He'd be glad when the week was over and Justice Marshall was back in his own home. As with most big events, there'd been excitement at first, hard work leading up to it, and then anxiety about what could go wrong.

He'd tried to foresee every danger but couldn't shake the fear he'd forgotten something. Worse, Blackburn no longer seemed interested in the job he'd insisted on having. Busy with other things, he assured Clay he was doing fine on his own.

Justice Marshall had arrived in town safely, and the first day had gone well. Clay found the Justice down-to-earth and personable as they went through the necessary briefing and last-minute changes. Travel for a celebrity was work. They didn't really get to enjoy the places they visited, since they were themselves attractions who had to be "on" every moment. Clay left Marshall with the night team at his hotel after a long day, sensing the great man was ready for some quiet time. He stopped at the office, assured that everything was set for tomorrow's itinerary, and left for home.

Hoping there'd be cooking going on, he cut across the block and approached the Parkers' house. Jake would start school on Monday, and since being the new kid was tough, Clay had decided to take her there in the Camaro. It would make a good first impression, and she was sure to get questions about it that would break the ice.

Leo answered his knock at the back door, looking like his mind was somewhere else. "Hi, Leo," Clay said, "is Jake here?"

A shifty expression appeared on Leo's face, totally unlike the man. "I'm sorry, Mr. Danner. Jake is out with friends." He'd opened the door just a crack, and he held onto it as if Clay might try to force his way in.

Jake had no friends as of yesterday, but he let that go. He asked about Leo's shop in the basement, which he usually liked to talk about, but he was barely polite. Finally Clay asked, "Is Libby around? She said she'd have banana bread to sell today."

"She's gone out too. With Memnet." Leo was terse and unlike his usual polite self. Clay left, wondering how he'd worn out his welcome. When he got to the sidewalk and turned toward home, Libby was on the front porch, sweeping furiously, her hands white on the broom handle. She didn't notice Clay, and he didn't speak. Obviously, they didn't want him around.

Back at home, Clay stuck a Salisbury steak TV dinner in the oven and wandered aimlessly through the empty rooms as it heated. For reasons unclear to him, Clay's great uncle had left him the rambling mansion. When Clay was assigned to the Chicago FBI, it made sense to make use of it, though he certainly didn't need the whole space. He'd closed the two upper floors, divided the downstairs in half, moved into one side, and rented the other out. A young couple from Gary had proven to be good tenants and good neighbors to boot.

Things had been good until the recent break-in. According to Jake, the guy had rifled his desk, but an unsealed envelope containing four hundred dollars was left untouched in the top drawer. If the intruder wasn't a thief in the usual sense, Clay wondered what he'd been doing there.

The break-in bothered him. Leo's cold reception bothered him. What was going on with everyone? Stopping at the desk in the hallway, Clay stared at it as if it could answer his question. He'd looked through all the drawers after the incident, trying to determine what was missing. He'd even turned them upside down and checked the bottoms. FBI training at work.

It occurred to him now that he hadn't looked at the bottom of the desk itself. It seemed important to leave no stone unturned, or desk either, he told himself. Tilting the piece forward onto a scatter rug, he turned it away from the wall so he could see the underside. On one side were dead insects and thick cobwebs, for which he knew he should be ashamed. The other side lacked both web and bugs, because someone had taped a large mailing envelope to the wooden bottom. It had no address or postmark, but there was something inside.

With a handkerchief over his hand, Clay removed the packet and set the desk back in place. The flap wasn't sealed, so he carried the envelope to the braided oval rug in the living room and dumped the contents. Inside were three typed sheets, none signed or dated. They appeared to be drafts of a letter, and he scanned the first one.

Sharon,

I don't know how to tell you how I feel about you. We've only met a few times, but from the first I knoew you were the woman I want to spent the rest of my days life with. We agree on so many things, the way we'd like to live someday, the direction the United States is heading (wrong) and even how we take our coffee (ha ha). It was great that you showed me there are others who feel like we do, but I have to say your wrong to think that things can change peacefully. Sometimes peaceful people get run over by those who don't understand reality. I'm going to do something to show you that I'm serious about changing things in this country. If it works, I will—

It ended there. The next sheet was a second attempt that differed only in syntax, a few added phrases, and the addition of a final line, *I hope we can see each other again soon.* The third was a clean copy, retyped without errors except for *your,* used in all three copies where *you're* should have been.

Along with the three sheets was a pamphlet called *The Threat of Integration.* Clay flipped through chapters titled "Racial Inferiority," "Corrupting the Gene Pool," and "Studies Link Negroes to Violence." It contained distortions typical of such literature, including the claim that God created the races in a sort of hierarchy with whites at the top. Checking the publication information, he found *Eagle Press, Pittsburg, Penn.* Sharon's "patriotic" publishing house? Disgusted, he considered throwing the whole packet into the fireplace. Then he changed his mind.

Someone had planted this stuff to be found during a police search of Clay's home at some point in the future. He was supposed to look like a racist, out to impress a beautiful woman who was also racist. *Why?* As he pondered that question, along with who was behind it, Clay's dinner burned to a smoking black mass.

Chapter Thirty-four

Once the black sedan was out of the neighborhood, Blackburn turned to examine Memnet. "Do you speak English?" She didn't answer. "Is there a telephone number where I can call your friends?" When she didn't reply, he said, "They'll come and get you if we call them."

She remained silent, unwilling to help these men catch the others. They drove on for a few minutes, the only sound the bump of snow tires on bare pavement. Blackburn kept glancing at her in the rear view mirror. "They'll get the message, one way or another."

The man who'd grabbed her was almost certainly the one Leo and Jake described. He was indeed pale, almost blue, as if he weren't fully alive. His eyes, however, greedily raked Memnet's body as he leaned over the folding front seat, measuring her for some future moment.

"Mason, you know what to do. Take her to the house then go back down to 100th and drop off the note. I have to get back to the office and play dedicated FBI agent."

"I got it. I'll see you tomorrow, downtown."

"Remember, once you finish, get out fast." Blackburn was definitely in command. "Drive at a reasonable speed. If you panic, I'll hear about it."

"Don't worry," Mason responded. "I've got a blond and a brunette for company tonight." Reaching into the back seat, he pinched Memnet's knee, making her stomach turn over.

"Focus on the job and leave the women alone," Blackburn

ordered. "Don't add a thing to what I told you, understand?"

"Don't get all uptight!" The man's tone turned whiny. "She's too dark for me anyway!"

"Last time, you screwed up and got caught. If you make a mistake this time you'll get a needle in your arm for aiding an assassination."

Mason seemed cowed. "Okay. I got it."

The candor of Blackburn's comments told Memnet he wasn't afraid she'd repeat what she'd heard. She wouldn't to live to tell anyone.

Blackburn drove to a small park, obeying speed laws and crossing intersections with care. The place was uninviting, the swings, slides, and benches deserted and snow-covered. The only sign of recent human occupation was a second anonymous black sedan parked at the far end. After a final warning to Mason to follow instructions, Blackburn got in the second car and left.

Sliding into the driver's seat, Mason drove away, muttering to himself. Most of it was inaudible, but at one point his voice rose. "Arrogant son of a bitch!"

Memnet watched street signs, trying to get her bearings though she knew it wouldn't help. She had no way to summon her friends, even if she figured out her final destination. Past 31st Street, she heard the blinker click on, and Mason turned right. After that, turns to the left and right came quickly, and she became totally lost. On a residential street, he pulled the car into a small garage and turned off the engine. "We're going in, and you ain't gonna make no fuss, understand?"

She remained silent, thinking it might be an advantage to pretend she didn't speak English. Mason got out and opened the back door. As she stepped from the car, he pushed her roughly against it and ran his hands over her body, his grinning face close to hers. Terrified, Memnet kept her expression blank, her eyes on the ground. Disappointed at getting no reaction, he released her and pushed her toward the house.

It was a large, plain structure of two stories, lap-sided in faded blue with moss-encrusted shingles and windowsills starving for paint. The yard had a tall, plank fence to separate it from its neighbors. A *For Sale* sign in the yard looked like it had been there for a long time. Up three concrete steps, Mason unlocked a characterless front entry door. The foyer smelled of old cooking grease, wet wood, and multiple dog accidents.

He pointed upward, and they climbed narrow stairs. At the top, a hallway led to three closed doors, each with a small metal number tacked at eye level. Mason unlocked the door with a *3* on it with a key he took from his pocket.

The room held only a bed, a dresser and a nightstand. An inner door opened into a small bathroom that had probably once been a closet. The only window was covered with wire mesh. Before Memnet had time to take in more than that, Mason closed the door, and she heard him lock it from the hallway. Seconds later she heard the car start up and drive away. Mason was leaving to follow Blackburn's instructions. He'd lead her friends into a trap with her as bait.

***

Roy was like a wolf Jake had once seen in a cage at the zoo, pacing the same track back and forth. He kept cracking his knuckles, and he heard little anyone said to him.

Jake felt terrible. Memnet was the sweetest person she'd ever known, and if anything happened to her... She didn't let herself finish that thought. Libby insisted if the men had wanted her dead they'd have killed her outright, which meant she was still alive. Jake didn't know whether that was good or not.

They talked on and on, getting nowhere, until the sound of something hitting the porch interrupted them. Leo peeked out the window then shrugged his shoulders to indicate he saw no one. "Small stones." Exiting the house for a moment, he returned carrying a note. Everyone gathered around as he unfolded it, so they all saw the words, lettered with a broad-tipped black pen: *If you want the woman, come to the Schmidt Museum at seven tomorrow morning. Second floor.*

There was no signature, but they didn't need one. Blackburn had Memnet and, it seemed, plans for all of them. Looking at Roy, Jake realized he would do as the note demanded. Leo would go too, but could they rescue Memnet and defeat Blackburn by themselves?

Clay came to mind. Maybe he could help. Roy would be mad if she asked, but who else did they have to turn to? Taking Leo aside, she made her pitch. Leo would listen to her, and Clay would listen to Leo, she hoped.

***

After examining the items in the packet several times, Clay put everything back into the envelope, still using his handkerchief, and slipped the whole thing into a second, larger one. This he mailed to himself in care of the couple in the other half of the house, putting every stamp he could find on it to assure delivery. He'd alert them to it later, but right now he needed it out of his hands. He had no way to prove he hadn't written those drafts in an attempt to find the right words to convince Sharon O'Hara she was the girl of his dreams.

Returning from the mailbox down the street, Clay found Leo and Libby on his porch. He invited them in but they declined, moving their feet nervously on the wooden floor. Leo's usual good humor was absent, and Libby was white and tense. They had something important to tell him.

"Mr. Danner, can we impose upon you to meet us somewhere, perhaps at that McDonald's you sometimes take Jake to? We'd rather not talk here."

In just over fifteen minutes they were seated in a booth, Clay with a large cheeseburger and a Coke, Leo and Libby with steaming cups of hot tea. He waited for them to tell him what was going on, but they both seemed reluctant now they'd gotten him there. Danner ate his cheeseburger while they stirred their tea and stewed.

Finally, Leo began. "Mr. Danner, um, Clay, we need your help. Your capacity as a federal agent makes you our best choice, and paradoxically, our worst. We need to tell you about a problem that has arisen, but we must of necessity limit the information we provide."

"I'm only going to get part of the story?"

"I assure you we are not criminals in whom the Bureau of Investigation would be interested. You have our word on that."

Clay noted Leo's odd phrasing. If they were criminals, lying probably wouldn't bother them. "Tell you what. I'll listen and let you know when I'm feeling too much in the dark."

Libby looked at Leo, who gripped the table edge with both hands. "We should add that our situation might involve you as well," she said.

Intrigued by the quaint old couple's contention that some

problem of theirs touched on FBI business and him personally, Clay asked himself if they might have had something to do with the material hidden in his house. He immediately rejected that idea. The Parkers simply weren't hateful types.

That brought the antagonistic Parker to mind. "Does Roy know you're here?"

They exchanged glances. "We said we were going for a walk. He hardly noticed."

"Okay. Tell me what's bothering you."

Looking once again at Libby for moral support, Leo began. "Memnet has been kidnapped."

Clay almost jumped out of his chair. "Have you called the police?"

Libby touched his arm. "We came to you, Clay."

Minutes later he had the story, at least as much as they were willing to tell. They'd witnessed two men killing a third. The murderers had seen Roy, Leo, and Jake clearly. When the police arrived, they'd run away for fear they'd be blamed. No word of the murder had appeared in the news.

Danner saw gaps in the story. The Parkers had something to hide, or they would have pursued the matter. He leaned forward, waiting for the rest.

What they'd witnessed would have stayed in the past, Leo explained, except Roy and Memnet had seen one of the men a few days later. They had moved to their present home to avoid him, but now the killers had found and kidnapped Memnet. They'd received a note demanding a meeting.

What was most preposterous about the whole story was Leo's conclusion. "One of the men is Charles Blackburn."

"Ridiculous!" Clay scoffed, but before he went on, he lowered his voice. "Agents of the federal government don't go around killing innocent people."

Leo took a deep breath, as if he knew he was going out on a limb. "We think the man you work for killed the real Blackburn and took his place."

"Why would he want to impersonate a federal officer?" Clay realized it was a dumb question as soon as he said it. There were lots of possible reasons, all of them bad.

Leo moved his cup to one side. "I suspect he intends to accomplish one important crime."

The cheeseburger turned to stone in Clay's stomach. Tomorrow morning at 10 a.m., the first black man ever to serve on the Supreme Court would travel through the Loop. If something happened to Justice Marshall, Blackburn could say Clay had planned the route, the stops, everything.

Pushing a hand through his hair, he said, "If what you say is true, Blackburn is setting me up to take the rap for something. My guess is it's the assassination of Thurgood Marshall."

Leo looked confused while he mentally translated the idiom. Clay went on, "I found stuff planted in my house that makes me look like a white supremacist."

"You mean like the men who dress in sheets on the television news?" Libby asked.

Clay nodded. "It looks like I'm desperate to impress a girl, so much so that I plan to do something horrible to show her how dedicated I am to the cause."

A recent event took on new meaning and he went on, "Blackburn had my address written on a notepad one day. He was talking on the phone about a 'little creep' he wanted followed." His expression turned angry. "I'm the little creep, and that's probably how they found you."

Leo seemed to need clarification. "This man intends to blame you for a crime he will commit?"

Clay ticked points off on his fingers. "The guy who broke into my house left evidence of my supposed extreme views. I recently attended a dinner at the home of a known racist, though I didn't know it at the time. Blackburn made a big deal about my excellent marksmanship to the whole staff, and he's got me on duty tomorrow morning." He slapped a hand on the table. "It will look like I used my place in the Bureau to set up the crime!"

They were silent for a few seconds as they absorbed Clay's words. Finally Leo said softly, "There will be an assassination?"

"That's my guess." A shadow passed over Leo's face, and Clay asked, "What is it, Leo? We need to share everything if we're going to figure out how to stop it."

"I don't know how to stop it," Leo answered. "I was only thinking that blaming you for the crime will be easier for them if you aren't alive to defend yourself."

"You saw them kill a man," he replied. "They want you dead too."

Movement caught his eye, and Clay looked up to see Jake in the doorway. Surveying the room, she located them and hurried to the corner where they sat.

"I couldn't find you, and I couldn't stop him! It was on TV then he was gone. I couldn't find you!" The low tone she began with rose toward a wail.

"Jake," Leo spoke calmly. "Tell us what happened."

She took a deep breath as he rested his hand on her shoulder, guiding her into the seat beside him. "Roy's gone after Memnet," she said, her chest heaving. "I was trying to watch TV, but I was worried…" She looked questioningly at Danner.

"Clay's going to help us," Libby said.

Jake began again. "When I heard what the news was saying, I went to find Roy. I thought he was in the kitchen. His cigar was still burning in the ashtray, but he's gone. I started walking toward the train station and saw the Camaro outside this place." Tears filled her eyes. "Roy's coat is gone, and I think a gun is missing from the shop. The door was open, and he always locks it unless he's in there."

Leo made a low moan. "He and I had sketched out a rough plan, but he's gone off to attempt it alone."

"Blackburn doesn't intend whoever goes in that museum to come out alive, Leo," Clay said. "Roy's trying to protect you."

"But he's put himself in great danger. There are at least two of them, and they'll be waiting."

"I'd better call the Bureau right away," Clay said. "We've got to warn Justice Marshall and send someone to intercept Roy before he gets himself and Memnet killed."

"But that's what I saw on the TV, Clay!" Jake grabbed the sleeve of his coat. "Your face is all over the news, and if I didn't know better I'd run if I saw you. They say you're a dangerous criminal. In fact, they made you sound like a raving lunatic!"

Chapter Thirty-five

Before Mason's car was out of the driveway, Memnet was searching for a way out. The room he'd locked her in had no openings except a heat duct less than a foot wide. She looked for something she could use to pry away the mesh on the windows, but again there was nothing. Frustrated, she searched the tiny bathroom. A stool, a sink, and a medicine cabinet, nothing else. She opened the cabinet. Empty. As she started to close the mirrored door, she heard a sound from the next room. A woman was crying, and the sobs were familiar. Charlene Dobbs was on the other side of the wall.

"Charlene? Charlene!"

Sniffling, then, "Who's there?"

"Come into the bathroom and open the cabinet." As in many apartments, the sinks in the two apartments were aligned to simplify plumbing. The medicine cabinets backed up to each other, so two thin sheets of metal were all that stood between Memnet and the curator.

"How do you know my name?" Though she stopped crying, Charlene still sounded whiny.

"I read about you in the paper. They're looking for you all over the city."

"Really?" She sounded almost pleased.

"I'm a prisoner too. Have you tried to escape?"

"Oh, I tried everything, even being nice to that awful man who brings me food. It didn't help."

Memnet considered. She could pry the cabinet out of the wall, but they'd still be locked in, unless—"When does he come to feed you?"

"Early in the morning and just after dark. Why?"

"See if you can pry your cabinet away from the wall."

"What good will that do?"

"When he comes back, he won't know there are two of us in one room."

A pause. "I could never squeeze through that hole."

"I think I can. Together, we will defeat him."

"Oh-h-h-h, I don't think I like the sound of this," Charlene wailed. Letting the idea sink in, Memnet went in search of a tool. She considered everything, but even the toilet paper roller fell apart when she removed it, its pieces hitting the tile floor with a tinny clang. There was nothing.

As she clenched her teeth in frustration she heard, "Stand back!" A crash sent the cabinet flying from the wall, barely missing Memnet. Charlene's pudgy face appeared in the hole.

"I used a fork left from breakfast," she said matter-of-factly. "Pried my side out then stood on the toilet and kicked your side in." She started to cry again. "It's so good to see an honest face!"

***

"I hate trains!" Roy muttered as he waited in the El station. Noting nervous looks from those nearby, he finished his tirade silently. *An American curse, even if I did make a good living off them for a while.*

A train had pulled away just as he approached the station. Now Roy paced and peered down the tracks, unable to remain still. This late there were fewer of them going into the city, and he berated himself for not making his decision sooner.

When the next train finally arrived he got on, his stomach feeling like it would eat right through to his belt buckle. Leo would be angry at being left behind, but Roy was unable to wait at home any longer, wondering if they'd be able to rescue Memnet. When the idea finally hit him that the kidnappers might not expect him to already be in the museum when they got there, he'd had to move. Surprise was his only advantage.

On the chance they had someone watching the house, he'd gone out the back door and crossed the yard in the dark. His plan was to get into the Schmidt, find a good hiding place, and wait for an opportunity. It was risky, but he figured Blackburn didn't intend for any of them to see another sunset.

As the train rattled along and the buildings became taller and closer together, Roy thought about Leo's theory that Blackburn was an imposter. The audacity it must take for him to enter the Federal Building every day and pretend to be one of them! They'd seen first-hand that Blackburn had a cool head and adapted quickly when circumstances changed. *But no real man picks on women, A guy like him wouldn't have lasted long in Butch Cassidy's gang.*

When the train stopped at State Street, Roy got off and made his way to the Schmidt. For over an hour he stood in the shadows, looking for signs of activity. When there was nothing, he entered the familiar alley and went to the bricked entry. With its customary click the door opened, and he ducked inside.

It was a small measure of comfort to be in a place he knew better than almost anyone else. After a quick stop at his favorite display for luck, he hurried upstairs, boots silent as he set them carefully on the marble risers. He had no idea where Blackburn intended to meet him, and he no longer had keys to the rooms. He settled into the recessed doorway of a conference room. Unless someone shone a light directly at it he wasn't visible, but he could see anyone who came up the stairs.

As he sat there, conserving energy for what was to come, Roy recalled how Memnet had looked that morning as she showed them her newest product, love beads. She'd noticed people wearing them everywhere and, in her usual industrious way, began gathering the materials for making them. Hers were high-class versions, artistic and beautifully done.

She'd smiled with pleasure as her friends admired them, but it wasn't pride in her accomplishment. It was happiness at putting her talents to use for the good of all. The image of Memnet, frightened or harmed by these men, was so upsetting that Roy had to get up from his hiding place and pace for a bit. A cool head was essential, because he'd probably have to kill Blackburn to save Memnet's life. He was willing to do that, even if it meant he died in the process.

***

"Often I've wished I were a man, but never so much as tonight!" Libby moaned as she paced the kitchen where they'd recently held a hurried council. Afterward, Clay and Leo had gone off to find Roy and save Memnet. She was left to guard Jake. "Why are females always left behind to worry?"

Jake was fidgety too, never sitting for more than thirty seconds. She'd get up, wander the kitchen picking things up and setting them down, then plop into a chair again. She kept wishing aloud they had a phone, though Libby couldn't think whom they would have called.

Shortly after ten there was a knock at the front door. At first they ignored it, but it became more insistent. Motioning for Jake to remain where she was, Libby went to the door. Through the sidelight window she saw two men in trench coats. Bending her back and trying to look feeble, she opened the door a crack and gave them a querulous, "Yes?"

"FBI, ma'am. We'd like to come in."

"I don't understand, officers."

"We need to ask you some questions."

She supposed they had the right as officers of the law to question people who knew Clay Danner. Opening the door, she ushered them in, letting in a blast of cold as well.

The agents were in their thirties. One was strongly built, with a nose that looked like it had been broken a few times. The other was slim and red-haired, with a smile she assumed was meant to reassure her. It didn't. They wore suits under winter coats, but she deplored their tailor's skills.

"How many people are home right now, ma'am?"

"Only me, officer. My husband went out, but he'll be back any minute."

"Where are the others?" Red-hair smiled again. The effect wasn't warm.

"Others?" They weren't after Clay. They'd come for them.

"We know there's five of yous. Now where are they?" This came from the large one. Red-hair gave him a look of warning, and he set his rather puffy lips.

"Ma'am," Red-hair said with mock patience, "we have a job to do. We know five people live here. Where are they?"

I wish I knew. Libby's distracted mind began putting together details she'd missed at first. The men had shown no badges, which the television police always did. They knew who lived here. And they looked wrong.

"I don't know." She must have given away her thoughts, because the men looked at each other. Tacit communication occurred, and they abandoned the charade. Large Man reacted first, pushing past Libby and heading for the hallway.

"You can't come in without a warrant!" she cried, but he paid no heed.

Red-hair took Libby's arm in a cruel grip and pulled her toward the stairs. "Let's see who's up there." His smile turned even less attractive, and he held a gun in his right hand. She said a silent prayer that Jake had had the sense to hide.

Red-hair pushed Libby ahead of him. Large Man made a lot of noise as he searched downstairs, but there was no sound from Jake. "No one's here but me," she told Red-hair.

He paid no attention, going through the rooms one by one then dragging Libby back downstairs to meet Large Man, who spread his hands to indicate he'd found no one. "Now what?"

"We ice her and wait till the others come back."

A terrible clatter arose from the kitchen as he spoke. *Oh, no, Jake!* Large Man was off, and a few seconds later she heard him make a sound somewhere between surprise and pain. With a disgusted grunt, Red-hair dragged Libby to the back of the house. "You go in," he ordered.

A push on the swinging door opened it only a few inches. Blocking it was Large Man, laid out flat on the floor. Beside him lay Libby's black cast-iron skillet, useful for browning meats, and apparently for other things as well.

Peering over her shoulder, Red-hair shouted, "All right, whoever you are, I've got the old lady here, and I'll kill her if you try anything."

The man was nervous, and in other circumstances Libby might have enjoyed his predicament. Still, she had no doubt he intended to kill her. "Run!" she called. "Get away *now!*"

Red-hair jerked her back down the hallway, stopping after a few steps to assure no one followed. The swinging door remained still. She fought desperately to get free, grabbing the door frame as they entered the great room, but he struck her smartly on the side of the head with the gun. She let go without meaning to, reeling from the blow.

Red-hair released her and stepped away, stooping to pick up a pillow from the divan. She noticed irrelevantly it was one Memnet had embroidered with intricate designs. Holding it over the muzzle of the gun, he pointed it at her chest.

Libby's mouth went dry, her mind cleared, and it seemed that time slowed to a crawl. Red-hair had regained his unlovable smirk. "A lady white as you shouldn't live with no A-rabs," he said reproachfully. "But then, where would you Brits be if we hadn't saved your bacon in Dubya-Dubya-Two?"

The front door flew open with a crash. Red-hair turned his head and therefore received full in the face the banana cream pie Libby had made that morning. Seizing her chance Libby stepped forward and delivered a vicious kick to his privates. Picking up a lamp, she whacked Red-hair soundly on the temple. He dropped to the floor, groaning, then went limp and silent.

Jake stood in the doorway, panting from her run out the back door, through the snowy yard, and around to the front. Her bare feet made wet spots on the scuffed wooden floor.

"Excellent work, my dear!" Libby said as they embraced. "But no time for congratulations. Home is no longer safe."

Jake sped to the hallway closet and got warm clothing for each of them. As she pulled on cotton socks and buckle-front boots, Libby donned her woolen coat and hat. Finished, she leaned down to speak to the prostrate figure on the floor. "I know little about modern wars, but the last one *I* directed, England won without help from you or anyone else!"

They left then, afraid one or both of the men would recover his senses. With fear as encouragement, Libby found she could easily keep up with Jake.

Chapter Thirty-six

Memnet managed to get the museum curator to tell everything she knew without revealing much about herself. After Charlene helped her climb through the hole in the wall between the two rooms, Memnet claimed she had no idea why she'd been kidnapped. They sat on the bed as Charlene, looking rumpled but still smelling faintly of Chanel #5, told her story.

"Leaving for work one morning, I think it was two days ago. Two men grabbed me from behind. They were so rough they tore a hole in my new mohair sweater!"

Her eyes teared up, and Memnet crooned, "How frightened you must have been."

She pulled herself together, gratified that someone understood. A strand of blond hair had fallen over her eye, and she smoothed it behind her ear with a practiced gesture. "They put me in a car and brought me here."

"Can you describe them?"

"One was skinny and red-headed with a smart aleck grin," Charlene sniffed. "He thought it was real funny when I asked him to go back and get the shoe bag I dropped when they grabbed me." She paused for a moment's reflection on the lost shoes then continued, "They took my keys. 'You're gonna be part of history,' they said. Then they laughed, but it wasn't funny ha-ha. More mean, you know?"

"Did they explain that? Becoming part of history?"

"No. They just said tomorrow will change everything. I think it has to do with the museum, because they asked a lot of questions about it."

"What kind of questions?"

"Hours and guard schedules." Charlene picked at the chenille bedspread. "They wanted to know if there were doors nobody used. See, we caught some people living in the museum last fall. We don't know how they got in and out, and these guys wanted to know." She looked up at Memnet." I'm the one who caught them. You probably read about it in the papers."

"I've been out of the city," Memnet lied.

Charlene seemed thrilled to have a new audience. "These people were living in my, uh, the museum I manage, actually living there! The FBI says they were big-time criminals."

"Really."

She pushed the wayward strand back from her face again and leaned toward Memnet earnestly. "Yeah. They're trying to destroy our government."

"Oh, my!" There was genuine dismay in her voice this time.

"Agent Blackburn says he ran into them before." Her expression turned pouty. "He wasn't happy I told the *Tribune* reporter that, but he never said it was a big, hairy secret!"

All it took to keep her talking was a sympathetic look from Memnet. "Anyway, he said not to talk to the press anymore, but some racist guy is planning something awful, and he's hired the gang that was living in the museum to help him. I promised I'd keep quiet." She waved vaguely at Memnet. "You don't count, since you can't tell anyone."

"I see." Memnet thought ahead as she listened. Marshall would speak at the B.R.I.C.K. building tomorrow morning. That was directly across the street from the Schmidt.

Charlene was suddenly suspicious. "Where are you from?"

Memnet spun a lie that would appeal to Charlene. "I work for the United Nations, promoting women's equality worldwide."

"Really?" Charlene dealt with the hair again. "That's cool!"

"Yes." It was true she'd come to believe in equality for women since meeting Libby.

"If I had a dime for every man dumber than I am who got promoted before me," Charlene said, "I'd be rich."

Memnet brought her back to the situation at hand. "We must think of a way to escape."

"I agree." She stood, causing Memnet to sway as the bedsprings rolled in response. "We have to get out and call Agent Blackburn right away, because I know the name of the racist guy. It's Clay Danner."

Memnet bit her lip. "How do you know this?"

"Mason keeps talking about how he has to check in with Danner. He must be scared of the guy, because he's said it more than once."

To plant that name in your mind. Charlene would warn Blackburn of their escape, believing she was doing the right thing. That meant she couldn't go free yet, though it was important for Memnet to get away. "I think we should change our plan," she said. "I should go back to where I was before."

"I thought we were going to attack him together?"

"But if he enters the other room first, he'll know something's wrong." Memnet explained what she had in mind, emphasizing the importance of Charlene's acting abilities.

"Groovy!" She gave Memnet an unexpected and unwelcome

hug, all heat and squishiness. "As soon as you're free, you can let me out."

"Of course." Peeling Charlene off, Memnet wriggled back through the hole in the bathroom wall, scraping her hips a second time. The pain of the tight fit at least assured her that Mason, if they could trap him in her room, would be unable to reach Charlene and harm her.

Charlene leaned through the hole in the wall, grasping Memnet's hand. "If this works, we'll be free soon." Memnet tried to smile. With luck, she'd escape, but her fellow prisoner would be staying right where she was.

***

Clay insisted if he could see the bureau chief, Winston Farner, the suspicions directed at him would be straightened out. Leo went along, hoping Clay could convince his superior to believe him and mount a rescue.

His doubts grew as they cruised an area off Lake Shore Drive while Clay searched for Farner's house. He said he'd know it when he saw it, but he didn't remember the number or even the street. At the point where Leo was almost sick with panic, Clay finally pointed. "There. I recognize the balcony."

It was a lovely home, with a large yard and a columned front portico topped with a rococo balcony. At a large door, side-lighted and solid, Clay knocked and waited. A woman answered, listened briefly, and then ushered them inside. Asking the two men to wait, she went down a hallway. Standing in the marble-and-oak entryway, Leo decided that either a bureau chief's salary was generous or Mr. Farner had married well.

Footsteps sounded, and a man came toward them with the woman who'd admitted them a few steps behind. He was about

Leo's age and size, his spine straight as a history book. He had the look of a man with no sense of humor whatsoever. His salt-and-pepper hair was wiry and expertly cropped, and though he was at home and presumably relaxed, he wore a jacket over a pale blue shirt with the last hole unbuttoned at the neck.

Farner seemed to be nearsighted, because he didn't recognize Clay at first. He raised a bushy eyebrow, pulled a pair of glasses from the jacket pocket, and put them on. "Danner?"

"I'm sorry to bother you at home, sir, but it's important."

Leo watched the old man, trying to guess how he would approach the situation. His choice was paternalistic. "Son, there are serious concerns about your behavior. You must turn yourself in and tell us what's being planned."

Clay took a step forward. "I'm not crazy, sir. I'm here because I know you're honest."

Farner seemed almost amused that a lunatic had confidence in his integrity. "I'm sorry, Danner. I'm placing you under arrest. I want you to—"

"No!" Clay sounded desperate, and his manner apparently lent credence to the rumors Blackburn had sowed. Farner frowned, and a look flashed between him and the woman. She turned and left the room.

Clay shrugged his shoulders, relaxing the tension. "You have to believe me, sir. Charles Blackburn is trying to frame me for a crime he's planning."

"Blackburn? Explain." Leo guessed Farner was humoring Clay, stalling.

"He isn't Blackburn. He killed the real one and took his place. He—"

"Clay." Farner put a hand on the younger man's arm and spoke distinctly, as if the young man were deaf. "I worked with Charles Blackburn two years ago in Florida. He's no imposter. Now get a grip on yourself."

The woman returned, and again the couple exchanged looks. Clay stood frozen, unable to take in what he'd heard. "But this man saw him—"

"Clay." Leo touched his shoulder. "We must go."

"What?" He looked at Leo in confusion.

"They've called for help."

Leo had to give Clay credit. He pulled himself together, straightened his shoulders, and faced Farner. "I've done nothing wrong, sir. Justice Marshall is in danger, and if you won't help, I'll stop them myself." He backed toward the door as he spoke. "Come on, Leo."

"Danner, this can all be worked out."

"We've both got guns." At least half a lie, since Leo had no weapon.

The old man took a step forward but must have known he couldn't stop them. At Leo's last glimpse backward, Mrs. Farner was holding her husband's arm. His days of physically chasing down criminals were behind him.

Outside, there were decisions to make. They couldn't drive Clay's car for long, since every cop in the city would soon have its description. Once they were away from the house, they parked it in an empty lot. After climbing through hard-packed snowbanks and crossing drifted backyards, they returned to the street several blocks away.

Clay made a call from a phone booth, and after a nerve-wracking wait, a cab arrived to pick them up. Clay pretended to be drunk, leaning against a lamppost with coat collar turned up and head lolling into it to hide his face. Leo took the part of the remonstrating relative, apologizing to the cabbie for his nephew's behavior. They needn't have bothered; the driver's interest seemed focused on chain smoking. The air in the cab was blue and foul-tasting, as if they smoked as well.

They rode uptown in silence, each with his own thoughts. Though he guessed Clay was desperate to stop Blackburn, Leo's concern was for his friends. While he was sure Justice Marshall was a fine man, Leo had, for the first time in his life, loved ones to protect. A Borgia or de Medici one might respect but not love. A parent one might love but not respect. His little family had Leo's love and his respect. His first allegiance was to them.

The two exited the cab a block away from the Schmidt in order to approach unseen. The street was dark, as it was now after midnight on a frigid January night. "We're here," Clay announced, rubbing his cold hands together. "What do we do?"

Leo had been thinking about that. Clay didn't know they could get into the museum, and though Leo trusted the young agent, he didn't know if it was wise to give up all their secrets. "If we wait and watch, we can get an idea of how many there are and whether Memnet is with them. If we sneak inside, we might meet Roy and be shot by mistake in the darkness."

Clay grinned ruefully. "He'd gladly shoot me. Roy doesn't like me much."

"Roy is coming to realize what Memnet means to him," Leo replied. If Clay wondered why a man wouldn't know what his wife meant to him, he didn't comment.

"If Blackburn has Charlene, he has keys to the doors," Leo

said. "I suggest we keep watch at the staff entrance, which they will no doubt use. If Blackburn comes alone that's good, but I expect that won't be the case."

"There have to be at least two others," Clay corrected. "He wouldn't have been in on snatching Charlene Dobbs, since it looks like she's going to be his witness. She'll insist you guys were helping me, and Blackburn will be the good guy who rescues her and kills all of us."

It was good, Leo thought, to have an ally trained in dealing with criminals. "Let's find a spot out of the wind." Taking two pairs of gloves from the voluminous pockets of his coat, he handed a pair to Clay. "There's an all-night diner a few blocks down. Tea is fine for social occasions, but I find in a situation like this, coffee suits better, don't you?"

Chapter Thirty-seven

Libby and Jake ran several blocks before slowing to a walk. Despite her fear, Jake was in awe of Libby's handling of her would-be murderer. She'd heard about disabling a guy that way, but how would someone her history book termed "the Virgin Queen" know it? Adults could be surprising.

Libby finally stopped in the shadow of a meat market. Peering at the sidewalk behind them, she patted Jake's shoulder. "How brave you were to attack that large man!"

"I didn't have much choice. They were going to ice you."

"That means to kill?"

"Yeah. I hid under the sink while he searched then I listened at the door. When they said that, I started throwing pots and pans around. I got your skillet and jumped up on the countertop. When he poked his head in, I swung that thing with both hands, like a ball bat." She shuddered, remembering how the pan vibrated as it connected with a living head. Still, it had been desperate necessity.

Libby patted her shoulder again, an awkward but heartfelt gesture. "You were marvelous."

"You weren't so bad yourself," Jake replied. "Kicking that guy in the crotch and then whacking him with the lamp. Where'd you learn that?"

"I suppose the swing came from tennis with my father. The other was instinctive, and we needn't mention it again." She turned to look behind them. "Now we must decide what's next."

What was next turned out to be Aletha from church. When

they knocked on the poor woman's door at midnight, she appeared in a floor-length, blue quilted bathrobe with gold piping on the sleeves and front. Her head was wrapped in a matching terry-cloth turban, and gold lamé mules showed beneath the robe's hem. Filling the whole doorway, she looked like an exotic alien queen.

"We need your help," Libby said, and Aletha went into action. Ushering them in, she clucked sympathetically at their need to be out on such a cold night, sat them in chairs in her cozy kitchen, and began bustling to make Libby coffee and Jake a glass of Tang. When she could get a word in, Libby explained their presence, following Leo's rule about telling as much of the truth as possible. Bad men were planning something downtown tomorrow, possibly the assassination of Thurgood Marshall.

That was all it took for Aletha to get mad all over.

"What they thinkin', killin' a man so good? He be helpin' people for years now, workin' for civil rights. Why, the NAACP wouldn't be nothin' without Mister Marshall." Setting fisted hands on her hips she added, "Use my phone to call the police."

Libby shook her head. "We can't prove what we say."

Aletha's nod revealed experience with doubting police officers. "What we gonna do, then?"

"We need a ride downtown. We can stop them if we get there in time."

Aletha's face fell. "I got no car, Miz Parker. But we can take the train."

Libby raised a hand. "You can't come. It's dangerous."

"Humph!" She set sugar and Cremora on the table with twin thumps. "Somebody put Mister Marshall in danger, they better be watchin' out for *me*, not the other way 'round."

When Libby pressed she admitted her five children made direct involvement problematic. "Ah know!" she said after a moment's thought. "My nephew Pinkie Ray gots a car!"

Reaching Pinkie by telephone, Aletha first asked, then coaxed, and finally ordered that he drive her two friends downtown. Her last resort was family blackmail. "Pinkie Ray, Ah ain't never said nothin' to my sister about how you out all night doin' things you shouldn't. Now, you do somethin' for me, before Ah change my mind an' break my sister's heart!

She hung up the phone with a decisive click, explaining for their benefit, "My sister Luletha lives in Arkansas—" She said Ar-KAN-sas, "—and she think that boy work in a factory." Aletha's muttered comments as they waited made Jake doubt Pinkie's character. Their pursuers might be watching for them at the train station, but Aletha's repetition of "Rapscallion" and "UH-uh-UHH!" were not confidence builders.

When he arrived, it was easy to get the Pinkie part. The nephew's car was a 1963 Chevy Bel Air, painted hot pink. With an extended nose and fins on the back, the car seemed a half a mile long. Inside were fake leopard seat covers, an ill-fitting ragtop bound to leak cold air like mad, and a picture of Diana Ross shellacked to the dashboard.

Pinkie Ray was himself a picture in a suit of shiny black fabric with a pink (of course) shirt and a skinny black tie. His shoes were shiny wingtips, and his socks were pink, but by the time Jake's gaze reached his feet, she wasn't even surprised. He wore a black hat she thought was called a Panama, with a pink hatband decorated with the feather of some exotic (pink) bird.

Handsome, with skin like a Hershey bar, Pinkie had warm,

dark eyes and gel-sculpted hair. The only thing keeping him out of the dreamboat category was the curl of his lip. He was not happy to be there, even when Aletha explained his important mission for "the people." It was clear helping two white women out was not high on Pinkie's list of personal goals.

Pinkie Ray obeyed his aunt's wishes, but he did it on his own schedule. Their trip to the Schmidt involved multiple detours in order for him to speak to outrageously dressed young women on various street corners. He spent only a few minutes with each one, but at four in the morning they still weren't even close to their destination. Libby's tight-lipped expression revealed she knew what Pinkie Ray was and did not approve.

Things went from bad to worse when a patrol car flashed its lights and stopped them. "Oh, man!" Pinkie Ray moaned. "How I gonna explain bein' out at four a.m. with a old white chick and a little kid?" Like the spoiled brat he was, he slapped the steering wheel with an open palm.

Libby spoke from the backseat in a regal tone. "Mr. Ray, I will handle this."

The policeman's serious expression turned to surprise when he looked in the back seat where Jake and Libby sat, smiling calmly.

"Good evening, officer."

"Ma'am." More comfortable with what he understood, the cop asked spoke to Pinkie. "What you doing out this late with these ladies?"

Libby gave Pinkie no time to reply. "Officer, I've hired Mr. Ray to drive me to my son's home on Lake Shore Drive."

"You hired Pinkie Ray?" The cop was doubtful.

Libby smiled ruefully. "Mr. Ray's aunt and I attend the same church. My son was supposed to pick us up tonight, but he must have forgotten."

"I see." His expression said he didn't.

"I am unlicensed to drive in your country, and of course you all drive on the wrong side of the road." She gave a haughty little laugh. "I hired Mr. Ray to take my granddaughter and me home. I've offered him ten dollars."

"You coulda had a cab for half that, and it wouldn't smell like Tabu."

"That's all right. Mr. Ray has been quite charming."

"Well, okay, then. Pinkie—Mister Ray," he purred. "Your taillight's out. Get it fixed *after* you take these ladies home."

Pinkie Ray drove off, using his turn signal and slowing for corners as long as the cop could see them. When they were several blocks away, he turned to them. "Did you mean that about the ten?"

Libby gave him her most withering stare. "Not a cent, Mr. Ray. And if you don't go directly to Roosevelt and State right now, I will call your mother in Arkansas myself."

***

It didn't take long to feel the cold. Despite gloves Leo provided, Clay had to put his hands under his arms from time to time to keep the blood flowing. It seemed like Leo had been gone a long time, but the weather and the situation didn't help. *Time slows when you're miserable.*

The doorway they'd chosen was across the street from the staff entrance, which Leo said led to the back staircase. He'd been to the Schmidt many times, he told Clay, being an admirer of old things.

But where was he? Clay wondered if he'd run afoul of Blackburn or one of his henchmen, or maybe gotten scared and took off. But no. Leo wasn't the type to run when his friends were in danger. A fine man, intelligent, creative, and artistic, but also good-humored and charming, he struck Clay as a perfect gentleman, maybe even a perfect human being.

Finally, a figure appeared. Seeing the long, dark coat and the brown paper bag the man held, he began to have thoughts of warm, sweet coffee. He rose from his crouched position to make room for Leo in the doorway. A hand held the bag out, and Clay reached for it. Too late he realized the man wasn't Leo. Something arced toward his head, pain burst through it, and he knew nothing for a time.

***

Though she shook with apprehension, Memnet was determined her plan would succeed. When Mason brought their dinner he came to her room first, shouting for her to back away from the door before he opened it. He peered in, alert for tricks, and entered carefully, checking behind the door. Under the bed, Memnet remained perfectly still, afraid he'd leave before she could turn her plan into action. Right on cue, though, Charlene's voice came from the bathroom, "Oh, I'm sick. I'm so sick!"

Mason stepped into the room, setting a cardboard carton with two Dairy Queen cups and what looked like hot dogs wrapped in waxed paper on the night stand. From her position Memnet could see all of him but his head. Charlene moaned again, and Mason moved toward the bathroom. As soon as his back was to her, Memnet rolled out, pushed herself to her feet, and scrambled into the hallway. Closing the door behind her she locked it, using the key her captor had thoughtfully left in place.

Mason's roar of outrage terrified her, even with a sturdy door between them. He pounded on it, cursing loudly. A few seconds more and Charlene added her voice to his, urging Memnet to hurry and let her out. Feeling like an insect, Memnet scuttled down the stairs, leaving them both behind.

There was no one else in the house. Outside, she avoided the front, where Mason was apparently wrenching at the mesh on the window. The two captive's voices rose behind her as they bemoaned their similar fates.

Memnet didn't know where she was, but home was her goal. She walked quickly, avoiding people and staying out of the light as much as possible. When she came to shops with Chinese characters on their signs, she sighed with relief. Libby and she had visited Chinatown a few times. Having figured out where she was, she made her way to 100th Street as fast as the transit system allowed.

When she turned onto their street, Memnet saw that the front door stood wide open to the winter night. Entering cautiously, she closed the door and listened. Jake's kitten peeked timidly out from under the stairs, making little mews of dismay. A splattered mess of something littered the floor. Pie?

She searched the house but found no one. The kitchen was a mess, with pots and pans strewn everywhere. She stood in the center of the room for a few seconds, trying to understand it. Finally, her need for order asserted itself and she began putting things back where they belonged. Though useless, she felt that the actions restored some sort of order to their lives.

Rising on tiptoe to hang Libby's skillet on its hook, she saw the note lying on the countertop. The others had been ordered to the museum to save her life. Checking her coat pocket, Memnet counted the change from the twenty she'd begun with that morning. Seven dollars and coins. Locking the doors, though that was probably folly, she started for the train station.

An hour and a half later she approached the museum, ducking out of sight whenever a car appeared. She watched the alley for a long time to convince herself no one was watching before sliding into the familiar darkness. Feeling her way along the rough wall, she found the hidden doorway and entered.

Inside there was only silence, and Memnet wondered if she'd done the right thing. Should she have gone to the police? Though they had manpower and guns, Blackburn was one of them. If she called anonymously and said there were bad people at the Schmidt, would they believe her? At the least, she thought, they'd have to investigate. There was a pay phone in the lobby. It was worth a try.

Moving through the dimness, she checked the clock over the door. Almost time for the guard's round. She'd have to hurry to make the call before he came by. As she turned, a voice spoke in her ear. "Memnet." She gasped, and a hand covered her mouth for the second time that day. This one was gentle, however, and the voice was one she knew.

"Roy!" she cried softly. His arms went around her and she clung to him, taking in his scent and his strength. She'd felt so alone these last hours. He held her until she recovered and could stand on her own.

"Are you all right?"

"Yes." It was hard to let go of him, but she stepped back to demonstrate she really was okay.

"Come upstairs. I've found a place to wait." They stayed to

one side of the stairway, keeping out of the light that slanted in from the street. On the second floor, Roy opened a door to a study room. As soon as he closed it behind them, she asked. "Where are the others? Are they all right?"

"Yes, but let's start with what happened to you."

She told him about her capture, Charlene's revelations, and her escape. When she finished, Roy pulled her close again.

"Oh, my poor, brave girl," he murmured into her hair. "I didn't know I could love you any more than I already do."

In the dark she couldn't tell if he realized what he'd said.

When he released her, Roy told his part of the story, ending with how he'd conquered the old-fashioned lock on the room they occupied with a laminated ID card. Memnet listened, her heart light despite the danger. He'd said he loved her! It took a moment to focus again when she heard Leo's name.

"Leo is here too?"

"He went to get Danner. You must have just missed him. Leo says Blackburn intends to kill Justice Marshall tomorrow and blame it on that young man, Danner."

"He's right, I think. Charlene insisted Clay ordered her kidnapping, which is ridiculous." She remembered her earlier purpose. "When you found me, I was going to telephone the police and tell them Blackburn is a bad man."

"Clay and Leo went to the FBI, but Blackburn has them convinced Clay's loco. We have to stop them ourselves." His tone changed. "But not you. We need to get you away from here right away."

"But if you and Leo are going to try to stop two killers—"

"Hey, we handled them once, right?" Roy gripped her shoulders. "This time we're a step ahead, and we have a real FBI agent with us. Knowing you're free makes it all a lot easier." He paused, no doubt remembering she'd found the house empty. "I wish I knew where Libby and Jake are."

Memnet repeated her argument. "We should at least try to get help from the police."

Roy's expression was grim. "We don't know what Blackburn's told them." After a moment's consideration he said, "Okay, make the call. Say Marshall is in danger, and tell them to eliminate the stop on Roosevelt. If the Chicago police aren't part of it, somebody might listen to you."

They froze at the sound of a soft footstep in front of the door. "It's me." Leo's silhouette showed in the half-light as he entered the room.

"Memnet!" Leo embraced her. "We were afraid for you!"

"You'll enjoy the story," Roy said, "but for now, tell us your news."

Leo sobered. "Clay has been captured. I saw two men carry him in through the staff entrance, either unconscious or dead."

"They plan to frame him," Roy said. "Since they brought him inside, the attack will come from here."

"They have Charlene's keys," Memnet said. "Was one of them the pale man? Blackburn calls him Mason."

Leo rubbed his receding hairline with a callused hand. "I'd never seen either before. That means there are at least four."

"Did they see you?"

"I don't think so, but they must know we're nearby."

"They don't know about our door," Memnet said. "That is one good thing, but there is more that is bad." She told Leo what she'd found at the house.

He groaned. "So they might have Libby and Jake too?"

"And Charlene Dobbs," Memnet added. "I should have freed her."

"She's safer where she is," Roy said. "Charlene's meant to be their witness against Clay, and probably us too." He stirred, signaling action. "Go make that call, somewhere far from here."

"I'll see she gets safely away," Leo offered.

The plan came to a halt when they reached the stairway and saw the glow of a cigarette near the landing. When they crept to the back stairs, the smell of smoke wafted toward them there too. Guards were posted at either end of the building, where they couldn't miss someone coming to or leaving the main floor.

Chapter Thirty-eight

Clay woke with a start, ducking to avoid the blow he'd seen coming at the last moment. That was before. Now he was in an unfamiliar office, and a dull ache in his wrists revealed he was handcuffed to the arms of a chair.

The room was handsomely furnished and very neat. On the highly polished desktop there was only a French provincial telephone, a nameplate, and a clove-scented pomander on a small crystal holder center front. The phone's cord lay on the floor like a lifeless serpent. The chair Clay occupied belonged behind the desk but now sat in front of it. He could read the nameplate: *C. Dobbs, Curator.*

He was inside the Schmidt Museum. The clock on the wall said two a.m. Clay wondered where Leo had gone, if he'd found Roy, and if they knew where he was. As he tried to gather his thoughts, which were still a little cloudy, the door opened. Clay tensed, ready to defend himself, but he quickly realized he wasn't going anywhere. The cuffs allowed only a few inches of movement. He couldn't even scratch his own nose.

His boss entered the darkened room followed by a second man. Blackburn carried a flashlight, which he used to assure Clay was securely fastened to the chair. They'd taken his coat but left his gloves on, probably to protect his wrists from cuff marks and hide the fact he'd been restrained.

"Hello, Danner," Blackburn said. "How's the head?"

"Hurts." Clay's vision hadn't cleared yet. The men looked like dark blobs with blurry edges.

"You have time to recover before the big event."

"When you frame me for assassination?"

If he was impressed that Clay had figured out the scheme, Blackburn didn't show it. "That's what you get when you stick your nose in where it doesn't belong."

"Isn't my job protecting the good guys?"

The other man spoke from the doorway. "You don't even know who the good guys are."

"I'd say a Supreme Court justice qualifies."

"That's because you don't see the big picture." Blackburn rested a haunch on the glossy desktop. His voice had an undertone of enjoyment Clay hadn't heard before.

"No guards in the museum tonight?"

"One, but he's handcuffed to a chair too. We made sure he overheard you named as the man who'll be on the balcony with a rifle this morning."

"I found the stuff you hid in my house. It's not there anymore."

"You found it?" The man's tone revealed he'd done the planting.

Blackburn shrugged. "It doesn't matter, Mason. There's more where that came from."

"So the story will be I killed Marshall to impress Sharon O'Hara?"

"She'll be shocked," Blackburn said. "She had no idea her doubts about racial integration would lead some lovesick dope to assassinate Marshall."

"I see. Sharon becomes famous, your organization deplores my violent solution but still collects converts, and the civil rights movement gets a big setback."

"Civil rights!" Mason broke in, his tone outraged. "What about white people's rights? Don't you care about your country's heritage?"

"You mean the idea of accepting a person on his ability and not his skin color?" Clay asked.

Mason frowned. "Certain elements have to be kept in line or civilization will fall apart."

"And you're going to help the elite citizens of the nation see that by killing an innocent man."

"Marshall is guilty as sin!" Mason's face twisted with hate.

"Of what?"

"Climbing above his natural place. He makes other Negroes think they can have good jobs and positions of power, and where will whites be then? Overrun with coloreds who'll ruin a nation white people built with their sweat and toil!" He was ranting now. "Patriots got to take action for the public good!"

"Mason, go get Charlene and bring her up to the room next door." Blackburn's tone was firm but not sharp. Glaring at Clay, the man retreated into the darkness.

When he'd gone Clay asked, "He believes that nonsense?"

"His views are more acceptable to a lot of Americans that you'd think."

"Nice friends you've got."

"And your FBI pals play with guns and politics while the country goes to hell in a hand-basket."

"So you're a real idealist and the rest of us are chumps."

"The leaders of our organization understand that for a dozen idiots like Mason they need one guy with a brain who can formulate and execute a plan." He straightened Charlene's telephone so it sat square on the desk. "I can accept the rhetoric as long as the pay's good."

"Are you really Charles Blackburn? Farner insists you are."

"My name really is Blackburn. Charlie was my cousin."

"And he's the agent Farner worked with in Florida."

His shoulders moved slightly. "We look alike—" He stopped. "We *looked* alike. Everyone said so. I figured the old man wouldn't pick up on the differences as long as I kept a low profile." He chuckled. "As soon as you left his house, Farner called me. The cab company was happy to help the FBI trace the route of a dangerous criminal."

"You shot your own cousin in cold blood?"

Blackburn had moved away from the window in order to light a cigarette. The match flare briefly illuminated his face as acrid smoke wafted toward Clay. "Charlie's daddy prepared him to move up in the world: government work, maybe politics once he got some experience." Blackburn exhaled smoke before going on. "My dad gave me a fist in the face and said the army would make a man out of me. I got to participate in our nation's current venture in Southeast Asia, where Americans fight and die for an inferior race."

He dropped cigarette ash into Charlene's ficus. "It wasn't all bad, though. Vietnam's where I met the men who pointed me in this direction." He turned toward Clay, and his voice betrayed belief in the cause despite his earlier cynicism. "The American people won't wake up until something terrible happens in their own back yard. They don't care what happens in faraway countries. Hell, they barely recognize there are other countries."

"The army made you an expert on American politics?"

Blackburn recovered his detached air. "As much as anyone else." He checked his watch, holding it up to the window to see its face. Taking another drag on the cigarette, he went on, filling the time until whatever was going to happen was scheduled. "While I was in the army, Cousin Charlie joined the Bureau. His dad said being a crime-stopper could get him into the White House someday." His tone was bitter. "He laid it all out, a real Joe Kennedy."

"So you decided to bend your cousin's career to your needs."

"Damned right. We'd been following his rise in the Bureau, and when they assigned him here last fall, we saw a chance for me to replace him."

"That must have taken some doing."

"I found a guy who was a genius at forgery, a real da Vinci with a document." Clay noted Blackburn's use of the past tense. "Charlie always thought we were buddies, even when I put snakes in his bed or left him in the woods to find his own way home. He wasn't the least bit suspicious that night until we grabbed him." His voice turned flinty. "Then your friends interfered."

"My friends?" Hoping to spare the Parkers, Clay tried to sound confused.

"Don't you think *Foreigners Involved in Assassination Plot* will make a great headline?"

Clay scoffed, "Libby? Memnet? Who'll believe they're assassins?"

"You're going to kill them once you didn't need them anymore. It's hard to tell how nice a person is when she's dead." He shifted his feet. "Elwell's on the street right now, hunting down the old man."

"You don't have to hurt them," Clay said, though he guessed it was useless. "They only want to be left alone."

Blackburn nodded. "That's what I said at first, but they keep showing up." He added almost to himself, "I thought I had the big guy once."

"They'll leave Chicago if you tell them to."

"They have to die," Blackburn said matter-of-factly, "because I've decided I like Charlie's identity."

"What?"

Tossing the cigarette butt to the floor, Blackburn stubbed it out. "The original plan was to kill Marshall and let Charlie take the blame. I'd go back to being Randy, and the cops would never know where Charlie went. But this new idea will allow me to accomplish a lot more."

"I can hardly wait to hear it."

"Once I get rid of you and this band of gypsy foreigners you're so fond of, no one knows I'm not Charles Blackburn. So when you assassinate Marshall, I get to be the agent who tries valiantly to stop you."

Clay saw it falling neatly into place. "You kill me."

"Seconds too late. Stricken with grief that our nation lost its first Negro Supreme Court Justice at the hands of one of my own men, I pledge to work even harder for the Bureau and the U.S. government." He chuckled. "I might run for Congress after they give me a medal for killing you."

***

Across the street, Libby stared at the alley. If Blackburn knew about the hidden entrance, she'd walk into a trap. Inside, how would she find Roy in the dark? She had to assume at least some of the plotters were in there by now.

Beside her, Jake stood shivering in the early morning chill. Making her decision, Libby said, "We need to keep Justice Marshall from stopping anywhere near the museum this morning."

"How?" Jake asked. "If we try to get near him, we'll get arrested."

"We'll need to be clever." Libby chewed her lower lip. "Something Shakespearean, I think."

***

By six o'clock, Blackburn had arranged things to his satisfaction. He'd warned the police about Danner's associates, three foreigners and a big cowboy. The Parkers would get no help from the Chicago police, even if they shook off their natural distaste for authority and reported what they knew. That meant they could do only two things: walk into his trap or run as far away as possible.

He was upset to learn that Mason lost the girl. When he was late returning, Tate went to the house and found him locked in the room where she should have been. In addition, Tate and Leskin reported they'd found the Parker house empty when they'd gone to eliminate the residents.

Blackburn didn't like snags in the fabric of his plan, but he shook off his concern. The Parkers could do nothing to stop him. Things would proceed, and his men would kill any of them that ventured out of hiding. He took satisfaction in knowing he'd included Mason's demise in the final details. That screw-up would be dead by 10:15. One less link to Charles Blackburn, FBI agent.

Chapter Thirty-nine

Near the museum's back entrance, Roy heard rather than saw what happened. The man on guard moved to open the glass doors, and a voice ordered a sniveling Charlene into the building.

"Heard you lost your little Arab girl, Mason."

"Shut up," the newcomer responded. "Chasing down old ladies didn't sound hard, did it, but I heard you couldn't find hide nor hair."

Silenced, the other man took up his post at the base of the stairs again, but Mason's entrance had distracted him long enough for Memnet, Leo, and Roy to slip past. They'd made it to the main floor, but they couldn't escape. There was nowhere they could go except the wardrobe room, but at least they were on the ground floor.

***

Clay heard voices coming upstairs: a woman and at least two men. He'd been trying to free himself with no success. The wooden chair had rollers, but he saw no advantage to that with his hands secured. He worked on the only thing that might pay off, jerking the chair arms loose from their anchor points. After what seemed like a long time one arm wiggled a bit, but not enough. He'd be all morning freeing one hand, and then what?

His concentration was interrupted by the re-entry of Blackburn, accompanied by Sharon O'Hara, looking beautiful but distant. Remembering his pleasure at the attention she'd given him, Clay felt like a fool.

Blackburn was more animated than Clay had ever seen him.

"Come on, Danner, it's show time!" Sharon stepped behind Charlene's desk and picked up a video camera. Expertly she loaded film and checked the battery's power level.

"I'll signal when I'm on the street and ready." She went off, leaving Clay confused. His captor was happy to explain.

"You're going to be a TV star, Danner. Every American— except you, of course, will see you on tape ten, maybe twenty times in the next month. You'll be as famous as Jack Ruby."

"Whatever you've got in mind, I'm not helping you."

"Oh, I think you will. You see, we've got the museum curator in the next room, and Mason is more than willing to take slices out of her until you do as you're told." Pleased at Clay's shocked expression Blackburn finished, "You're dead either way, Danner, but she gets to live if you do as you're told." After a pause to let Clay's dilemma sink in he added, "The irony is that she'll die whispering your name to the cops."

Clay knew he was beaten. "What do I have to do?"

"It's starting to get light outside." Bending behind the desk he picked up a rifle, checked the chamber to be sure it was empty, and snapped the bolt into place. "I'm going to release you. You'll step out onto the balcony, and Sharon will tape you holding this Remington 700." As he spoke, he released Clay's wrists, leaving the cuffs attached to the chair arms. "My part comes later." He smiled. "I'm the mystery guest."

"I get it. You get video of me standing on the balcony with the gun. Sharon tells the world she filmed it just before Marshall was shot."

"She'll panic and drop the camera before the shots are fired, but there will be a clear image of you on the balcony holding the murder weapon. Who's going to question that you pulled the trigger? Now, trade your gloves for mine." Blackburn pulled a pair of thin cotton gloves from his pocket and handed them to Clay. "I used these to fire the rifle recently, so they have gunpowder residue on them."

Pointing his service weapon at Clay, Blackburn handed him the empty rifle. Clay saw no alternative but to step onto the balcony. In order to have any chance at all to stop this, he had to remain alive. But how long did he have? Only until Marshall appeared. Blackburn would kill Marshall and then kill him. Ten o'clock, maybe a few minutes after.

As he stepped onto the balcony, the cold Chicago wind hit him like a slap, and he instinctively lowered his face. Sharon stood below on the sidewalk, already filming. He held the gun as Blackburn ordered, cradled in his right arm. He was nervous and stiff, which didn't help a bit. In fact, it made him look exactly like a man waiting to assassinate someone.

The whole thing took seconds, but the visual evidence would be damning. This early on a weekend day, the downtown was quiet. A single car crossed the intersection on his right, but the driver looked neither right nor left. A shuffling form, hunched against the wind, stepped out of an alley farther down, but he didn't have time to get more than an impression before Sharon signaled success. Ordering Clay back inside, Blackburn relieved him of the gun and nodded at the chair. Clay sat, and he was cuffed in place again.

Checking his watch, Blackburn said briskly, "It's time for me to report to work." He patted Clay's shoulder. "Don't worry. I called Rhein to replace you on protection detail. They've been warned you're out somewhere plotting murder, but they won't see a thing till it's too late."

Clay went back to work on the uncooperative chair arm. How could he stop this? Would anyone ever know he didn't kill Thurgood Marshall? Remembering the figure down the block, he wondered if he really had seen Libby on the street below. Even if he had, Clay didn't see how she could help him now.

***

Libby saw the whole thing. Her attention had remained riveted on the museum for hours, though she'd sent Jake to get food. "We'll be no good to anyone if we faint from hunger."

They'd rehearsed their plan several times to get the timing down. Libby had given Jake the less dangerous part. If the ploy failed, she was to melt into the crowd. She'd promised that if things went wrong, she'd go home and take refuge in the attic until one of the others returned.

When Jake brought back two cups of coffee, a cheese Danish, and a jelly-filled doughnut, Libby didn't tell her what she'd seen on the balcony. The girl was scared enough without knowing her hero's life was in danger. Libby hoped Leo had found Roy, and they had a plan of their own to save Clay. She would do her best to save Justice Marshall.

After they ate, Libby gave Jake everything she carried that might identify her. "If I'm taken to—Alcatraz, is it?—you must find a way to free me."

Jake tried to smile, but the smile was even weaker than the joke. "We'll be okay," she said, though her chin wobbled a little. "We've got to be."

***

Memnet slipped out first, at about 9:15. They had no watches, and it had been nerve-wracking to keep peeking out at the clock in the

308

main hall, but timing was important.

She wore a coat of soft leather with fur inside, a matching hat, and mukluks. Making her way to the Eskimo exhibit was tricky, but they'd chosen it for its proximity to the back stairs. She knelt in the center, beside a mannequin of an Inuit man wearing fur pants and a sealskin coat. Nearby was a sod house, low-roofed to represent that it was half underground. Memnet sat, bending as if tending the cooking fire. Soon she heard a sound to her left and a whispered, "Go!"

In response, she began a clicking sound with her tongue, repeating it every few seconds at varying intervals. It took a while, but finally the skinny, pimple-faced man standing guard at the back of the main hall came to peek into the cubicle. Though apparently perfectly still, Memnet continued the noise. He stepped closer, examining the display for what might be making the clicks. When he bent to touch Memnet, Roy stepped from behind the scenery and hit him sharply with the wig stand he'd chosen as his weapon. "Fits nice in my hand," he'd said.

Roy caught the man as he fell, half-conscious, and Memnet stuffed a wad of batting into his mouth and tied a strip of cloth over it. Roy trussed him hand and foot then tied the two ropes together tightly, rendering him unable to move. They dragged him into the sod house, out of sight.

As they finished Leo appeared, wearing robes of velvet and a hat that looked like a bad soufflé. Memnet tossed her furs aside, and they worked their way toward the front of the building. It was daylight now, and the sun was beginning to peep in at the east windows, turning the main hall to gray. To avoid it and Blackburn's men, they wove through the displays, passing silent mannequins who obligingly looked the other way.

At the medieval display, nearest the front staircase, Leo moved into the scene, joining the lifeless guests at the table of a great lord by scooting one of them down a bit. He took a pose, appearing to concentrate on a trencher supplied with plastic venison and papier-mâché figs. After Memnet and Roy hid themselves behind the cubicle wall, Leo began tapping the underside of the table at varying intervals.

It took longer this time. Leo looked at them once with a question in his eyes, but Roy motioned for him to continue. Finally Mason appeared, looking around suspiciously. Leo sat like a stone, face averted. Seeing nothing to explain the noise, Mason turned to go. Leo tapped again. The pale man scanned the entire display, then, to their dismay, left.

Leo looked up and mouthed "What?" at the other two. Hurriedly they stepped back to their hiding spot as they heard footsteps. Mason had sent two others to investigate. They stopped in the doorway for a few seconds. Then the large man entered while the red-haired one waited, holding a gun.

As the man circled the display, coming closer and closer to Leo, Memnet looked at Roy questioningly. They'd hoped to subdue their enemies one by one, but the fact that Leo was no mannequin would be discovered when the man got close. Touching her arm, Roy pointed down, indicating she should stay there, while he turned and disappeared into the exhibit behind them. She guessed he intended to circle and come up behind the man with the gun. But what about the other man?

When she thought Roy had enough time to get into place, Memnet made a decision. Pulling off her blouse, she stepped into the dimly-lit display, smiling seductively. The appearance of a beautiful woman wearing only blue jeans and penny loafers caused both men to freeze in surprise. Their hesitation provided just enough time for Roy to thump the redhead soundly behind the ear, dropping him without a sound. At the same moment, Leo brought his wooden trencher up under the big man's jaw, spinning him sideways with the force of it. He didn't go down, but a vicious rap from Roy's wig stand finished the job.

By the time Leo and Roy had the two men tied and gagged, Memnet was fully clothed again. No one mentioned her helpful diversion.

Chapter Forty

At 9:48 a.m., Justice Marshall's escort pulled onto Roosevelt's east end. A crowd had gathered, and TV news teams were setting up. Reporters chatted idly until the show got going, and among them, Sharon O'Hara stood with the rest, ready to film the event.

More officers had been added to protect Justice Marshall, since the deranged Danner was still at large. The justice had chosen to stick with his schedule, assured by the agent in charge that they were prepared and vigilant. As the cars stopped before a small stand erected for his use, Marshall stayed inside, as advised, while Agent Rhein, several other FBI men, and the police searched the area. They found nothing unusual.

Rhein spoke to Marshall. "A few minutes, sir. Agent Blackburn advises by radio he is on site, checking things out."

"I appreciate that," Marshall responded.

***

Blackburn entered the museum through the back door, playing his part as the diligent team leader. The place was empty, but he expected that. Only Mason and Elwell were supposed to stay for the main event. Elwell would arrange the scene, and Mason, though he didn't know it, would join Danner as evidence of Blackburn's attempt to save Thurgood Marshall.

When Blackburn entered Charlene's office, Mason unlocked the handcuffs from Clay's wrists and dropped them into a duffel bag. He forced Clay against the wall next to the balcony door, holding him there with a gun under his chin. Elwell, a man Clay recognized as Sharon O'Hara's supposed cameraman, scanned the room for remaining signs of their presence. He removed Blackburn's cigarette butt, dumping the ashtray into the bag and wiping it clean with his shirt-tail. He made a final check of the room and then, satisfied, picked up the duffel bag and left.

Clay still wore the gloves they had provided. It appeared that only he had been in the room. They had him on film holding the gun that would soon become a murder weapon. Marshall sat in a car below, waiting to meet the people of Chicago. Everything was as Blackburn had planned it.

Putting on his own gloves and pulling a mesh hood over his head, Blackburn stepped to the balcony door, which had been cut in half horizontally. Crouching, Blackburn opened the bottom half and crawled through to where the rifle lay, loaded and ready. Clay noted the decorative awning, which would hide him from the sharpshooters on nearby rooftops. "This is a turkey shoot for him," Mason told Clay proudly. "He can hit a bottle cap at a hundred yards."

Blackburn's head appeared in the stunted doorway. "As soon as I kill Marshall, shoot Danner in the chest. One bullet, then hand the gun to me and get out." Mason nodded. Blackburn picked up his two-way radio, pushed the button to connect with the FBI men on the street and said, "All clear. Proceed."

***

On the street below, Rhein opened the door for Justice Marshall and spoke, his eyes watching the street. "All right, sir, you may step from the vehicle."

At that moment, a voice rose from the crowd. "'Beware the ides of March!'" Rhein turned to see a woman in a black coat with wildly disheveled red hair.

"Ma'am?"

The woman poked Rhein in the chest with a bony finger. "'Who would fardels bear, to grunt and sweat under a weary life, but for the dread of something after death?'"

"Ma'am, you can't stay here. We have a man who—"

"'A man, dear lady, why he's a man of wax!'" Her thin face lit with a smile.

Drunk, high, or maybe senile. "Van Stee, will you escort this lady—"

She grabbed his lapels in both hands. "'I see their knavery: this is to make an ass of me; to fright me, if they could. But I will not stir from this place, do what they can: I will walk up and down here, and I will sing, and they shall hear I am not afraid.'" Releasing him, she began singing "Greensleeves" in a strong, clear voice.

"Ma'am," shouted Rhein over the racket, "We will remove you if you won't leave voluntarily."

The woman sang on as if she hadn't heard a word. Then she stopped suddenly, and her demeanor changed again. "'I am not merry,'" she intoned seriously, "'but I do beguile the thing I am by seeming otherwise.'"

Two city police officers approached and took firm hold of the woman's arms. As they ordered her to come with them, she turned to the man in the car. Though his lips twisted a bit, Justice Marshall nodded gallantly. In response she curtsied, perfectly and with dignity. The crowd began to applaud the woman and boo the police, who were hardly popular figures.

Rhein raised his voice. "Sorry, folks. Justice Marshall will speak shortly."

The two cops pulled at the woman's arms, but she stood still as a stone. "'Double, double, toil and trouble!' 'Something wicked this way comes!'" Holding their faces expressionless, the officers finally picked the old lady off her feet and carried her off, to the cheers and jeers of the crowd.

Rhein had not a second's respite before the sound of sirens split the air. In the process of moving toward the car where Marshall sat waiting, he stopped again, his hand on the door handle. Three fire trucks careened around the corner, sirens and lights on full. They stopped at the front entrance of the Schmidt, and firefighters alit from all sides.

If Rhein were more observant he'd have seen the woman smile. Jake had done her part.

"One moment more, sir," Rhein said. His voice indicated a realization that this was going to be one of those assignments where nothing good happened.

Marshall chuckled. "Hey, this is what makes the job so fascinating, right?"

"Right," Rhein answered, his tone unconsciously copying Bill Cosby's version of Noah.

***

Sharon O'Hara didn't know what to do. She'd faked mechanical difficulties to prevent having to tape anything before the assassination. To the piece she already had of Clay on the balcony she'd add a wildly swinging shot of the crowd in panic and Marshall falling to the pavement. The video was supposed to be confused, like the one of JFK's death. With footage of Clay on the balcony and Marshall dying on the sidewalk, she would be the most famous reporter in America.

However, things weren't proceeding as planned. Rhein kept

Marshall in the car. Sharon watched as an agent approached the fire trucks. Glancing unobtrusively at the balcony, she saw no sign of Blackburn, but then, she wasn't supposed to.

Firemen gestured at the building, which looked peaceful from the outside. Police officers ringed the car where Justice Marshall sat waiting. As they conferred, the doors of the Schmidt opened and Agent Blackburn stepped out, his expression irritated.

"What's going on, Rhein?" he demanded.

"Sir, first we had a crazy woman then these trucks showed up. They got a call there was a fire."

"Obviously that's not true."

Rhein looked confused, but Blackburn said reassuringly, "I've been over the whole block. I'll check the Schmidt one more time, but I haven't seen anything to indicate trouble."

Rhein spoke to the fire chief, who ordered his men to replace the equipment and pack up.

When he returned Blackburn said, "Let's get the Justice back on schedule."

"Are you sure, sir?" Rhein asked. "With all this, I've got a bad feeling."

"Marshall is a popular man," Blackburn said reasonably. "If we stop it now, the press will claim the FBI can't do its job."

Rhein shrugged. "It's your show."

"Go ahead with the speech. If Danner had plans for Marshall, we've scared him off. I'll finish my sweep and get back before you're ready to head to the next stop."

As Blackburn walked away, Sharon shouldered her camera. Things were back on track.

Chapter Forty-one

From their position under the stairs Memnet, Leo, and Roy watched Blackburn step outside. "That leaves one man up there with Clay," Roy said. "Time for you and Memnet to get out, Leo. Wait in the alley till it's safe then fade into the crowd."

"We can't leave you and Clay here!" Memnet protested.

"If Danner's alive, I'll free him. Get her out of here."

Memnet resisted at first, but Leo took her arm. When they were out of earshot, he whispered, "I'll be right behind him as soon as I see you safely out of this place."

They moved toward the back, heading for their secret exit. Leo took off the cape and hat he'd used for his disguise and laid them on a bench. When they'd descended to the secret entrance, Leo asked, "Do you have money? Take a cab home and wait there. Any of us who can will return, and we'll decide what we can do to help the others."

Memnet turned to Leo with tears in her eyes. This might be the end of their family. Who might already be dead, who'd been caught, and who would soon be in danger?

Though Leo was thinking the same thing, he smiled and gently kissed her forehead. "Do as I ask. We will do better knowing you are safe." With that he turned and went back up the metal stairs.

As Memnet stepped through the secret door, a hand grabbed her, pulling her out into the alley, where she fell to the ground. The man who stood over her wore a badge that said *Press*, but he held a gun, not a camera. "I knew you people had to have a door nobody knew about."

Pulling Memnet up by her shirtfront, he put his face close to hers. "Back inside. Move." He shoved her toward the entrance. As she climbed inside he pushed her, and she fell to her knees. Having gained time to climb in after her, he put a heavy hand on her shoulder and pulled her up once more. "Up the stairs."

There was only one chance for escape: a tight spot just inside the door where they had to maneuver around the ductwork. Being taller, her captor had to duck to pass though, and his hold on her slackened a little. Seizing her chance, Memnet vaulted the handrail and landed hard on the steps that lead to her former home. Ignoring the pain in her ankles, she ran as the man thundered after her.

Instinctively Memnet headed for the room she knew best, Storeroom C. The door was unlatched, but once inside, she despaired. It was empty, and the slam of the metal door hitting the wall echoed in her ears.

Their false wall was gone, making the open space even bigger. She turned to close the door, to try to keep her pursuer out, but his strength made it impossible. After the briefest scuffle she staggered backward and he stood framed in the doorway, glaring at her.

Above Memnet heard a tinkling sound. Only once, but it kindled hope.

"No more tricks," he growled. "Upstairs, or I'll kill you where you stand."

Memnet obeyed. "I won't tell anyone about you," she said as he fell in behind her.

"We'll see to that," he replied. "One less foreigner dirtying up our country."

She turned to face him. "Your country? I think there were others here before you." Though his bigotry angered her, more important was distracting him in case help was on the way. "Were there not American Indians?"

"They never did anything with the land. It was whites who tamed it, built the cities, and made it what it is today." His words sounded rehearsed. "You foreigners come along wanting a piece of the American dream. Why don't you go back where you came from?"

"Believe me, we've asked ourselves that question a hundred times," said a voice. At the same time, a heavy velvet cape floated over the man's head, at once blinding him and pulling him backward so he lost his balance. Strong hands—sculptor's hands—grasped his wrist as he stumbled, twisting until the gun dropped from his fingers. Memnet scampered to get it as Leo twisted the cape tighter, cutting off his opponent's air. Handing the gun to Leo, who let his prisoner feel its barrel on his back, she said, "The old room is empty. There is nothing there to help him escape."

Retracing the route, they pushed the man inside. At the sight of the empty room Leo said, "Charlene has plenty of space to store Christmas decorations now."

He closed the door with its padlock, brushed off his hands, and turned to Memnet. "You've had trouble of late arriving at your destination. This time I'll escort you to a cab myself."

***

As soon as Memnet and Leo left, Roy crept silently upstairs to the offices, holding the Luger he'd brought from his gun shop. It was too bad he had no ammunition. "What I wouldn't give for a couple sticks of dynamite," he muttered as he ascended.

Listening at the first door he came to, he heard movement but no conversation. Opening the door, he saw Charlene Dobbs, tied to a chair and gagged. Charlene's blue eyes got wider when she saw the gun. Putting a finger to his lips, Roy signaled quiet. The gesture was unnecessary, he realized. She wasn't telling on anyone in her present condition.

Closing the door, he started on to the next room, but the sound of someone coming up the steps stopped him. Darting back to where Charlene sat, he closed the door behind him and waited. The steps went by.

Looking more closely than before, Roy noted the room was under renovation. Materials such as insulation and ceiling panels were piled at one side, awaiting installation. The next thing he noticed was that voices in the next room sounded unusually clear. Looking around, he saw an opening in the wall, covered only by a sheet of plastic. In the next room he heard a slightly ruffled Blackburn tell someone, "I've got things under control. I'll have to change my story, but it will work. Let's do it."

***

On the street, Rhein apprised the Justice of Blackburn's advice, and Marshall agreed they should continue. The crowd had thoroughly enjoyed the whole circus, but now it was time for the guest of honor to appear. Once more, Rhein opened the door. Once more Marshall leaned out of the car. Then glass crashed overhead and a piercing voice from above screamed, "Oh, my god, he's got a gun! Oh, my god, oh my god, lookout!" Charlene Dobbs, whom Roy had released from her chair, had thrown a hammer through the window. Now more than half of her was thrust through the opening, screaming for all she was worth.

Rhein sprang into action, pushing Marshall back into the car as a bullet whizzed over his shoulder. Panic reigned as people reacted. Some ran; wiser ones hit the ground and crawled to cover. The shooter fired twice more, in frustration, it seemed, because Marshall was no longer visible. Bullets hit the store window behind them, shattering it. Rhein slammed the car door closed, tapped the outside twice, and the driver pulled away, following emergency protocol. Within moments, agents located the source of the shots and headed into the Schmidt.

***

As Blackburn fired, Mason pointed his gun at Clay, ready to do his part. Clay stood helpless, both angry and scared. He was about to die, and he'd be branded a bigot and that most cowardly of criminals, the assassin. Behind his would-be murderer, he saw a flash of movement. He was almost as surprised as Mason when Roy made a flying tackle, simultaneously grabbing Mason's gun hand and putting a shoulder into him as effectively as any Bears lineman.

Clay turned to Blackburn, who was crawling back inside the room on hands and knees, swearing as he came. Clay kicked the rifle out of his hand, and it skidded off to one side. He launched himself at Blackburn, but he pulled his sidearm from beneath his jacket and rose to one knee. Just as Clay hit him Blackburn fired, and Clay dropped to the floor, twisting sideways as a searing pain hit his shoulder.

Roy and Mason struggled near the office door. Mason looked to Blackburn, his expression beseeching assistance, as Roy gripped him from behind, trying to choke him unconscious. Over Mason's shoulder he saw Blackburn raise his gun again. Roy pulled Mason backward, twisting his body around the corner to put a wall between himself and the bullet. He heard Mason cry,

321

"Don't!"

Blackburn fired anyway, hitting his confederate in the torso. Mason slumped forward, and Roy released him, letting the man slide to the floor.

The crash of the doors below being forced open blended with Charlene's screams as she fled into the arms of waiting police. Running footsteps sounded on the stairs, and Roy slid into the room she'd vacated just as several men joined Blackburn in Charlene's office.

"I got two of them, but one got away," he told them, still out of breath from struggling with Clay. "You two, check this floor. Everyone else, search downstairs. He'll be trying to get to an exit."

As the others retreated, Blackburn told the two officers who remained, "Start at the far end of the building and work toward me, and we'll trap him between us. If you see him, don't hesitate to shoot. The guy is a killer."

Knowing discovery was imminent, Roy looked around the room for a place to hide. The half-remodeled office offered only the door and a window, and both led to discovery and arrest. The construction paraphernalia stacked in a corner offered no help. Pulling the lower edge of the plastic sheet away from the wall, he found hope. A three-by-three hole in the air shaft was exposed, presumably for the installation of air conditioning.

Removing his socks and beloved boots, Roy stuffed them inside a roll of pink insulation. As steps sounded outside the door, he climbed into the shaft and disappeared.

Someone entered the room. Roy traced the sound of steps as a man walked around, moving any object big enough for a man to hide behind. After exhausting the possibilities of the room itself, he pulled the plastic aside, stuck his head into the airshaft, and peered down. Roy saw only a dark form; the other apparently saw nothing at all. The head disappeared, and after a final slow turn around the room, he left.

After the door closed Roy climbed out, arms and legs shaking from the effort of suspending himself above the opening in the shaft. Putting his prickly socks and boots back on, he settled behind the rolls of insulation to wait out the search.

Chapter Forty-two

Clay lay motionless on the floor of Charlene's office, feigning unconsciousness. Blackburn stood in the doorway for a few moments, waiting until the policemen were gone. When he was satisfied they were far enough away, he nudged Clay with his foot. Though the pain was intense, Clay didn't respond. Bending down, Blackburn bent to check for a pulse.

Seizing the opportunity he'd awaited, Clay kicked Blackburn's legs, sweeping them from beneath him. When he hit the floor with a grunt Clay rolled onto him, using his body to pin him down. With his good arm he beat Blackburn's hand against the floor, trying to knock the gun free. Holding on fiercely, Blackburn struggled to point the weapon at Clay. Though the wounded shoulder hurt like nothing he'd ever felt before, Clay used his body like a wrestler would, keeping his opponent pinned down. With his free hand Blackburn flailed at him, sending jolts of pain through his torso that almost made him lose consciousness.

Desperate for an advantage, Clay moved his good hand onto Blackburn's wrist and pressed his thumb into the soft underside of the joint. With his nail he dug into the nerve between the chords, interrupting the signal that allowed Blackburn to maintain his grip. A final, sharp blow sent the gun spinning into a corner, out of reach of either man.

The move helped Clay and hurt him at the same time. Blackburn could no longer shoot him, but he now had two hands free while Clay's whole left arm was useless. Still using his body to hold Blackburn down, Clay pummeled his face with short, vicious punches as Blackburn continued to pound Clay with both fists. The pain was terrible, and Clay knew he had to finish the fight before his waning strength failed completely. Soon his body would become unable to respond to commands, and he would succumb to unconsciousness.

You have to win, he told himself. Remembering that Memnet and even Jake might be dead because of this man, Clay opposed the pain with a final burst of anger. He kept up the jabs to the face, over and over, though his arm grew weaker and his fist felt like it was being hammered rather than hammering. Finally Blackburn's arms dropped and he lay dazed. Still sitting on his chest, Clay watched him, exhausted but wary. "You're under arrest. You have—"

"Forget it, Danner." He turned to see Sharon O'Hara standing in the doorway. She had picked up Blackburn's gun, and she was pointing it at him. "I told the officers they were needed downstairs."

"Shoot him!" Blackburn's speech was slurred, but he knew what he wanted. Sharon raised the gun, though Clay saw hesitation in her eyes. "Do it!" Blackburn snarled, but he was too late.

***

Hearing the struggle in the next room, Roy had left his place of safety. Just as Blackburn gave Sharon the command, he came up behind her and reached around to snatch the gun from her hand. With a mumbled, "Sorry, Miss," he spun her around to face him and punched her in the jaw—more gently, he'd claim later, than he'd have done if she were male. As she collapsed Danner hit Blackburn once more, rendering him silent again.

Grimacing in pain, Clay staggered to his feet. Every move

made him wince. His jacket was stained with blood. Roy handed him Blackburn's gun so he could guard their prisoners while he took Clay's handcuffs from his belt and secured Blackburn's hands behind his back.

"Charlene was in the next room." He gestured at the plastic that hid the open air shaft. "They didn't realize it, but she heard everything they said."

"Then she knows I was set up?"

"Yes." Roy peered at Clay's white face. "Are you okay?"

Clay gave him a shaky smile. "No, but I'll live till the cavalry arrives." Taking Blackburn's cuffs from his belt, he handed them to Roy, who cuffed Sharon's hands.

Sounds below indicated they wouldn't be alone for long. "Go, Roy," Clay said. "I'll handle this."

Roy didn't hesitate. "Tell the rest I'll be home for supper, will you?"

"If I get home by then. Paperwork, you know." Clay indicated the prostrate Blackburn.

"Nice work, kid," Roy said. Then he was gone.

***

On the street below, Libby sat in a police car while two officers argued. "She's locked in," the younger cop said. "We can leave her for a few minutes to see what's going on."

His more experienced partner gave him a disgusted glare. "What if she's part of this mess and we lose her? Your ass would be grass and the lieutenant would be the lawnmower. Stay here. I'll go see what's up." He took off in the direction the rest had gone, leaving the younger man to pout.

As he stood on tiptoe, trying to see what was going on down the block, a girl approached. "Hey, officer," she called. "Are you arresting that old lady?"

"Maybe." He was in no mood to chat with kids.

"I saw her drop a purse over there earlier." She pointed down the street then went on, apparently feeling she'd done her civic duty.

The cop looked in the direction she'd pointed. They'd frisked the crazy old bat and found nothing. If he learned her identity, he'd have something to contribute to the investigation. Somebody would notice him.

He considered the odds. It would take thirty seconds to retrieve the purse, maybe less. The woman had gone quiet once they locked her in. With a last glance around, he crossed the street. Sure enough, a cloth purse lay inside a storefront recess. He hurried over, picked up the bag, and opened it. Empty! Returning to the car, he pounded the hood in frustration. The woman was gone. Someone had released her from the back seat.

***

Libby and Jake were first to get home. Once they were away from the Schmidt, Libby hailed a taxi. Though Jake could hardly believe she'd spend that much money, Libby pointed out it was the fastest way to travel. When they arrived Jake served as hostage while Libby went inside to get money to pay the fare.

Leo and Memnet came next, both upset and frustrated. Seconds after they'd stepped out of the alley, a patrol car with two officers pulled into it, blocking the entrance. Leo was unable to get back in to help Roy.

Several ambulances had arrived at the museum, they

reported. Clay was taken out on a stretcher, wounded but conscious. The man called Mason, also on a stretcher, was unconscious but apparently alive. Each of their conquests was led out in handcuffs, first the three they'd tied up in the display rooms and later the one Leo had locked in the basement. An attractive woman was escorted to a police car in the custody of a female officer. Leo said she'd looked angry as she shielded her face from the cameras with her coat.

They'd also seen Blackburn, stone-faced but refusing to bow his head, led away by Agents Marks and Van Stee, who seemed a little dazed to have their former boss in custody. The guard, Jake's old pal Stosh, walked out under his own power.

What they hadn't seen was Roy, either under arrest or on a stretcher.

"We must hope he got out during the melee," Leo said.

Memnet was a wreck, and Jake tried to console her. "Roy will make it if anyone can. He's like Superman." *At least I hope so,* she added to herself.

The nightly news informed them that Agent Clay Danner was a hero who'd single-handedly taken out a gang of assassins. Several suspects were being questioned by the FBI. Leo mused, "I wonder how much the agents will believe of stories of mannequins that move."

Just after ten o'clock they heard a key in the door. Roy entered with both arms raised like a prizefighter, proclaiming, "Here I am, all in one piece." They ran to greet him, and he hugged each in turn. When Memnet exclaimed at his cuts and bruises, he assured her they were nothing. Jake thought he was pleased at her concern though.

"What happened, Roy?" Libby urged. "We know bits from

the news."

Plopping himself in a comfortable chair, Roy began pulling off his boots. "I have to hand it to your friend Danner, Jake. He's tough as nails." He related the details, Blackburn's plan, his own intervention, and Clay's heroic struggle. After they'd congratulated Roy on his success he mused, "The interestin' part is Danner seemed to know I didn't want to be found there. Why's that?"

"We told Clay we'd must remain anonymous, but we didn't explain why," Leo answered.

Roy nodded. "Well, when the shooting was over, I waited in this little hole-in-the-wall..." He smiled at his own joke "...while police crawled all over the Schmidt, collecting bad guys and evidence."

In his first foray into the ductwork, Roy explained, he'd noted a horizontal turn a few feet above the entry point. "When I climbed up in there the second time I went around that bend, so I didn't have to hang like a spider in a drain-spout."

Once the FBI and the police had gone, the museum crew came in to clean up, so he'd had to wait again. "It took a long while, but finally things quieted down, and I was able to leave by our door in the alley. A pretty exciting day, for once."

Memnet slapped his arm in gentle admonition. "We want no more days like this ever!"

After his story, each of the others told the events from their viewpoint. Roy was appalled at Memnet's second brush with danger and amused at Libby's antics and Jake's rescue of her afterward. "Looking at the whole experience," Leo pronounced, "we are lucky to have come through it alive."

Around midnight they retreated to their rooms, overtired but still wound up from excitement. Jake managed to fall asleep sooner than she expected to and slept until full daylight. As she entered the kitchen, Roy was explaining something to the other three. Jake saw surprise on Libby's face, disapproval on Memnet's, and interest on Leo's.

"And how does one accomplish this?" he asked.

"As far as I can tell, we just hang out a sign," Roy answered. "There isn't much to it, though I'd get a license to make things official."

"License for what?" Jake asked, sliding onto a chair and taking a piece of toast. She was getting used to Libby's way of preparing it, letting it cool and buttering it later.

"Roy thinks we could open a detective agency," Memnet said, her voice carefully neutral.

"Cool! I'll do the stakeouts. No one will suspect a kid."

"You will be in school," Libby said firmly. "And we haven't agreed to it yet."

"We did rather well as a team, Libby," Leo reminded her.

Roy tried flattery. "It sounds like you were great as a crazy old lady." At her withering look, he lapsed into silence.

"Libby might prefer to do the office work," Leo suggested. "Now that you've mastered the telephone, you'd be the center of the operation."

"And me?" Memnet asked.

"The beautiful spy!" Jake guessed.

"Not exactly." Roy grinned. "I notice women understand things men don't. Memnet puts people at ease, where I scare them, right, Jake?"

"You don't scare me anymore," Jake contradicted.

"Anyway, Leo is a whiz with gadgets and such, and I'd do the rest. With some training, we can make it work." He added as a sort of olive branch, "We'd continue the jobs we've been doing. This will be additional money."

"I don't know," Libby began.

"We'll have to discuss it, Roy," Leo put in. "This is not something to be decided lightly."

Jake read Leo's mind: *At least he's given up the idea of robbing a bank.*

"Of course," Roy replied, apparently happy to leave the possibility open.

Chapter Forty-three

At mid-morning a car with the FBI seal on the side pulled up outside the house, scaring Libby half to death. Out of it stepped Clay, his upper body wrapped and strapped and his coat draped over his shoulders. Peering out from the curtain at the door, Jake heard him say to the driver, "Thanks, Bill. I need to let my neighbors know I'm okay. They'll see that I get home all right."

The car pulled away, and Clay was soon among them. After a great fuss over his injuries, they again exchanged stories of what each had experienced, putting the whole thing together. They sat, as usual, around the kitchen table. Libby served mincemeat pie, though she groused that pie is never any good the second day. Clay said he didn't mind, since he'd eaten nothing but a few doughnuts in the last forty hours.

"Blackburn is in big trouble," he told them between bites. "Mason turned state's evidence. Sharon isn't cooperating, but the DA thinks he can get her on conspiracy charges. She's connected with racist groups in about a dozen ways."

"You're lucky to be alive, Kid," Roy commented.

"Does this Ballard command the assassins?" Libby asked.

"Probably, but we won't be able to prove it. Blackburn and Sharon know better than to implicate him."

"So he will not be punished for his crimes?" Memnet's forehead puckered in irritation.

"They won't stop either." Clay set his fork down and pushed the plate away. "Killing people who stand in your way is easy if you have guys like Blackburn to do the dirty work. They didn't get Marshall, but they'll look for other chances to kill."

"We haven't come far from the Borgias," Leo said sadly.

There was silence as his words sunk in, the meaning clearer to some than to others.

Clay approached the subject they all knew must be settled. "Thank you," he said soberly, "for my life. I came to tell you I will keep our friendship separate from what I do for a living."

"We appreciate that, Clay," Libby answered. "You should know we've done nothing that compromises your position at the FBI. Without saying more, we appreciate your keeping us out of your account of yesterday's events."

"Yeah," he said with a grin, "as far as I know, the Green Lantern stopped by and helped out." He yawned, covering his mouth with his good hand.

Roy rose from the table. "Kid, you look like you could use some sleep. Let me walk you home." Bundling Clay into his coat like a big brother, he escorted him out.

"It seems Roy has taken to Clay," Leo observed. "But why does he call him Kid? Isn't that a term for children?"

"Probably reminds him of an old friend," Jake guessed. "The Sundance Kid."

Later that day, she found Roy paging through her book on ancient Egypt. "What're you doing?"

"Looking at pictures," he replied. "Egyptian ladies didn't wear tops to their dresses, did they?"

Memnet had told Jake and Libby how she'd distracted the two goons in the museum. "In my country, breasts are not shameful, but Roy does not look me in the eyes today. I'm afraid he thinks I am a bad woman." Lowering her head, she'd added, "I think we are too different to ever be together."

Libby and Jake had wiggled their eyebrows at each other. It seemed Memnet had finally decided what she wanted from life.

As she thought about how to answer Roy's question, Jake guessed he didn't disapprove of Memnet's action. He was trying to understand, maybe for the first time, who Memnet really was.

Though she didn't know everything there was to know about love, Jake wanted to help. Pointing to a picture in the book, she explained, "Sometimes they wore just a skirt with shoulder straps, like that. I bet Memnet would show you how she used to dress if you asked her."

Roy blushed. He actually blushed. "That is no fit thing for a young girl to be suggesting, Jerilyn Kay. Sometimes I don't know what comes over you."

"And sometimes you sound just like Libby," Jake flung at him. She left him with the book—and his future—in his own hands.

++

Other Books by Peg Herring

4 Simon & Elizabeth Mysteries-Historical, Tudor Era
Her Highness' First Murder/Poison, Your Grace/The Lady Flirts with Death/Her Majesty's Mischief

4 Dead Detective Mysteries-Paranormal
The Dead Detective Agency/Dead for the Money/Dead for the Show/Dead to Get Ready—and Go

3 Loser Mysteries-Contemporary Mystery/Suspense
Killing Silence/Killing Memories/Killing Despair

Stand-alone Mysteries
Shakespeare's Blood-Contemporary Mystery/Suspense
Somebody Doesn't Like Sarah Leigh-Contemporary Cozy
Her Ex-GI P.I.-'60s-era-Mystery

Caper Novel
Kidnap.org-Contemporary Humorous Crime

Historical Romance-Medieval Scotland
Macbeth's Niece/Double Toil & Trouble-

Website: http://pegherring.com
Facebook: http://facebook.com/Peg's News

Visit Peg's alter ego, **Maggie Pill,** for a cozy series, The Sleuth Sisters Mysteries